DEATH IN THE GARDEN

Edwina, Cassie and Alice, three young women who had become an inseparable trio, shared a birthday, success in their respective professions and a belief that nothing could change their relationship. Then Edwina's lover Tim, father of her unborn child, died in a road crash. All three received anonymous telephone calls and at the reception for Edwina's father's second marriage their publicity agent drank poisoned whisky, dying in agony. They found themselves sharing at least one more experience—that of being murder suspects.

DEATH IN THE GARDEN

Jennie Melville

A Lythway Book

CHIVERS PRESS
BATH

19.50

First published 1987
by
Macmillan London Limited
This Large Print edition published by
Chivers Press
by arrangement with
Macmillan London Limited
and in the U.S.A. with
the author
1988

ISBN 0 7451 0668 4

Copyright © Jennie Melville, 1987

88 B9442

British Library Cataloguing in Publication Data

Melville, Jennie
 Death in the garden.—(A Lythway book)
 I. Title
 823′.914 [F]   PR6063.E44

 ISBN 0–7451–0668–4

DEATH IN
THE GARDEN

CHAPTER ONE

Inside every murderer is a lover trying to get out.

This truth, a truth for her, for truth can come in all shapes and sizes and there is a truth for everyone, was discovered by Edwina Fortune the summer of her father's second wedding and her own crisis.

A time when she was pregnant, and alone, and hunted.

*   *   *

Three months before that terrible period Tim Croft and Kit Langley were travelling south from Edinburgh in adjoining sleepers. Young barristers in the same chambers, they had both been working on a prolonged public enquiry in Scotland.

Kit was woken up in the middle of the night by shouts from Tim's compartment. He lay for a minute listening, half awake, half asleep. Then Tim shouted again: a dark, throttled sound from the back of his throat.

Kit knocked at his door. There was silence, then a sound of movement and Tim called out:

'Come in. It's not locked.'

He was sitting on the edge of his sleeper with

1

his head in his hands.

'You all right?'

Tim raised his head. 'Yes. Just a nightmare.'

'Oh well. OK then.' Kit made a move away.

'No, don't go.'

Kit sat on a suitcase and looked at Tim. 'You look rotten. Have some whisky—I've got a bottle next door. Old Baggers pressed it on me.' Baggers was his noble Lordship, Lord Baggally: one of Her Majesty's judges. He had presided in Edinburgh.

'I think he fancies you,' muttered Tim. Kit laughed. 'No, no. He's my godfather. Married to my mother's cousin—I thought you were being strangled.'

'Not me, no ... It was a rotten dream. The worst ever—I was strangling someone.' He looked at Kit. 'I thought I was strangling Edwina ... She's got such a lovely neck and I had my hands right round it, squeezing.'

'Knowing Edwina, she fought back,' said Kit lightly.

Tim did not laugh. 'Yes, yes, she did. I could feel her hands pulling on mine. But I killed her all the same. I strangled her.' He shuddered.

'Oh come on, Tim. You're in love with the girl. You won't kill her.'

'No.' Tim put his head down in his hands. 'You don't understand. Women worry me, people hang on so.'

'Do you mean Edwina?' Kit was prepared to

2

be defensive.

'No.' He hesitated. 'Not Eddie. Forget it.'

'I'll get the whisky.'

When he came back, Tim's hand was trembling as he took the drink.

'I'm a bloody murderer.' He spilled the whisky. I know, Kit thought. But he did not say it aloud. He took the glass away.

Later, lying on his narrow bed as the train swung along the east coast route to London, he wondered what to do.

There had been blood on Tim's hands from scratches as if he had clawed himself in his nightmare. Somehow this made it serious, something not to be brushed aside.

Should he tell Edwina? Was that the right thing to do? But he was more than half in love with Edwina himself, which put up a barrier. Besides, he *liked* his friend Tim.

Tell Alice then, who was Edwina's close friend? But he guessed that Alice was more than half in love with him. Cassie then, her other close friend, the third in the triangle? But Cassie's tongue was suspect and her discretion not absolute.

He decided to say nothing, nothing at all.

Two weeks later Tim was dead, and Kit was glad he had not spoken. Tim was dead, killed in a car crash on a winding Perthshire road. The Procurator Fiscal examined the evidence with the police and called it an accident. No details were ever made public. In fact, he had been dead for some days before anyone except his mother in Northumberland knew. It was a shock to them all. Their first intimation of the way life can, without warning, rub you out, leaving no message behind. It was hard to believe Tim was dead. It seemed almost as if he was not.

A few weeks after that, when Tim was buried and while he was at a wedding, he thought that, after all, perhaps he should have said something.

★　　★　　★

It was the wedding of the year, the wedding of the decade, some said it was the wedding of the century. A small, intimate wedding for family and friends. Just one thousand of them shut into a converted warehouse in Covent Garden, eating smoked salmon, drinking champagne and shouting. There was laughter too. There was always laughter when those three entertained: Edwina, Cassie and Alice. It was they who were giving the wedding for the bride, Lily Dex, who was marrying Edwina Fortune's noble father, the Lord Bulkley. The warehouse was being converted by Cassie Ross, architect, into her offices, drawing room and living apartment combined. She would live on the job. The wedding itself had taken place in St Godrun's church in the tiny ancient parish no more than three streets square. It was a glittering social occasion.

Five kings were dancing at the wedding. Have you ever seen five kings all at once, let alone dancing on nimble feet? King Edward VII once led five kings to church at Sandringham and a fine sight it must have been, but that was a long while ago.

The kings were Peter Lloydd who was playing King Lear at the National, Pip Cardew who was King of Hearts in the new ballet at the Garden, and Eddie King, the rising young comedian. The other two kings were actors from the Cardboard-Cut-Out Theatre that performed from a travelling booth in the Piazza of the Garden, several days a week. Cassie had hired them to perform because she had heard the Sandringham story and wanted to make up the number. They were wearing long robes, masks and glittery cardboard crowns, glitz personified, and had promised an amusing act with silver balls. But since no one seemed to be watching them they soon ceased to juggle and quietly joined the party. They popped up everywhere, yet so cunningly that at least one person wondered exactly how many of them there were and felt bemused. Five kings, a three and a two, with different claims on the name, but all important. The whole designed by Cassie so she could have her joke. At the time she thought

5

what a marvellous publicity hook for Luke Tory to use. Afterwards, of course, she saw things differently, even wondering if the idea had been fed to her without her realising it. Bee Linker smiled at her nephew and shook her head so that he thought it was time to go home—Bee couldn't stand too much noise—and he wondered if Janine Grandy, her part-time secretary, would be with them that evening. She was so good with Bee. Involved. He had an idea that Janine always did, but never wanted to, get drawn into people's lives.

'Mine eyes dazzle,' thought Cassie, catching sight of a clown; she was slightly drunk on champagne and on the occasion. As so often the three of them stood together in a group. Perhaps they were unaware how frequently they stood together just so, but their friends noticed it and called it their trademark: the three of them together, studying the world. Perhaps a hint removed, even superior? Their enemies hinted as much, but they need not have been envious. The world was about to strike back.

Kit Langley, who liked them all, stood watching. He was tall, clever and ambitious, but sometimes, in their successful femininity, they made him feel like some strange animal from another species. This was such a time.

He studied Edwina whom he loved: beneath the party glitter her face looked strained. He'd heard a bit about her lately. She did attract the oddities of life, some people did. She always had done.

He had known Edwina since childhood and it had been Edwina who had almost caught fire on her own Guy Fawkes bonfire, and Edwina who had very nearly been hanged in the dormitory at school.

Should I have spoken? he asked himself. To arm her, to protect her?

Could you protect her?

Oh, you three, he thought.

At the moment they were admiring the picture presented by their friend Lily, now the new Lady Bulkley, departing for her honeymoon in natural silk tussore and a froth of blonde curls. 'Goodbye, my trio of darlings. Edwina, remember I am a wicked stepmother, not the good fairy.' There were kisses all round and with a wave she was gone.

'The beauty,' murmured Alice appreciatively. 'She does wear clothes so well.' Wearing clothes had been Lily's profession as a much-photographed model. If she produced the heir Lord Bulkley longed for, then Lily had promised to dress the child in clothes designed by Alice and to be photographed herself with him. As she said: what was good enough for the Princess of Wales would do for her.

The noise of Kit Langley's laughter and the happy voices shouting pieces of really monstrous gossip floated out through the open

7

windows where it joined the music from Tuttons and the shouts of the children watching a Punch and Judy show, full of matrimonial fighting. Or rather, Punch beating Judy and the baby, for that was the nature of the game and one which Edwina watched, marvelling at the way the children loved the violence. It said something about human nature she'd rather not dwell upon.

Some of the guests had been drinking wine at Tuttons before they came on to the wedding, others had come from the Savoy, or the Ritz; the guests were a nice social mix. There was also a little grey cat, belonging to Cassie, who had sampled the champagne from someone's glass and was now wandering around, unsure of paw and quite tipsy. Tomorrow it was going to have a hangover of human proportions. Another hangover was coming the way of Miss Drury and Miss Dover, the middle-aged ladies known to the Garden as Ginger and Pickles, whose travelling Help-Yourself-to-Health food stall set itself up in the Garden twice weekly, and who spent the rest of the week repairing the health of the outer suburbs of Staines and Chertsey. They were popular figures and glad to be asked to the wedding: Lily was one of their best customers. So was Canon Linker who had conducted the wedding service in his tiny ancient church of St Godrun's, a stone's throw behind St Paul's, Covent Garden. He was in company with his illustrious Aunt Bee. It was the Canon's champagne the little grey cat had tippled. If he had known, he would have been glad to share, for he was a generous man, a great expert on Anglo-Saxon poetry, which made him an appropriate choice for Rector of Şt Godrun's. Also present was Dr Fisher, the local GP who got into everything. So they were all there, bar one person, who could not come and was not invited anyway; but who was there as a familiar or evil spirit.

Janine, who worked for the trio and also for Canon Linker's aunt, had stood in the sun, unobserved, outside St Godrun's to watch the bride arrive. Lily was a real beauty whose intelligence and integrity shone through her professional glossy poise. Everyone loved her, and even Janine, a cynical spirit, responded to her charm. But she would have gone to the church anyway. She often went to church, especially to St Godrun's, and in a funny kind of way she liked weddings. There was a theatrical side to church ritual (and St Godrun's was very High) which pleased her. She liked a good production, with attention to detail. When the problem with the flowers for the wedding came up—cut flowers, no flowers or false flowers—it had been Janine who, making no fuss, had solved it, knowing exactly where to go to get the artificial flowers put together naturally. Left to themselves, she thought, those girls would have

9

had the place full of bushes like jokes out of Davenport's. A joke is always welcome, her Thespian father had said (he had often shopped for jokes at Davenport's himself) but you don't want it thrust in your face. Especially at a wedding. It was amazing, Janine's thoughts continued, how wrong that talented trio could get things.

As well as the champagne the wedding cake was going around, a deliciously rich cake with an icing not too hard to take a good bite, but hard enough to leave a toothmark in it when you had bitten into it. It was too rich for one guest, whose stomach was a little queasy and who put it aside on a ledge.

It was a fantasy wedding, not the sort to end in death, but perhaps they should have been warned. It had been in the horoscopes for all three hostesses. A bad day, it had said, after which time things will never be the same again. The little grey cat was going to live to bear witness to that.

There were no flowers and not a single bridesmaid. Lily Dex, now Lady Bulkley, did not approve of cut flowers (nor of real fur, though real diamonds were all right) so all the floral decorations, all the roses, peonies and lupins that formed great splashes of colour against the white walls like a Dufy painting, were of paper, real paper, although you would never have known it. The few guests who

10

noticed or cared said lovingly that it was just ike darling Lily. One woman who was allergic to the peppery smell of peonies sneezed away happily just as if they were real.

Lily's bridal bouquet was of creamy-yellow silk. What about the silkworms before she gets her silk? Did Lily know what happens to a silkworm after it has made its silk? Or mind? No, Lily did not mind about the silkworms, all her wedding finery had been borrowed from the collection of antique wedding gowns owned by Alice Leather, and the silkworms had done their job and paid for it over a century ago. Even Lily could not weep over them.

Luke Tory represented all three girls for publicity purposes, and so the matter of the flowers was grist to his mill. It could make a paragraph in *Harpers and Queen* if he handled it right, and a splash in the *Evening Star* where he was on special terms with a gossip columnist. Luke always had an eye to the main chance, whether for himself or a client, translating that chance into money in the pocket as soon as he could. Luke liked money. He also liked information. He was a great gatherer-up of gossip and valuable to the three women on that account also. The love affairs, quarrels and shifting alliances of Chelsea, Knightsbridge and Belgravia could be important professionally to Alice and Edwina, if less so to Cassie, but even she liked to know who might be thinking of

11

endowing an extension to an art gallery or running up an office block. Amongst the very rich it was as well to know what your feet were treading in. Luke helped them to watch their step.

Luke's two interests combined in what he knew about his three principal clients. He knew more about them and their finances than they guessed. He knew that Cassie, who had left the large firm where she had won prizes and commendations, to set up her own business, was very short of money although high in contracts. He knew that Alice was working on a very tight cash margin and that her bank manager was not her best friend. He knew that Edwina had sold all her inheritance to invest in her gallery.

He also knew the great capital of inner resources and talent each had to call upon; he regarded them as bankable. They were in the fast lane.

Luke would have been on the job now, talking to the editor of a famous magazine, bussing, in his sexless way, a well-known beauty and party girl, if it had not been for a strange sensation.

'You're getting randy, dear.' He was surprised at himself. 'It must be the effect of the wedding bells.'

But it couldn't be. He knew himself too well. Nevertheless the feeling did not go away. Mild, but positive, it remained with him. He felt unreal. Floating, not happily either.

He moved round the room, talking to the right people and seeing they talked to the other right people, all the time feeling increasingly unusual. Perhaps it was aggression he was feeling. Perhaps that was what masculine aggression felt like? But he knew himself; he was not an aggressive man, nor strongly sexual.

He tried to reassure himself. 'Lovely party. Just like the dear girls to give Lily a bash like this.' He banged against one of the kings in a paper crown. 'Oh sorry, dear.'

The king did not answer, but raised a bony hand in mock salute and drifted away, leaving Luke feeling no less unreal. In his opinion all the kings had been a mistake. He liked the Cardboard-Cut-Out Theatre and was very glad for them to earn a little extra money but now they should huff off to Deptford Broadway or Woolwich Arsenal where they also set up stage to perform their carefully composed mimes and mini-plays like the strolling players of the past. The company of three men and three women existed, when they existed at all, on a small grant from the Arts Council and patrons like Edwina and Cassie. They also passed the hat round and took other jobs as they came along, to keep them going. One of the kings was passing his crown round at this moment.

To his fury, Luke saw a tenner being dropped in, and another, and not a penny taxable.

Another king appeared with a tray of drinks. 'Sorry.' Luke refused the offer. He had the uncomfortable feeling that the kings were taking over the party. 'Can't take champagne, doctor's orders. Gives me gout. Have to stick to whisky.' He held up his glass. 'Got my own supply.' Cassie's actually. She had laid on a special decanter of malt and left it in her pantry for him to help himself.

It was hard to be affable when you felt unwell. Luke made up his mind to leave the party and go home. He usually took the tube, but he might rise to a taxi tonight. 'A really supreme party,' he murmured with an effort, as he made for the door. He just managed to catch Cassie's eye.

'Yes, isn't it,' she said politely.

But the real party came afterwards when everyone had left and there were just the three of them.

As in the beginning.

*   *   *

In the beginning there were just the three of them: Cassie, Edwina and Alice. They added a couple more friends on the way up but these were not founder members and, subtly, were allowed to understand so. The two friends that were added were Lily, whose wedding had just been celebrated, and Tim. He had had his funeral.

It had been a quiet funeral, truly quiet, and had not been attended by any of the three. After the crash, his mother had travelled from Northumberland where she lived and taken his body back with her to bury before any of them, even Edwina, had known about it. No one had been happy about that but there had been no way of stopping her. So perhaps that was one reason why they had put on such a show for Lily now. 'He was a super man,' Cassie had said sadly, 'I would like to have seen him buried.'

'He wasn't willing to die,' said Alice. 'He didn't want to and I wish he hadn't.' She looked at Edwina who said nothing. Nothing at all.

At that point she did not know what lay ahead of her in full. A bit of it, certainly, a very important part, but not all. She had married her father off to Lily and that would work, for both of them, she was sure of it, and now she must face what was coming to her.

Ten years ago they had all three met at the university, enrolling in the same year and on the same day but in different faculties: Cassie Ross, Alice Leather and Edwina Fortune. It was in the act of enrolment that they found out that they had all been born on the identical day in November 1954. They were a perfect match. It was what started them off as a group. But they soon discovered they had a lot more than birthdays in common.

'Decision day,' Cassie had said happily on that day as they enrolled. She took it easily, she knew her course and saw her future clearly, but the other two were more tentative. Was it right for Edwina to study history and fine art? Was Alice making a good choice when she settled for design as her final aim in art school? Who could be sure?

But they had time to think about it. The large city university which had taken them on allowed movement within disciplines if you'd made the wrong choice.

As it turned out, they had not. Cassie became an architect and made choices all the time. Some were bad, but most were good because Cassie had talent, genius even. It was part of her job to make judgements and not to fret over them too much. Since she was an architect her choices took shape in bricks and concrete and cantilevered roofs. If she made the wrong decisions then her roofs leaked and the floors sagged beneath the weight of the bodies on them. But this did not happen often and Cassie's buildings soared upwards in confident splendour.

Their contemporaries awarded them prizes for initiative and spirit. Natural achievers, their friends said. Those three witches, said those who did not like them.

By the end of the decade they had behind them one broken marriage—Alice; a many-times-broken heart—Cassie; and one impregnable fortress—Edwina. Or so Edwina had thought.

But even their enemies admitted they were generous. They took a lot out of life but they gave a lot back. They were alike in everything but their backgrounds. Cassie came from middle-class Liverpool. Alice from the London dockland and Edwina from a beautiful shell of a house in Norfolk.

They also had success. Success expressed in solid material terms like their own businesses, pleasant places in which to live, and designer clothes.

And one death.

Not that the death was talked about much, but it was never forgotten. Only that day, in a lull between greeting guests at the reception, Tim had made his presence felt.

Alice had said to Cassie, 'He's not quite gone really, has he? That's how I feel. He still hangs around.' Like now, but this she did not say.

'Oh come on, Alice.' Cassie was brisk. She looked around the room, assessing the scene. The party seemed to be going well. Edwina looked peaky; she'd been off-colour lately. Understandable, of course, and she would not be helped by remarks such as Alice's.

'You know it's true. There are still bits and pieces of his possessions around, for one thing. I've got a book he left. He was a great leaver-

17

around of his possessions. The book's got his name in it. Makes him feel so close.'

'You've had too much champagne.'

'No. Not me. What happened to the rest of his things?'

'I don't know.' No one had wanted to involve Edwina. 'I think Kit managed that side of things. Gave stuff away. I think Jim Linker took the clothes for charities. He'd know what to do.'

Cassie, remembering this conversation now, and looking at Edwina, thought that her friend was bearing up well but not enjoying life.

'Well, my new stepmother was in very good nick.' Edwina was sitting on the floor with her shoes off, the party over, the guests sped away. Now they could talk. Alice was reclining on the only piece of furniture you could sit on in Cassie's huge bare room. Living area, she called it. Alice had her shoes off too, and her feet curled under her on the great sofa of pale Italian leather. Cassie was in her high-tech kitchen where the shining pipes crawled up the wall and a bright red Aga hummed with gas-fed heat. 'I don't know when I've seen her look better. The old man's in luck.'

'I think Lily's in luck too,' said Alice. 'I could go for the Lord myself.'

'Yes, he's always been one of the great beauties of his generation.' And it was true, Brogden Fortune, Lord Bulkley, was remarkably handsome. Edwina examined her

18

own face in the silver-gilt compact from Cartier that had been her father's present to her that day. She had inherited her own mother's round-faced, healthy look and was not a beauty, but by sheer hard work she had imposed great style on herself. She was very paintable. There was usually a portrait of her in the gallery she owned in Covent Garden. She exhibited only women artists and it was her habit to commission a portrait of herself from the best. These were not for sale. She was forming a collection which would be unique: one woman's face, late twentieth century, painted by the foremost women artists of her day. She was going to New York soon to be painted by Libby Tolam, probably the best young portrait painter of her generation. Edwina claimed to be unlike her ancestors, but in having her portrait painted she was right in line with them.

Alice said: 'Pour out the champagne, Cass. This is our private party. Us. Our own. It's very quiet, Cass. Aren't the caterers clearing up?'

'I sent them off. Told them to come back on Monday ... Put away the champagne. I have something much better.' Cassie produced a bottle, handling it carefully. 'One of the best clarets ever put down. You and your ancestors taught me to like claret, Eddie; when I came to Bulkley and had my first taste of the good stuff, I really grew up at that moment.'

She started to pour the wine and Edwina

uncurled herself and came forward for her glass.

'I always love this bit after a party when we talk it over,' went on Cassie. Once she would have said: when we have the post mortem, but one didn't talk about post mortems in front of Edwina these days. She glanced at Edwina. The girl wasn't limping any more. It had always been more of a psychic limp anyway. The doctors said there was nothing wrong with her leg. Edwina just didn't want to walk straightforward into the future, and Cassie could understand that even while she deplored it. You had to remember that Edwina had not been hurt physically. A miracle, really, because in that sort of accident she could have been killed. On hearing of Tim's death she had taken a large drink of whisky then fallen headlong down the stone stairs where she lived. Miracles did seem to happen to them. But it wasn't all up, they had their downs too, indeed they did, although outsiders never believed them.

Then she got down to the part that really amused her. 'Come on now, girls. Accounts, please. Profit and loss. Alice?'

'I don't really like doing this at Lily's wedding . . .'

'We agreed.'

'All right. Well, I have to admit it wasn't entirely a wasted occasion, businesswise . . . Louise says there's another royal baby on the way, twins this time they think, and I am being lined up to provide another christening gown since they only have the one genuine article. Not much money, but good for sales. I shan't be named, of course, but everyone will know.'

'Luke will see to that.'

'Right. What about you?'

Cassie sipped her claret. 'Must get back into the kitchen and bring the mousse through . . .'

'Tell. Don't keep us in suspense. What is it, do they want you to build a new wing to the Tate? Or the Fifth Terminal at Heathrow?'

'No, I'm not in that league yet, although I intend to be. No, the Standishes have asked me to build their new house . . . It's to be the first big country house built since Lutyens, just about. Nothing suburban or twee. It's to be grand, elegant, beautiful, that's the remit. Think of it. What a compliment.'

'What about you, Eddie?' Alice was laying the table, a great round piece covered with a red damask cloth so that you felt you were inside a Venetian painting. On it Alice was setting out a selection of battered forks and knives. Cassie had not yet got round to buying any table silver and possibly never would. Alice hoped there was some china to eat from, she had seen no sign of any in the kitchen. She removed a small pile of freshly typed letters, evidence of the recent activity of Janine Grandy, their part-time secretary.

'Oh I don't know, nothing much,' said

Edwina absently. 'It wasn't my day, I suppose. One of the Agate brothers said he might look into the gallery. Might have a sale ... Luke'll be pleased. He's always wanted an in with the Agates ... Didn't think he looked well. Odd. Did you notice?'

'No.' Cassie dismissed Luke. 'Do you like the mousse? It's structural.'

People who did not know Cassie well assumed that she was called Cassandra or Lucasta, but such an upper-class name would not have come with her background; in fact, she was called Priscilla and had given herself the change of name when it suited her.

'Delicious.'

'Eat it then.' Edwina was not eating enough lately, hadn't been doing so for some weeks, and her lovely plumpness was melting away so that you could see now what Edwina would be like when she was an old lady.

Alice was sitting there quietly like a good little girl, which was not what Alice was at all. You don't build the kind of business in the rag trade which Alice was building now by being good. Alice was hard-working, aggressive (when required to be) and lucky. She knew she was lucky and counted it her greatest asset. After a spell in a factory in Manchester to learn the ways of mass production, she had gone to Milan for a year to work in an Italian design room and returned with an Italian gloss on her streetwise

London spirit, but otherwise unchanged.

When she came back she found a hole in the fashion world and set about filling it. She designed and had made in her own workrooms beautiful clothes for beautiful, and rich (that was important), children. She went to the Victoria & Albert Museum to examine what children had worn in the seventeenth, eighteenth and nineteenth centuries. She studied paintings of the Italian Renaissance and went to look at Renoir's little girls in the Louvre. From these studies she drew ideas and created clothes which were not copies but modern, wearable clothes of great charm and some little nostalgia. These clothes were beautifully made and very expensive. Then, six months later, copies of these expensive clothes were mass produced, under franchise, with Alice taking a royalty, in a factory in South London. The couture clothes were labelled simply 'Alice'; the cheaper editions were called 'Alice in Wonderland', and that was where the real money was, but you couldn't have the one without the other.

Alice's showrooms were round the corner from Edwina's gallery and next door to Cassie's warehouse. United in their birthdays, they were still sticking together in their workplaces. Only Cassie lived in the Garden, however, for Edwina's home was round the corner in Packet's Place and Alice lived in Lowndes Square.

'Lily made a beautiful bride,' said Edwina. The food tasted like nothing in her mouth. It was funny lately the way food did not taste. 'I'm worried about Luke. Let's ring him up.'

'You were late today,' said Cassie. 'Only just in your seat before Lily arrived.'

'I know. I had to see the doctor.'

'Your leg again? You've seen the doctor a lot lately.'

'There are other reasons for seeing the doctor,' said Edwina quietly. Cassie looked at Alice, then they both looked at Edwina.

'Yes, I'm pregnant. And yes, of course it's Tim's child. And yes, he did know. Just. I told him a few days before the accident. And it was an accident. He didn't crash on purpose.'

'Of course,' said Alice quickly. Perhaps too quickly.

Cassie turned away. She did not believe, and never had, that the car crash in which Tim had died was an accident. But she had no real evidence one way or another, all was buried in Scottish mist. Tim had never been accident-prone although, in her heart, she had thought him a danger to others. Very attractive, but dangerous.

Tim's death remained a mystery. News of the pregnancy did not solve the mystery but it certainly added to the pain of bearing it.

'Why didn't you tell us before?'

'I think I just needed to be private with it for a

24

little while.'

'The first of us to produce a child,' said Cassie. 'We've been slow, Alice. Congratulations, love, the second generation of Us. This is our baby.'

'My baby,' corrected Edwina. 'You have your own.'

'Share?' Cassie held out her hands hopefully. 'We always do.'

A faint resentment stirred in Edwina, the first time she had felt such a feeling with her friends. They did share. Always. But she did not wish to this time. This was a baby. Not a property.

'I miss Tim,' she said.

'He was a lovely man,' said Alice sadly. 'I loved him. But not in the way you'd mind. Isn't it lucky we never fancied each other's men?'

'Speak for yourself,' said Edwina. 'I fancied your Peter like mad. But I held back when I saw you were serious.'

'I wish you'd taken him.' Alice's marriage had been a short-lived, if hilarious, disaster. She still saw Peter, who was a successful, cheerful, drunken journalist, prematurely bald.

'You've gone quite white.' Cassie was concerned. She stood up. 'Let me get you some whisky. I don't think Luke took it all.'

The telephone rang. Edwina said, 'Don't answer it.'

The girls had been receiving anonymous silent telephone calls. The invasion had started with Edwina, spread to Cassie and moved on to Alice like an infection.

The calls were irregular, might come at any time but were recognisable as from the same source by the way the caller always rang twice within the half-hour. It was as if that caller wanted to establish an identity.

Cassie hesitated about answering the telephone now.

'*Don't.*'

'It's just breathing. Silly stuff.'

Edwina said, 'He's started to talk. Yesterday he spoke.'

'Saying what?'

'The usual thing. What they usually say. Then he said he was someone I knew.'

'They always say that.'

'Might be true,' said Alice. 'We're all ex-directory. How did he get our numbers?'

Edwina shrugged. Who knew? Did it matter? And how could they tell?

'Should we tell the police?'

'I already have,' said Edwina.

'And?'

'Not much use. Not interested. Too much of it about. They were polite but not helpful.'

'I suppose it *is* a man?' Cassie was thoughtful.

'What do you mean?' Edwina was surprised.

'Suppose it was a boy? An adolescent. That would make it no more than a nasty kid's trick.'

Edwina thought about it. 'No. I'll tell you

why. I heard background noises. Sounded like a pub. I don't think a boy would do that. Kids ring from home when Mum's out and they're bored. Only a man would ring from a pub.'

'Someone doesn't like us.' Alice was light, deliberately so. Alice thought of her husabnd and Fanny Eisler who had been at design school with her. Fanny was dead now, of course ... Cassie thought of the ,assistant she had dismissed. Edwina thought about Tim's mother.

'Someone *hates* us.' Edwina stood up. They had enemies all right, enemies they had made on their journey to success. 'And I think we ought to be careful.'

'Oh, it's just a joke.'

'Is it? There's sex and violence behind the calls. I can feel it, I tell you. Perhaps it's just for me. I feel it is.'

Fear had crept in. They who feared nothing, who had sped about the city, about the world, intent on their own business and afraid of no one, now knew fear. They were worldly, intelligent young women, not to be alarmed by an obscene telephone call, but the stranger had opened up a crack and let the virus in.

Alice hesitated. 'You don't think ... it couldn't possibly ...? It couldn't be Luke playing some game on us?'

'Funny game,' said Cassie. 'A sick joke.'

'He's looked sick lately,' said Alice.

'He doesn't eat properly,' responded Cassie, an ardent disciple of healthy foods and a keen shopper at Ginger and Pickles' stall. 'All that fuss about wine not suiting him and having to drink whisky instead. That's his trouble. I can't see him upsetting us. We're business, and you know how Luke feels about that.'

'It's not Luke,' said Edwina, as if she knew.

They looked at her.

'I've seen him. At least, his back view as he walked away and it wasn't Luke ... He came into the gallery while I was out. Dougie spoke to him.' Douglas Clark was her assistant. 'He was tall, sallow, wearing dark spectacles and he asked for me. By name. Tell Edwina.' She stopped. Dougie had described the voice: harsh, high, whiny. That was it.

'Tell Edwina what?'

'That I'm looking for her.'

'You'd better answer that phone,' said Alice.

'It stopped some time ago,' said Cassie.

Then it began to ring again. That made the twice.

*　　*　　*

Luke had taken a taxi home. He had given his address then crawled into the cab, opening the window. He needed air.

'Don't let the rain in.' The driver loved his cab. 'That leather you're sitting on is new.'

28

'It's not raining.'

'A storm coming any minute.'

There's a storm inside me, thought Luke, raging around. He could feel the turmoil rise to a crest within him.

Someone had left an evening paper on the seat and his eyes fell on a headline.

POLICEMAN IN ROBBERY PLOT

Police Constable Edward Miller, aged 22, living in Wilberforce Street, WC, and James Meckendorf of Hounslow, were jointly charged in the conspiracy to commit a robbery in Slough.

Luke pushed the paper away and groaned. 'All I needed. Oh, the bloody fool.'

Feeling even sicker, his symptoms now including a terrible burning sensation in his guts combined with an inability to swallow, Luke lay back. Every organ, inside and out, seemed to be swelling and taking on a life of its own. He ordered the taxi to the nearest hospital.

This turned out to be the Skin Hospital, off Shaftesbury Avenue, and it was another fifteen minutes by the time he arrived at St Thomas's Hospital, Lambeth.

By this time the storm had broken. But it was not water that was staining the taxi's leather.

The taxi driver had been proud of his cab but it wasn't on his mind now. 'Poor little bugger, poor little bugger,' he kept repeating.

And his passenger had been muttering something. Tell Eddie, had it been? Well, it could have been, and he had to hope that whoever Eddie was, he would find out.

*   *   *

When Luke arrived in hospital, barely conscious, the young doctor who received him speedily called in his senior.

Luke could still talk, just. The doctor listened, and made out what he could. 'Yes, I think I've got what you want. I'll do what I can. Calm down, feller.'

He was a bright young man, but glad when his experienced registrar appeared.

'He's had violent diarrhoea with a big haemorrhage. He's bad.'

The registrar made a quick examination. 'My guess is an irritant poison of some sort. Can he say? Suggest anything?'

Luke could not, he was a bit beyond giving them much help. He tried, but could remember nothing he'd eaten or drunk that was special. But he wanted someone to tell Edwina.

The registrar gave a number of swift orders. Luke was hurried into the Intensive Care Unit.

This was at 10.30 p.m. At intervals the young doctor tried to phone the number Luke had given him. No one answered. At 12.30 a.m.

Luke slipped into a coma from which he did not emerge. It would have to be the police.

★   ★   ★

The evening ended sooner than their evenings usually did. When Edwina said she was tired and was going home to bed there was no argument. In her condition she needed rest. The other two conceded this.

The telephone had rung twice more, with short intervals, but had remained unanswered. Cassie had found this hard to bear. She was a girl who usually rushed to answer the telephone, longing to know.

Alice got into her car to drive away to Lowndes Square. Edwina was going to leave her car where it was parked and walk across the Garden and round the corner to where she lived. She'd drunk too much to drive, she said. They all knew she was nervous of driving these days.

Before she left Alice said to Cassie, 'Do you think there's anything in this telephone business?'

Cassie shrugged. 'Might be.'

'Or just Eddie being imaginative.'

'She's not usually.'

'No.' Alice considered. 'But then she's not been pregnant before . . . I suppose that's true?'

'Alice!'

'Yes, sorry. Forget I said it. But she was very

31

upset over Tim, even more than she showed, I think ... We ought to look after her. She's very vulnerable. Agreed?'

It was the first time any one of them had used that word to describe themselves. Or even thought it could apply to them.

Cassie nodded.

'Right then, it's up to us.'

'About these telephone calls—' Alice began.

'Yes?'

'There's Kit Langley,' said Alice. 'He's in love with Eddie if I'm any judge. And he didn't like Tim any too much.'

'He's not a creep.'

'No. Probably not.'

'*No*,' said Cassie.

★　　★　　★

While they were still talking Edwina gave them a brisk goodbye and set off home. She walked carefully and slowly round the open square then turned the corner into Packet's Place. As she passed she could see the lighted windows of Alice's shop where an Edwardian perambulator was draped with a lace christening robe. A few yards away was her own gallery where the beautiful Thistlewaite landscape was held in the light of a single spot.

The square was quieter now, emptier, but a few pedestrians and the odd taxi were on the move.

There were always ghosts in the Garden, but Edwina loved them. To begin with there were the ghosts of the old market porters. You could still smell the odour of rotting vegetables and overripe fruit when the air warmed up. But as well as these, Edwina could imagine the ghosts of opera stars and actresses from the past. Tetrazzini, Melba and Callas walking together, then Mrs Siddons on her way to Drury Lane, while Ellen Terry rattled past in a cab to her home close by. They were all there in the Garden.

There were two other ghosts, too. Newer ones. The ghosts of a happy Edwina walking home holding Tim's hand.

She missed Tim. It was all very well being a solitary parent, but you needed the man. She did, anyway, and it was a revelation to her that pregnancy could make her so weak. She'd always been the stronger one.

Now she felt vulnerable, as though not only might terrible events befall her, but she might even attract them. This was one of the extraordinary by-products of pregnancy and one she had not expected. Yet it had been a feeling of fear, a cold tremor in the pit of her stomach, that had announced her pregnancy to her.

As soon as she had felt it one morning on waking, she had sat up in bed and said, 'That's it. I'm *enceinte*.' She didn't need any tests or any doctor to tell her. She told *him*.

Edwina lived on the top floor of a tall old house. On the ground floor was a jeweller's shop, above that offices, and above that Edwina. She had done the conversion herself and it was total. Like Cassie she wanted space and you opened the front door into one great light room where the canvases that Edwina had not displayed in her gallery were hung in lines or propped up against the wall.

She had more furniture than Cassie and her spoons were silver but otherwise you could tell that they were young women of similar tastes who were likely to be friends. Alice was different. She lived in a cosy clutter.

Edwina unlocked her door and let herself in. One light shone at the end of the room, a spotlight on her favourite picture of the month: she always had one. Later, she would sell it.

This month's picture was a tiny seascape of the Clyde estuary by Lizzie Macalinden.

Not a flat to bring up a child in, she thought as she closed the door behind her. I'll have to create a nursery.

On a table at the end of the room stood her telephone answering machine. A machine that had just lately become an enemy to be feared. There was another in the gallery and that was an enemy too. She switched it on: better to do it sooner than later. Unthinkable to go to bed and let the secret voice whisper on unheard.

34

The first message was a business appointment.

She made a note of it on a pad: lunch at the Connaught. Good, she loved the Connaught, and this American collector of paintings was about to buy one of her most valuable pictures: a country scene by Anne Redpath.

The second message was from Lily. 'Darling stepdaughter,' said that light, cheerful voice. 'This is to tell you how happy I am. Also your Dad. I'll look after him, Eddie, and love him. Promise.'

The last message had come through at twenty-three hours and twenty-three minutes precisely, because the speaker said so.

Edwina looked at the clock on the wall. The hands were coming towards the half-hour. Less than ten minutes since the call had come in. She had been on her way from the Garden to Packet's Place.

The voice said in its harsh, high whisper, 'I want you to know, Edwina, that I am coming close to you. You, Edwina. I shall be close. Pretty close, Edwina. You can tell the others. They are out of it now. Only you. Goodnight.'

There was no second call. The voice obviously meant what it said.

Reluctantly, Edwina got herself ready for bed. Somehow, she did not fancy tomorrow. Another bloody day.

Edwina slid into that deep, heavy sleep that seemed to be her way at the moment. Perhaps it was something her body demanded. Or possibly it was a way of escape.

Either way her sleep was sullen and heavy. But dreamless. In her sleep Edwina was neither loving nor loved. Just a mindless sack in which another body grew. That was how it felt when she woke up, as if night was a growing time.

Cassie slept lightly and peacefully as was her wont. She had strong nerves and an imagination harnessed to practical things. She never ever dreamt of a roof falling in on a building of hers; her roof never would. She claimed she did not dream at all. Nevertheless, she was troubled. The tiny seed of disquiet that the telephone caller had planted was growing even in her sceptical soul. But she was heedless of the débris of the wedding party: glasses, plates, empty champagne bottles lay all around. The wedding, or what was left of it, still stood in unprotected splendour. The cleaners would be in on Monday, the caterers would clear away. Till then Cassie could forget it. So she slept, ignorant that the disorderly room spelt trouble.

Alice was curled in her pretty brass-and-white enamelled bedstead, trimmed with muslin and blue bows, which was so much more practical than it looked. As was Alice herself. She was half asleep and half awake. All the time she was thinking. Alice always said she could think in her sleep, and her friends believed she could. Anyway, she often woke up with her decisions made. Now she was thinking about Edwina whom she loved but for whom she feared. She was certain it was on Edwina that the trouble centred. All right, they were all contaminated now, but it had started with Edwina. There was something about Edwina at the moment that made her attractive and yet vulnerable at the same time. Edwina felt it herself and Alice accepted it. Being pregnant was part of it, but Alice felt there was something else.

Edwina was still mourning Tim. Mourning is magnetic, attracting and repelling at the same time.

Alice had no doubt that sex came into it, somewhere, but she did not propose to question Edwina. Although they were so close as a group, they respected each other's privacy and did not ask questions. So about Edwina's life Alice could only guess from what she saw. Certainly Edwina had loved Tim. But there might have been other men on the edge of her life. Alice could think of a few, even name them. Mark Darbyshire, the painter; Alec Farmer who was a successful barrister and Johnny Dishart who seemed to do nothing at all and had the money to do so. But she couldn't see any of *them* ringing Edwina (not to mention the other two) with silent lust.

The telephone caller seemed to have mixed feelings about Edwina, hating her and yet being attracted. And why did Alice feel sure that the caller was not just one of those poor, dismal beings who get a kick out of making obscene calls? Alice asked herself that question as she came fully awake.

Because Alice knew something that the other two did not.

She too had seen the caller.

A week ago she had watched Edwina walk across the Garden to her gallery. Behind her had stalked a tall figure in a dark suit. Alice had noticed but thought nothing of it at the time; now she remembered with alarm that figure flitting behind the oblivious Edwina.

Canon Linker was in bed but awake. He was an insomniac with no real talent for sleep. So he amused himself with reading theology and crime in about equal shares. Tonight his reading would be divided between the Bishop of Durham and Miss Elizabeth Ferrars. He settled back comfortably, sure of a treat.

Before going to bed he had settled Aunt Bee for the night and arranged all the objects around her that she liked within easy reach: her piece of amber to hold, the rose to smell, and the silver Thermos of tea. He had made the tea himself, but it had been Mrs Grandy who had placed the tape recorder ready where it was in case Bee felt like getting on with Chapter Eleven. He believed it was Chapter Eleven. Every day he thanked heaven for Janine who gave Aunt Bee such comfort and help. She was a perfect secretary, coming when she was wanted and melting away when she was not. She operated from a small typing and secretarial agency she had set up for herself, called Mrs Grandy's Agency.

Two years now since Bee had finally admitted it, and six months since she had come to live with him. 'See you in the morning,' he said to her as he closed her bedroom door. He still found it hard to accept that Aunt Bee was blind.

Before getting himself and Bee home from the wedding he had superintended the homeward journey of Ginger and Pickles who had had a touch too much to drink. They had wobbled off happily in the old van. He hoped the police did not find them. They were happy, though, and had thrust a carton of special Bulgarian yoghurt as a thank-you present into his unwilling hands. He hadn't put it into the refrigerator yet, he remembered, it was still sitting in his car. Be pretty ripe in the morning.

But he was not really thinking about Aunt Bee just then, although she came into it. In a way he blamed her for his anxiety. She had a way of opening windows in the mind that you could never afterwards close. In this instance, she had reminded him of the old nurserymaid who had sent a series of vicious anonymous letters around the village before drowning herself. 'There was a cloud of darkness hanging over that girl, darkness made visible, and one of us should have spotted it and done something to help her. Not you; you were only a child.'

He did not remember the nursemaid, or whether he had seen a cloud of darkness, but he had seen blackness himself that day as he had entered his own church when it was full of flowers and lighted candles ready for Lily's wedding. Ahead of him he saw a tall thin figure, back towards him, sitting in a pew.

The head was bent forward, but somehow not in the attitude of prayer. No, this person was sitting there in unhappy thought. A cloud of darkness seemed to hang about the figure. It was an emotional and mental darkness rather than a physical one. He couldn't say he actually *saw* it, but it was certainly there: the mind recognised it.

He stepped forward to say something when he was interrupted by the verger, come with some problem about the organ. When he was free again, the figure had gone, taking the darkness with it.

Now that he thought about it, he knew the episode had frightened him. It was a kind of spiritual loitering with intent. He recognised it without knowing what to do about it, or even knowing what it meant.

40

Poor soul, he said to himself. Poor soul.

Something, somehow, had to be done. He gave that little lift of the shoulders that meant that, unconsciously, he had accepted responsibility.

Ginger and Pickles, Miss Drury and Miss Dover, slept noisily because they had drunk most champagne at the wedding and enjoyed the party most. They didn't get out much, the demands of their Help-Yourself-to-Health life were considerable. Both were dedicated but Pickles was the theorist and intellectual of the two. 'Our philosopher', as Ginger admiringly called her. She was also far and away the more adventurous. Miss Drury, Ginger, was content to get most of her supplies from a hygienic factory in Hertfordshire, adding to them a few simples made up by herself from her herb garden. Camomile tea, peppermint cordial and feverfew tablets were her specialities.

But Pickles' imagination took in a wider stretch reaching to India, China and South America from whence she imported such remedies as Dragon's Breath, Elephant's Ear and the Energy of Man, Potions One, Two and Three. She had a busy market for the Energy of Man, although she usually advised caution in the use of strength Number Three. Afterwards, she saw that the other side of a warning is encouragement. It all depended on what you wanted. She was told to take her share of blame

41

when it came to be handed out.

Pickles got up just after midnight to stumble to the bathroom. She too had seen the tall thin figure, but had not noticed the cloud of darkness, wouldn't have known it if she had seen it but, perhaps unconsciously responding to it, had put extra force into the warning on Energy of Man, strength Number Three. You need it, Chummie, she had thought. She knew what the dark spectacles meant, didn't want to be recognised, now or ever. As if she cared, but they always thought she did.

While Ginger had made their cup of acorn coffee (she always hated the customers that Pickles called 'Chummie' and kept well away) Pickles had watched her customer skirt the Cardboard-Cut-Out Theatre, cross the Garden and go towards the car park behind the Duke of York. This Chummie knew his way around the Garden, that was clear. You had to be local to know where to park.

Pickles went to the kitchen to pour some water down her parched throat. She looked out of the window: rain was pouring down, she felt like death.

It was quiet with her as with all those named: Edwina, Cassie, Alice and Canon Linker. Quiet and dark.

Unlike the brightly lit, organised frenzy of the hospital where Luke lay.

CHAPTER TWO

At 12.50 a.m. Luke slipped into that deep coma from which he did not emerge. Eight hours later he died.

At eight o'clock on Monday morning the police were on Edwina's doorstep. They had taken twenty-four hours to get there; but they had had to discover her. She represented the end of a chain.

When he was taken ill Luke had been wearing morning dress with a pretty white rose they later discovered to be made of silk in his buttonhole. The white rose had blood on it. In a breast pocket he had his wallet with his name and address. In another pocket he had his house-keys; the taxi driver had added the evening newspaper which he had folded up, and thrust into yet another pocket, believing it to be Luke's and feeling a superstitious, even primitive, need to rid himself of any personal possession of his unlucky passenger.

The doorbell rang and Edwina sleepily opened the door in her dressing gown.

There were two policemen in the new mould: Detective Sergeant William Crail in a soft white shirt, short blue jacket and blue jeans, and Woman Detective Constable Elsie Lewis, also in a soft white shirt and blue denim skirt. They

43

looked neat, clean, polite and classless. Sergeant Crail knew how to be menacing and overbearing but he did not often have to use these gifts, just to hint that he had them in reserve; WDC Lewis knew how to be tough and persistent and she used these traits all the time. They made a good pair bcause they liked each other enough but not too much.

Their first call had been to Luke's own flat, small, cosy. Bijou seemed the word. No one had answered the bell, so they looked at each other and opened the door with Luke's own key. On the hall table was an engraved invitation to Lily's wedding. They made a note of that: they had reason to be interested in where Luke had been in the hours before his death and where he had eaten and drunk. They might have gone straight round to Cassie then, but for the letter they found in a prominent position on Luke's desk, as if he wanted to be sure to find it.

On writing paper boldly headed with Edwina's name, her private address and her gallery address, she had written:

Dear Luke,
Yes, if you want a meeting although I can't think what you have to say about Tim. Monday at ten sharp at Packet's Place as I have to get off to Edinburgh on the shuttle.
Eddie

44

Back at the station, running a quick check before being on their way, the computer turned up Edwina's name and her report of the telephone calls.

So for the sergeant, the anonymous telephone caller and the death of Luke were firmly knitted together in his mind from the beginning.

Edwina knew they were police without being told and at once she thought of the telephone calls.

'What's happened?'

'It's about Mr Tory, I'm afraid. He's a friend of yours? I'm afraid he's, well, he's dead, Miss Fortune.' The sergeant had her name off pat, Edwina did not fail to notice that. 'He died in St Thomas's early yesterday ... We found the invitation to the wedding with your name and address on it ... We're trying to trace his next of kin. We thought you might know.'

Relief that it wasn't the tall stranger for the moment removed all shock and surprise about Luke and she was able to answer rationally that as far as she knew he had no living relatives. Nor many friends, she added after a pause.

'He works for us,' she said. 'For the three of us: me, Cassie and Alice. And others, publicity, PR work, that sort of thing.'

'So you don't really know much about him?'

Edwina shook her head. 'He knew more about us than we ever knew about him. How did he die?' She was still trying to take it in.

45

By now they were all in Edwina's living room. No one was sitting down but standing stiffly in the centre of the room.

'Ah.' The sergeant was not committing himself. 'Well, we're not sure yet. About the next of kin now . . .'

'I can't tell you that. But I can give you the address of his solicitors. I've got it somewhere. I haven't got it here. It'll be in my gallery among my business papers, but I know it was a City firm. Oldgate Street, I think.'

'Your gallery, miss?'

'I have an art gallery in Covent Garden.'

'Ah.' It was his favourite word at the moment. Or seemed to be to Edwina. She wished he would change it. Then she realised that it was not a word, just a means of retaining control of the conversation.

'He was at a wedding reception on Saturday? Yes. You'd be there too?' Edwina nodded. 'It was held at Miss Ross's address? I think a call there is indicated. Do much eating or drinking at it, did he?'

'Why are you asking me that?' Edwina's voice was sharp. 'What is all this?'

'Now, Miss Fortune,' said Elsie Lewis in a placatory way. But she didn't push it because she recognised in Edwina's voice the imperative, inherited from generations of the ruling class, and, against her will, responded by going quiet.

'It looks as though he was poisoned, Miss

Fortune,' said the sergeant. 'Shall we go and see Miss Ross? And would you come too? I think it would be appropriate.'

'Do you mean deliberately poisoned or by accident?'

'We don't know yet. It has to be established.' The sergeant kept his voice neutral. 'But we have to find out where he took the poison, and one of the last places he ate and drank before falling ill was the wedding reception. I take it he did eat and drink there?'

'Yes, as far as I know he did.' Luke had certainly drunk.

'And your reply to his request for an interview—what did he want?'

Edwina said bleakly, 'I have no idea.'

'It was about someone called Tim?'

'A man I was going to marry. He's dead. He was killed in an accident about two months ago.'

Sergeant Crail apologised. 'I'm sorry. I can see it's painful for you. But it might be important. Let's leave it for now and go round to where the wedding reception was held.'

'Just let me get dressed.'

Edwina reappeared very soon in pale summer colours and white shoes. 'We might as well walk, it's as quick as driving.'

At the door she paused. 'Luke ... I can't take it in. And poisoned. No, it doesn't seem possible ... I really ought to make some telephone calls. I'm supposed to be going to

Edinburgh.'

'Later please, Miss Fortune. Let's get round to Miss Ross now, if you will.' Then he said, 'No more unpleasant telephone calls, Miss Fortune?'

'You know about those then? No, not today.' Then Edwina went quiet as they walked round the corner to Cassie's.

It was a calm, hot morning, the sort of day that Edwina normally loved; there was a delicacy and gentleness about the day that suited her. It would have been a good day in Edinburgh and her pictures would have sold well, but Luke's death altered all that. It was still hard to believe.

Canon Linker saw them walking towards Cassie's door as he strode through the street towards St Godrun's. He had no difficulty in recognising that there was trouble. He knew the policeman to begin with, but he did not rush across to offer his help. Experience had taught him to keep out until asked in. You didn't have to wait for words, he knew how to tell when he was needed and this moment was not it.

Miss Drury and Miss Dover, just opening up their stall, also saw Edwina and the police, and were passionately interested without feeling the least desire to go forward with a sympathetic smile. They had no love of the police, had had a brush with Sergeant Crail over some drugs that had been imported, and didn't like his style.

Innocence got you nowhere with him.

Janine Grandy saw them as she circled the Cardboard-Cut-Out Theatre which was not yet stirring for the day. She looked at Edwina who, to her acute eye, seemed to be carrying her anxiety as if she was carrying a suitcase. She shook her head and hurried on to Miss Beatrice Linker who was her employer for the day. Janine only undertook casual, daily work. It suited her better that way and she was self-employed anyway. She noticed that in spite of her undoubted tension Edwina was dressed in a silk-twill jump suit of melon pink and looked delightful in it. Putting on weight, though. That would never do. So she smiled at Edwina who gave a tense, abstracted smile back. Janine had done temporary secretarial work for all three friends since Bee recommended her. Not their business affairs, of course, just social and personal letters.

Edwina hardly knew she'd smiled, except that there was nice Janine Grandy and she mustn't be rude. Noblesse oblige. She remembered that Luke too had employed Janine once or twice: she would have to be told he was dead. Damn. Dear Luke. She didn't want to be the one to write his obituary. She turned to the sergeant.

'Here we are.'

He nodded. Of course he knew. But it was her hand that pressed the doorbell, choosing the one marked 'House' and not the one below the brass plate that read: 'C. Ross, Chartered Architect'. Not for Cassie the discreet initials, ARIBA, she put her craft big and plain.

Round the corner Edwina could see that the caterer's van from the Maison Blanchette was parked. So they had arrived to clear away the débris.

'Must have been a lovely wedding,' said the woman detective, volunteering an independent remark for the first time. 'Lily Dex. I saw her walk into the church.'

Lily had gone in at a fast trot, unwilling for once to be photographed. This was her life, private, no pictures, please.

'I saw her picture in the Sunday paper next day. Of course, she'll have lots of other weddings, I suppose.' A tiny trace of spite.

'Oh I hope not,' said Edwina. 'It's my father she married, this time.'

Cassie opened the door. The little grey cat was with her, both were yawning. Cassie had on a striped linen skirt that emphasised her height.

'Early, aren't you?' Then she saw the policeman and her face changed. 'Edwina, what's up? Are you all right?'

'No. Yes. Let's come in.'

As Cassie stood aside, a young woman with a crest of purple and yellow hair set in a cockade above her brow bounced up. She wore a white tabard overall with the words *Maison Blanchette* splashed across. Behind her were two other young women.

'Hi. Millie Cane. We've arrived to do the chores. Super party.' Her accent was pure Sloane Ranger. 'Bit late. Sorry about that.' She gave a radiant smile. 'Was at the Windsor Horse Show last night. Kept it up a bit. Definitely fragile this morning.' She didn't look it, she looked as strong as one of those horses she so much admired. 'Must get to work.'

'Go ahead,' said Cassie. 'The door at the head of the stairs is yours.'

'Right.'

'No, don't,' said Sergeant Crail sharply.

Millie Cane opened her big eyes wide so that the black kohl that ringed them showed to full strength.

'Look here,' said Cassie.

'Everything's to be left undisturbed.' He faced Cassie. 'Mr Tory died of poison. By the timing he could have taken it in at this wedding reception.'

Cassie drew back, her eyes met William Crail's on a level. She was about his height. 'I'm confused.' But her eyes did not look confused, he thought. Only sharp and observant. She motioned them forward. 'Come on then, up the stairs.'

Millie Cane padded up behind them. 'I'm being paid, you see.'

Cassie said to William Crail, 'You needn't look me through and through and up and down.

51

I'm a woman. Another look will confirm it.'

'I know,' said William Crail. And he did. So Cassie was the second of them to learn about the death of Luke.

Alice was the last of the three to hear of the death. She heard when she went into her shop to start the day. Her assistant, Nesta, a tiny Welsh girl, had already opened up.

'Telephone,' said Nesta, handing it over. 'No,' she said as Alice raised an eyebrow. 'Nothing of that sort.' Nesta knew all about the telephone calls. 'It's Miss Ross.'

She had watched cracks begin to appear in the solid wall of her employer's friendship with the other two. She was one of those who had found their strong bond annoying, perhaps she envied them. Now she was surprised how sad it made her feel to see the tiny splits opening; one appeared now as Alice slowly picked up the telephone. Once she would have hurried.

'Alice here.' She listened. 'That's terrible. I'll come right round.' She sounded shocked.

She got up and went to where her diary rested on Nesta's desk. A meeting with her accountant, a call from an American buyer, luncheon appointment with a big manufacturer.

'Cancel all that, please.' She closed the book. 'I don't know when I'll be back. I'll be with Miss Ross. Get me there if you have to.'

'It's Mr Luke, isn't it?' asked Nesta, bright of eye.

'Yes. How did you know?'

'Word gets around.' Nesta was not willing to admit that her source was a certan taxi driver whom she was seeing a lot of these last weeks. It might be something or nothing, their relationship, and to talk about it could bring bad luck. Sometimes her dark Welsh blood stirred beneath her London chatter.

Alice strode the few yards to Cassie's establishment. She was very frightened. She had a strong feeling in her guts that something bad awaited her. In her own way she was as superstitious as Nesta and that morning she had seen a blackbird on her bedroom windowsill, perched there staring at her as she made up her face. Worst of all, she had first seen it reflected in her mirror. That was really bad. She was too sophisticated to admit this to herself, but it was there, and behind it all she heard her grandmother's voice saying to her, aged ten: Never walk on the left-hand side of the street on a Thursday, and spit when you see a blackbird. Come to think of it, it was her grandmother's wincey petticoats and tucked muslin blouses that had influenced Alice's first collection. Or the second, anyway, the first had been different.

Even as Alice got to Cassie's door a police car drew up behind her and three men got out and were past her and into the house before her. Cassie met her on the stairs.

'Come on up. It's open-house day.' She

sounded resigned.

'And what are they doing?'

'Searching . . . Glad you've come.'

'I ought to be working,' said Alice.

Edwina appeared silently at the head of the stairs. 'No work today. I ought to be in Edinburgh, Cassie was going to design a country house, but the police say No.'

'You make it sound easy.'

Now they were all together it was easier for them to face whatever there was to face.

They had faced terrible things together before. It had been bad when Cassie had been sued by an assistant for sexual prejudice and unfair dismissal, with enough truth to make Cassie cringe. When Alice had been accused of copying another designer's model; stealing, that had been called, but it had not been true, and Alice with many a pang of conscience (Alice had suffered then not for this, but for things done earlier) had brazened it out. Yes, they had gone through bad times together.

One of the worst had been when Tim died and his mother swept in taking him away for burial, in a way that seemed like a condemnation of them all, and Edwina in particular. That still wanted looking into.

'Poor Luke,' said Edwina. 'Poor Luke.'

'It was in our horoscopes,' said Cassie gloomily. 'Remember? After Saturday it was never going to be the same again. It won't be.'

'He wanted to see me,' said Edwina. 'He said he wanted to talk to me about Tim. This morning it would have been. About now.'

'I wonder what he wanted?'

'I shall never know.' Edwina kept her voice level. 'Not now.'

'We could consult our horoscopes.'

'Don't, Cassie. It's not funny.'

Alice said, 'You two know more than I do. You've seen the police, they've talked to you.'

'Not much.'

'Tell what you know,' she commanded. 'So Luke is dead. He was poisoned. What sort of poison and how?'

Edwina and Cassie looked at each other and it was Cassie who answered. 'They don't say much but Luke died of a dose of an irritant poison. I think they have had a guess at what it may be, but they did not name it while I was listening. Funny note in the voice, though, as if it meant something odd to them. Almost jokey, damn them.'

She paused. 'And now they are looking to see if they can find traces of the poison here. Going through every glass and dirty coffeecup, I suppose.'

'I wonder if they expect to find anything that way?'

'Oh, I suppose these forensic scientists have techniques. Perhaps they just use their noses to begin with. Or the sense of taste.'

Edwina said, 'I'm going to see what's going on.'

She went out of the sunlit room, up the short flight of stairs and through the big double doors to the room where the wedding party had been held. She saw the police squad spread around the room, not tasting the remains in every glass and dish—that had been entirely a flight of Cassie's fancy—but instead neatly packing away everything that had contained food and drink in flat containers ready to be removed for forensic study. The reality of it all hit her then. Until that moment it had been a horrible dream, but now the total professionalism of what was going on carried a worse conviction. This was not only real, it was threatening. She felt the threat, she felt menace in the air.

She turned her head to where she could get a view of Cassie's kitchen. Sergeant Crail was in there doing his own inspection. He had his gloved hand on the decanter of whisky and was sniffing a glass. His gaze was on Edwina. If she expected him to make some comment or offer an explanation, none was forthcoming.

'Can I make some coffee?'

'Not just at the moment if you don't mind, Miss Fortune.' There was no hint of mirth in his voice. Some people made jokes about Edwina's name. This he would never do, not his style at all, but he managed to convey that he felt her name to be strange. He never tried to put people at ease. Rather the reverse.

Edwina returned to her friends. Alice was smoking and Cassie was on the telephone, characteristic drugs in both instances. Cassie seemed to be having difficulty in making her call.

'Who's she phoning?'

'A journalist chum. If there's any publicity she only wants the best for us.'

Edwina shrugged.

Cassie emerged from her tussle with the telephone. 'Annoying. She's out.'

'Just as well. I don't think Sergeant Crail would be pleased.'

'Oh him.' Cassie dropped her voice a tone.

Edwina recognised the note in her voice. My God, she likes him. Her friend never ceased to amaze her. It could be mutual, too. Cassie rarely mistook her market.

'I tried to make us some coffee but the sergeant wouldn't let me in the kitchen. They're all over the place out there. You ought to take a look.'

Cassie got up. 'Yes. I might do that. They didn't ask permission. I suppose the police never do.'

'We ought to be thinking about Luke.' Alice stopped smoking and put out her cigarette, as if it seemed bad taste to smoke.

'I am thinking about Luke. And about us. And I'm also thinking the police must believe we poisoned him.'

'You're joking.' Alice put out a hand for her cigarettes again. 'Oh God, I shouldn't smoke so much, I'll kipper all the layettes...'

'No, Cassie's right,' said Edwina in a decisive tone. 'If he was poisoned, and if he took the stuff here, never mind how, then we are bound to come into it.'

'But murder...'

It was the first time the word had come out between them.

'I never said murder.' Edwina's voice was cool.

'No.' Alice had taken out a cigarette and was holding it, unlit. 'I wish I hadn't.'

But the word was out.

'Let's think about this,' said Edwina. She felt as if someone hard and calm, outside herself, had taken control.

'Go on.' Cassie gave her a nod.

'Luke has died of poison. We don't know of what poison. Possibly the police don't know yet, but I think they have made a guess. By the timing (which the doctors must have estimated) he took it on Saturday at the reception we gave Lily and my father. Before he died Luke had asked to see me today to talk about Tim. I don't know what he wanted, but the police are bound to start thinking.'

'It all depends,' started Cassie then stopped.

'Yes, it depends if Luke took the poison by

58

accident. Or left any indication he might kill himself. Because of the note to me and because of what we all know of Luke, I think suicide is out.'

'So do I,' said Cassie.

'I agree. Luke would never have killed himself. He was frightened of the dark.' Alice sounded sad. 'I am, myself, so I understood. We used to talk about it. People like us would never risk the dark.'

'So it's accident or murder. And on our ground.'

A dark shadow appeared at the door, blocking out the sunlight. It was Sergeant Crail who moved into the room and the sense of darkness was gone. You're being imaginative, Edwina told herself. You're seeing too much light and shade.

'Miss Ross?'

'Yes, Sergeant?' Cassie stepped forward.

'Miss Fortune, Miss Leather? I should like to speak to you all, please.'

They moved together and stood in their characteristic grouping. 'Of course,' said Cassie.

'No.' He was in charge. He could meet Cassie on her own ground and hold it steady. 'No, not together. Not here. In the next room, separately.'

★　　★　　★

An hour later, all three of them were together again. Edwina was the last to be interviewed and she emerged to find the other two waiting for her.

She took in a deep breath. 'Are they still going to be around?' *They* were the police. No need to name them. 'For long, I mean?'

'Just finishing up.' Cassie spoke with more confidence than she felt. Privately she had the feeling the detective force were like mites or rodents; once you got them in they were hard to get out.

Edwina steadied her breathing. 'Let's go to Tuttons for coffee, then.'

The restaurant was just opening for the day so it was empty, quiet and cool. There was a distant thread of music in the background but the volume had not yet been turned up.

Cassie poured out the coffee. 'So what did he ask you? I'll tell you what he asked me. Where I was all Saturday? What I did on Sunday? What I'd had to drink at the reception. Who served the food and drink? Had I noticed what Luke had?'

She stopped. She stirred her coffee, first clockwise and then widdershins, and watched it swirl.

'He's not stupid. Not totally nice, but not stupid,' she went on, as if conceding a point.

'I suppose he asked us all the same questions,' said Alice. 'I got much the same.'

Edwina nodded. 'Same here.' Perhaps he had looked her over as if he had wanted to press her about the reference to Tim in Luke's letter, but he had not done so. He was waiting.

They studied each other over the coffee cups. They knew that what they had been through had been a short, cursory examination, none the less menacing for that, and perhaps more so. There was more to come.

They were intelligent women and it was obvious to them that the sergeant had, to a certain extent, already made a picture in his mind, and that he would be back for more.

'I wonder if I can get some breakfast,' said Cassie. 'I haven't had any breakfast and I won't get anything with that lot swarming over my kitchen.'

'Oh, they'll have gone,' Alice murmured soothingly.

'Think so?' She went off and presently reappeared with a waitress carrying a tray on which rested rolls, butter and fig jam, together with another pot of coffee.

They all had some more coffee, then Edwina joined Cassie in eating a roll. She began to feel better, less physically sick, and the colour returned to her cheeks.

Alice and Cassie, who had been worried about her, relaxed a little. For all three of them, real sorrow and grief for Luke began to surface through the first sense of shock.

61

'Poor old boy,' said Cassie. 'We shall miss him.'

'Mmm.' It sounded as though Alice was agreeing, but she might just have been biting into the roll she had seized. Cassie gave her friends a thoughtful look.

'Don't choke yourself,' she said.

Edwina kept quiet. She was still making up her mind how she felt about the death of Luke. He had left a question mark hanging in her mind with his request to talk about Tim. What could Luke have had to say about Tim? They had hardly known each other.

Or had they? Holes seemed to be opening up in the ground all around Edwina.

Cassie reached out and took her hand. 'Calm down, love.'

'I am calm. You have no idea how calm I am. But I'm entitled to think. There seems to me a lot to think about.'

As if to bear out her words, the sun was blotted out again by the tall figure of Sergeant Crail.

'I thought I saw you come in here, ladies. May I join you?' He accepted a cup of coffee poured by Cassie. 'I'm sorry to have invaded your house, Miss Ross. I'm afraid we shall have to keep you out of your kitchen for a bit longer.'

He made it sound almost a medical matter: Miss Ross, your kitchen has a serious infection. Perhaps it had, for all she knew.

62

'Nice place here,' he said absently.

'Yes,' agreed Cassie. 'I eat here quite a lot. Handy, you see, if I'm busy.'

'You don't use your kitchen much?'

'Not too much. Not a lot of time to cook. And I've only just moved in.'

He finished his coffee. 'If you wouldn't mind coming back I'd like to have one last word with you. Won't take long. But you'd better hear it from me.'

He kept his word. Within a very few minutes he had told them that they had found what he believed to be poison.

'He asked me if I drank whisky,' said Cassie. 'I said No.'

'I told him I didn't, either,' said Alice.

'He asked me too,' said Edwina. 'I said I did sometimes. When I felt the need.'

Cassie summed up the situation: 'It looks as though there is poison in the whisky decanter that we set aside for Luke. If the tests confirm it, then that will be where he got the poison. You see where that leaves us.'

'Oh yes,' said Edwina. 'One of us did it. We three are the best placed to have put the poison in it.'

'There is an alternative,' said Alice. 'One of *us* was meant to drink it.'

It did not rule out the idea that one of them could have put the poison in the decanter of whisky, but added a gloss to it. It was like a tiny

63

spore of some dangerous mould settling on their relationship.

'I'm the only one who ever drinks whisky.' Edwina took up the idea, examined it and found it unpleasant. 'You two hate it.'

Another poisoned seed planted, as if by chance, in the back yard of their friendship.

'Damn,' said Cassie. 'So we can choose, either victim or poisoner.'

'It could be someone from outside.'

'And I know whom you mean,' cried Edwina. 'The dark-coated gentleman who's after Edwina.'

'That's enough,' said Cassie. 'Calm down, Eddie; shut up, Alice. That couldn't happen.'

For a moment they were a trio again.

It seemed quite easy for them, at that moment, to slip back into their ordinary lives.

They parted, Alice and Edwina striding off, the one to her shop and Edwina to her gallery.

Sergeant Crail, just driving away, saw them both.

★   ★   ★

Sergeant Crail looked at Edwina and remembered that she had complained of obscene telephone calls. Coincidence? Or was there a connection to be made? He might have to make it.

Behind a sober, even sad, appearance he was a

lively-minded young man who liked to feel life was growing all around him into interesting events in which he could partake. He found the trio, Cassie, Edwina and Alice, long known to him by repute, fascinating.

He was reluctant to admit it, even to himself, but he admired them all. And for Cassie he felt something much stronger, a decided attraction. If they had met under different circumstances he would already have been making his move. Not to be rejected, either, if he was any judge. True, she was a rising young architect while he was only a junior detective but they were equal in ambition and energy. Besides, from his sources, he knew how vulnerable Cassie's financial position was, as well as one or two other little problems. No, they could have made it, but for this bloody murder.

He believed Luke's death was murder. But there was something in the nature of the poison used that introduced a doubt. He had not told the girls what the poison was thought to be: or that it was an aphrodisiac ...

That was nasty, wasn't it? Introducing sexual undercurrents; that had to be thought about.

Edwina had been the one to whom Luke Tory had sent a letter asking for a talk about a man who was dead.

Always it came back to Edwina.

Edwina saw him looking at her from the car window, and although she could not read his thoughts her own ran strangely parallel.

It was all very well for those two, for Alice and Cassie, but they weren't at the end of the telephone which brought such unpleasant calls. They had had silent calls, but for her, there had been words and threats.

As she walked into the gallery she thought: I won't be a victim. I will *not* be a victim.

★　　　★　　　★

The gallery was warm with the sunlight flooding through the big window and it smelt of paint and new wood. Her assistant, Dougie, had already opened up in case of an early buyer; he had sorted the post and put on a pot of coffee.

Edwina felt she had had too much coffee already and her stomach gave an angry swirl.

He came in with a steaming mug while she was standing there. 'I thought you were in Edinburgh.' He took a gulp. 'Kit Langley's been ringing and ringing. I told him that's where you were.'

'I should have been.' Briefly she told him about Luke's death, passing as lightly as she could over the police investigation. No point in alarming him. Dougie had been hired because he had a wide range of contacts in the world of people who bought pictures, and a beautiful selling manner with them. The other side of the coin was that he was a gossip who could be relied on to spread a tale and improve on it. He would get to know what was going on, of course, but he could wait. 'Poor old Luke. Who'd have thought it? He looked as if he'd go on for ever. What a shame.' Dougie looked sad. He hadn't known Luke well, but death was brushing close. First Tim (whom he had loved and admired) and now Luke. 'What can I do to help?'

'Ring up Giles Mackintosh and explain I've been prevented from coming. Apologies, of course, but don't say too much.'

Dougie put down his coffee. 'Sure. Then I've got to push off to see Rosemary, I suppose I'd better do that still? I promised. She's got someone lined up who might buy the big Tosh pastel of the women bathing. Got a dance studio. Thinks it might do for the entrance hall.'

Rosemary was a go-between much used by both artists and gallery owners to effect a sale. She took her percentage from both seller and buyer. For some reason no one objected and Edwina had never been sure why. It must have something to do with charm, of which Rosemary had her share. Or the good wine which she poured out lavishly.

'You do that, but don't drink too much claret.'

Dougie gave a hoot of laughter. 'Chablis this month and a good year. Strawberries too if I'm lucky.'

'Sell that picture,' commanded Edwina. 'And

don't let Rosemary beat you down.' Hard bargaining was the other side of Rosemary's charm. But the gallery wanted to shift the Tosh panel.

'Some coffee before I go?' He waved the pot.

'*No.*'

'Ah,' he looked at her with sympathy. 'Got that nasty squirmy feeling, eh?'

Dougie was still talking in that soft, almost feminine voice he had on occasion, alternating with much deeper tones. People's voices didn't always show their sex, did they? But they did reveal their emotion. Dougie was fonder of her than she'd realised. Poor Dougie.

A moment passed, then Edwina said, 'So you know? I've been wondering when to say. How did you know?'

'Oh, my sister had a baby last year. And the year before that, if it comes to it. A really keen breeder.'

'I don't think I am.' Edwina was rueful; she was surprised at the waves of malaise that swept over her. Her body had been invaded by an alien force that was growing in strength all the time.

'Not to worry. You'll find I'm a very good nanny. Ask my sister.'

'Thanks, Dougie.'

'Don't mention. I'll be off then.'

When he'd gone, Edwina got down to some work. How odd that of all the people she had told so far it should be Dougie who was the most warming and the most comforting.

She put her hand where she supposed the baby must lie.

Nothing to feel: it was still too small and too secret. A pity to invade its privacy with tests and scans.

Shut up, Edwina, she told herself. You are going to have a child, a normal, healthy child. This ought to be the most important thing in your life just now.

Only sometimes life itself seemed to be full of menace.

She bent back to her work; she was determined to survive and raise that child.

She was putting together the catalogue for her autumn show on Angelica Kaufmann. She settled down to work, soon becoming engrossed, and worked on for some time in peace. When the telephone next rang she stretched out her hand, absently.

There it was, that low, gravelly yet strangely demasculined voice. Damn it, she thought, I feel as if I could know that voice if I tried harder.

The voice with its message. The voice *was* the message, Edwina thought.

'Edwina?'

She didn't answer.

'I know it is you; I know you are alone. Do you know why I ring?'

Edwina wanted to put the phone down, to cut

off this horrible call, but she couldn't. A dreadful fascination held her, and stayed her hand.

'I want to teach you to love. I have taken means to bring you up to scratch.'

'What do you mean?' Edwina found her heart bumping so that the words were in gasps. 'Explain that.'

But the voice had delivered its message and was gone.

A voice looking for a victim, Edwina said to herself.

I won't be a victim.

But how can you help what you are?

CHAPTER THREE

If you are not to be a victim, then you must take action. Thus Edwina decided. A couple of days passed normally enough, if you overlook the death of Luke. Edwina, Cassie and Alice did not meet, but talked as usual on the telephone, saying nothing much, but enjoying the contact. They were a group still in spite of everything; that mattered. On the wall in front of her was a rack of keys, one to the gallery, one to her flat, one to Lily's flat (entrusted to her by Lily before her wedding), all clearly labelled; Edwina hated keys that did not announce their identity:

useless. Everyone knew how Edwina felt about keys, so Lily had put a big red label on hers.

She came to her conclusion as she spent a normal working day. She talked on the telephone to the Edinburgh gallery, the Elton, promising to fly up later, she called her doctor at the clinic and confirmed an appointment she had to see her later. She had a light lunch with Dougie who had returned triumphantly from his outing. He had sold the Rita Tosh panel. Edwina was glad to see it go. She had liked it once, might like it again if she had a rest from it, but now she was bored by it. And the money would be useful.

'Tosh is coming in tomorrow,' Dougie reminded her. 'Wants to talk to us about a new exhibition.'

Rita Tosh, always called Tosh, was a brawny Scotswoman, famous for her forceful views on the place of women in society and her quick temper. Her works were very large, and strong, like she was. Lately she had begun to sell very well. Once you had seen a Tosh, you always knew another Tosh. For some people this had an attraction. If you could say knowledgeably, That's a Tosh, it sounded good. Dougie was suggesting mounting a spring New York show for her at the Rutherford Gallery in which Edwina had an interest. Edwina thought it was a bit too early as yet. Build up Tosh here first.

'We'll talk about it when she comes in,' she

promised. It was as well to have an agenda ready with Tosh. She was not a girl to want to waste time. Edwina could stand up to her, as so could Dougie in his way, but it was better to be prepared. She was uncertain how Tosh would react when her pregnancy became apparent. Probably withdraw her custom. She was known to favour virgin birth.

All the time she was working through her day, Edwina was thinking things over. A quiet undercurrent of discussion was going on inside her.

From her desk placed strategically near the big window with a fine view outside, she saw Cassie come out of her door and get into her car. Business as usual there, obviously. The small pastel-blue and white car with ALICE written across it in gold, which was used for deliveries by Alice, passed round the corner and drew up outside the shop entrance. Alice herself came out and started to load it up with packages in her pretty blue and white boxes.

Both her friends seemed enviably detached from the drama that must still be being played out wherever the police investigation was centred. It was as if the death of Luke had nothing to do with them. Murder, suicide, accident. No concern of theirs.

Or they could pretend so. Edwina knew better. Probably she too looked just as self-possessed. Dougie acted toward her as if she did. He was gossiping away about the party he had been to in Dorset the night before and the one he would be going to in Pimlico tonight.

'Gerald Road, no less, just opposite where Noel Coward used to have a studio and not far from the police station.' His eyes lit up. There was no doubt that although he genuinely lamented Luke's death, he was enjoying himself.

He was an onlooker, Edwina knew she was not.

Dougie might be prodded into an active part, though.

She sprinkled cheese over the minestrone. 'Dougie?'

'Yes, love?'

'You know that man who came in asking for me? Remember?'

'Think so.' Dougie looked vague.

'Would you know him again if you saw him?'

'I expect so. Depends what he was wearing. Different suit and I might not. You know how it is.'

'You've got a good eye, Dougie. You remember unusual details. What was he like?'

'Tall. Thin. Lanky kind of chap, I'd say.'

'Face?'

'Only really saw him for a minute. And I wasn't concentrating. Come on,' said Dougie regretfully. He started his lasagne. 'Tell you what, though.'

Edwina waited. Dougie had a way of holding on to little nuggets of information that could be quite maddening. 'So?'

'Saw the chap walking off. He was going one way, and you came round the corner. You came into the shop, but I went on looking out. I think he went over to Ginger and Pickles. He may even have bought something there. Why don't you ask?'

*   *   *

In the private area behind their stall where Ginger kept a kettle on a little spirit stove and a teapot, and where Pickles kept her crystal ball with her astrological tables (it was she who had predicted the trio's dire day of change, for she regularly did horoscopes for her friends), the two women were drinking acorn coffee and discussing the news about Luke.

'Of course, we didn't know him very well,' said Pickles. 'No,' agreed Ginger. 'Hardly at all, really.' She pulled at the little red cap she wore when cold to keep her head warm and which made her friends dub her 'Little Red Riding Hood'.

'Well, a little bit more than that,' said Pickles who rarely agreed with her partner if she could manage not to. Sometimes, of course, she had to: Ginger had a maddening way of being right more often than not. 'This coffee's worse muck

74

than usual, Ginge.'

Miss Drury grunted. She did not like criticism of her stock, even when justified, and this was justified. 'Good for the kidneys.'

'What does it do for sex?'

'Lavinia?' Ginger was alarmed, her use of Miss Dover's name revealed how much. 'What do you mean? Do you hanker?'

It had been accepted between them that they did not hanker, that they enjoyed their sexless lives. To have it otherwise might be rather daunting.

Also, she did not like the question for other reasons. Sometimes an arrow shot abroad goes whang between the cracks in the armour.

'*No.*' Pickles went back to her coffee and her crystal ball. 'Don't know why I said it, really. Just joking.'

Telepathy she's got, thought Ginger. I pretend to have it, she's really got it. A nasty little listener into other people's thoughts. Put like that it sounded akin to a dirty telephone call. She shook her head, as if to shake the thought out.

'Imagine me hankering,' pursued Pickles. 'Mind you, I've had my thoughts like everyone else, but on the whole I prefer a quiet life. I decided that years ago and I've never seen reason to change it. But I've always wondered about Luke, haven't you? Seemed to me he did hanker, but wasn't a doer. Think so, Ginger?

When I'd done his horoscope, I might have helped him. But he never asked.'

'Only you don't believe in it,' said Miss Drury scornfully.

'Three pounds for a depressing horoscope, five pounds for a happy one. Penny plain or tuppence coloured,' agreed Pickles. She had her own quiet tariff, you got what you paid for. 'I do and I don't. That's the answer. You get to believe even in a game, as well you know.'

The stall about them bore witness to that fact. Years of selling their products and nostrums and promoting their efficiency had made them believe in what they preached. They *did* believe in eating plenty of roughage, and that a minute dose of a herb that produced a headache could cure a headache and that dock leaves could cure almost everything. Their learnt sincerity made their money for them. Believing paid.

'So what do you see in the ball?'

Miss Dover took a long look. 'I see waves breaking on a cliff. I see a dark stranger. I see a cloud of black beetles. Nasty things. There, a trio of predictions. Somewhere there must be something true. I wonder which?' She sounded carefree. It was deliberate; she knew the effect, had worked at it.

'Sometimes you madden me, Pickles.'

'Only sometimes, Ginger?'

'Damn you, Pickles.'

The day was wearing on, they were getting on

76

each other's nerves; they always did in the afternoon.

'Oh and there's something else, just flashed into my mind's eye: a funny little thing like a tadpole.' She sounded surprised. 'Well, I never.' She knew what she was seeing, she remembered her biology. Sometimes she amazed even herself. Maybe she did have a gift, after all.

They had heard the full story about Luke, knew a good many details (how he had taken a taxi, gone to hospital, collapsed and then died), some of them untrue, but decided not to talk about it. A visit from the police was not something they fancied. The taxi driver was a local man and if they wanted to know more they could ask him, but otherwise they meant to keep their heads down.

Edwina walked in. 'Got something for morning sickness?' She might as well come right out and be blunt. They'd know soon anyway. 'All-day sickness, really.'

Pickles flushed with pleasure. 'There. So I was right. I am a clever girl. No, don't worry, Edwina, I know I'm talking nonsense but it means something to me. A baby. Oh you are lucky, I've always wanted one.'

'That's simply not true,' said Miss Drury. 'Or you'd have had one. You do talk rubbish.'

'It is true. I've fancied a mink coat but I've never had that either. You can't have everything you want. Edwina, I'm pleased. We both are.'

'That's true enough,' said Miss Drury. 'Take no notice of us.' She got up from her seat near the little stove and moved to a display cabinet. 'I think you might find peppermint tea quite soothing. It is carminative, you know.'

'Would you like me to do you a horoscope?' volunteered Pickles, making her contribution. 'I'm in the mood today. I could do the baby if you like.' It was true the baby was not yet born, so as yet having no birth-time, but it would be interesting to use the date of conception and see how that worked. She wondered how to phrase the question. Of course, girls these days never minded being explicit but Edwina, however, might. There was a reserved dignity to her that could make her hard to approach.

'Thank you, no,' said Edwina. 'It's going to have enough to contend with, this baby, without knowing its future as well.' Or me either for that matter.

She was wondering how to ask them if the dark stranger had called here. She wanted to phrase it so that Pickles did not get out her crystal ball. She was obviously in one of her psychic moods today, when she was convinced she really had a power. This conviction came and went. Once she had thought she could control electricity and had nearly caused a fire while experimenting, besides breaking a great many lightbulbs. Ginger had her fantasies too,

78

you never knew if either of them really believed what they claimed.

'I'll have the peppermint tea. Thank you. Yes, I'll go back and try some. I suppose it's not dangerous at all . . . ? No, sorry I asked. Forget it.'

'We never sell anything dangerous,' said Ginger with dignity. 'Not knowingly, anyway. And we test everything ourselves. Almost everything that is.'

Pickles said nothing, but silently took Edwina's money and wished she would go away. Her head was starting to ache. Also, she could tell that Ginger was getting above herself and getting into one of her moods. She might start levitating soon. She had tried that before now and broken an ankle. She limped yet.

'A week ago I had a visitor at the gallery, a tall man in dark spectacles. He was asking after me but didn't wait. Did he come on to you? Is he anyone you know?' Lamely she ended, 'I wouldn't want to miss a sale.'

If that was what the dark stranger had in mind, of course.

Pickles shook her head. Obviously her gift was not working in retrospect. 'Sorry. Mind's a blank.' There was a sort of mystery to her in having a blank mind, because she always wondered what would fill it. She felt that there were infinite wonders waiting to enter her imagination.

Edwina looked at Ginger. 'I can't help you,' Ginger said. 'We get such a variety of people that a person would have to have two heads to be noticed.' She looked at Pickles.

'Not one of your weirdos?'

'I do *not* have weirdos.'

'Special cases,' amended her friend falsely helpful. Even Edwina, preoccupied with her own worries, could see that Ginger was deliberately baiting her friend. But Ginger guessed that Pickles was hiding something. It could only be that she had sold something noxious and knew, or guessed, to whom. Pickles with a guilty conscience was unmistakable.

'No,' went on Miss Drury. 'Sorry, Edwina.' Then she thought again. 'I know.' Ginger banged her forehead. 'Ginger's had an idea. Why not ask Miss Linker? Bee Linker. She was around the Piazza almost every day last week, getting local colour for her new book about Nell Gwynn.'

'But she can't see.'

'She can hear, though. And she had her tape recorder going. Never know what might have been picked up. If it's important.'

Ginger was patently curious. In the end Edwina might tell her about the telephone caller, but for the moment the baby would have to be enough news.

'I might have a word with Bee Linker.'

It didn't seem likely that Bee would be able to

help, but Edwina always enjoyed talking to the writer. She would call on the Linker household later on. She knew their habits well enough to know that the best time to find them both in and relaxed was in the early evening. About now Bee would probably be dictating her next chapter ready for Janine to type.

Janine might be a good person to talk to. She always seemed so calm and wise. Of course, she might not be, you couldn't always tell what went on inside.

'Edwina.'

She turned round, knowing whom she would see. Kit Langley. Alone among her friends he never called her Eddie or Ed, never shortening her name in any way. Hardly used it ever. He seemed to get by without.

'You've been avoiding me.'

'Mmmm.' She considered saying No, or What rubbish, or inventing an excuse, and, instead, came out with the truth: she had been avoiding Kit.

'I want to talk.'

'Should we?'

'It's time.'

Yes it was, she would certainly have to tell him about the child. Unlike Dougie he had not guessed, but he knew she was distancing herself from him.

'Come into the gallery and we'll have a drink.' As he hesitated: 'Dougie won't be there.'

'No. You dig yourself in there. Neutral ground for me. Come to the Duke of York and have a drink and a sandwich?'

'I must check the gallery. See what's going on. Tidy up for the day.' It was after six o'clock.

'Since you are supposed to be in Edinburgh today I can't see that what is going on needs your personal attention.'

'You keep a check on my movements.'

'It was the last excuse you gave me,' he said grimly, 'and that was passed on by Dougie.'

'It was true . . . but something came up.' She looked at him. 'You don't know? It's Luke. He's dead. He was poisoned.'

Suddenly it all caught up with her, the shock of Luke's death, the tension since, with her own private and personal worries on top of it all, and she swayed.

Kit put his arm round her quickly. 'You want some whisky. And I did know about Luke. Who didn't? It was in all the papers. Come on—a drink.'

'Oh, God no, not whisky.' Never whisky. Luke had taken whisky. She might have drunk some herself that day if it hadn't been for the baby. She steadied herself. 'I'm all right now. The Duke of York it is, then.' She drew away from Kit. 'Whoops, I'm better now. I think I could manage a dry sherry.' In fact the idea suddenly seemed very tempting. She was hungry, too, ravenous. She was getting used to these sudden bursts of appetite and accepted it as part of what was happening to her. 'Thanks, Kit.'

They had once been close friends and very nearly lovers, but then Tim had appeared on the scene. The changed situation was now part of her life, built into it immovably, but she was not sure if Kit had ever accepted it. He gave no sign of it at the moment, but walked her round to the Duke, looking cheerful as if he had scored a point. She saw his large intelligent eyes studying her with interest. Damn, he was so quick and clever. One should never underestimate what he might know or work out.

In a dark corner seat near the bar she found herself telling him about the poisoning of Luke. How the three of them might be under suspicion. Or perhaps thought of as victims. Then she told him about the telephone calls. She heard herself talking about the man whom she thought was, somehow, following her. To her surprise it did not sound melodramatic but stark and cold. A nasty but credible exercise in human behaviour.

What did surprise her was his reaction to it. He was angry, and fierce.

'You're always picking up a demon lover.'

'That's a terrible thing to say.'

'Yes, I shouldn't have said it. But you bounced me into it. Still, it's true. You do attract men who are going to be devils to you. I could list them.'

Edwina looked at him eloquently.

'No, not me. I'm the exception.'

'My life's *not* like that.'

'You think so?'

'Tim,' she began defensively.

'Yes, even Tim. Tim even more so. It's time I said so.' He was angry. 'He wasn't good enough for you. He'd have let you down in the end and probably before ...' He had something to tell her about Tim.

Then he stopped, realising he had gone far enough. Too far probably. Tim, his rival for ever, had put himself out of reach by being dead. Why had he used the phrase 'demon lover'? It wasn't his style at all. But somehow it had come into his head as being true for Edwina at that time.

It didn't stop her being attractive. In fact she was more appealing to him at this moment, with her slight air of being lost, than ever before. It wasn't how you usually thought of one of that successful trio. It was new for Edwina.

'Give me that whisky.' She reached out a hand for his glass and poured its contents down her throat. 'There now. I'm as tipsy as an owl.'

'Darling. Oh darling,' he said helplessly. Helpless not because he could not help her, he knew he was going to, somehow, but because he loved her so much.

Then Edwina told him about the child.

Kit started to say, 'But—' But in his dreams Tim killed a girl, and he thought it was you. He called himself a bloody murderer.

'But nothing. I'll look after you, Edwina, if you'll let me.' There were times to keep a still tongue in your head and this was one.

*   *   *

Sergeant William Crail was also taking a drink in the Duke. It was not his local, but for the duration of this investigation it would be so. He had found it paid to drink on the spot. You never knew what you might pick up.

For instance, he could see Edwina and Kit Langley.

Kit Langley was a new face to record and fit in to what he knew already about Edwina, this was a plus.

But it was not the reason he was feeling pleased. He had found a way to get on terms with Cassie Ross which, although devious, was practical. He had nothing against deviousness. He was going to claim to be a friend of a friend of hers at university. He did not think it beyond his power to find out the name of a contemporary.

However, even this was not what he was chiefly thinking of at the moment. He was beginning to sniff out undertones in the character of Luke Tory, deceased.

In police possession, stained with Luke's vomit and blood, had been a newspaper. An item on page one recorded that Constable Miller had been charged, together with another man, with conspiring to commit a robbery. This may have been one of the last items read by Luke Tory before he became past reading anything.

Well, no mystery about Detective Police Constable Edward Miller. He had been corrupt. He was an example of what was coming to be a phenomenon of the new police: an early burn-out. He had been the best cadet of his intake, he had really put his back into his work at first. Overkeen, really, was Bill Crail's serious thought, and how different from his own colleague and working partner, WDC Elsie Lewis, who never bent her back an inch beyond what was demanded of her. But for DC Miller, in spite of exams passed and cases solved, promotion had not come quickly. Or not quickly enough. He'd been under investigation for dirty dealing for some time.

So, no mystery about DC Miller. But a note in a diary found on him had named Luke Tory. By the side of his name a sum of money was written. There was more than one such entry.

To Bill Crail, meditating over his beer, this suggested blackmail.

Whether Luke Tory was collecting the blackmail, or paying it, he was not as yet sure. He inclined to the view that Tory was the

86

blackmailer. It would explain DC Miller's headlong flight into crime, the poor sod.

God knows what Tory had on him or how. But blackmail provided a motive for murder, although why the powdered shells of agaric fly was used was something else again. Perhaps it was the only poison the killer could lay hands on. Motive, opportunity and means of killing were the three heads you looked for.

Bill Crail sipped his beer. In the end he would have to share his thoughts with his superiors, would wish to do so, but for the moment they were his alone.

He began to think about Cassie Ross who attracted him a lot.

*   *   *

Kit took Edwina's hand.

'You're in trouble, love. Let me help.'

'I can hack it. I want this child.'

'Of course you do. What happens next?'

'I suppose the police will question us again. We're under suspicion all right, we three.'

'No, I meant about the baby.'

'Oh, go to a clinic or something,' said Edwina vaguely. 'It's in my diary. I have a date. I'll get there.'

The clinic was in Ladybird Lane, near St Thomas' Hospital, not the smartest of areas but her doctor had booked her there. When she told her father he would no doubt suggest a private hospital somewhere. But Edwina thought that she and this child had better start as they meant to go on. They would both have to earn their own living. Besides, Ladybird Lane suited her mood at the moment.

'What's it for?'

'Oh, tests.' She was vague again, not really wanting to be explicit. To show the baby's normal, but she was not going to say so.

'Let me come with you.' He hated the thought that this was Tim's child. All the normality would have to come from Edwina, if the genes had anything to do with it. He didn't call Tim normal.

'No.' If she took any man it would be Dougie, there was a soothing feminine side to Dougie that would fit in.

Across the room William Crail, who had been aware of them all the time, got up and walked across. Everything about Edwina Fortune interested him at the moment. He had sensed that Edwina was the centre of that group of women. Cassie might be the most vibrant, and Alice the most talented (and the coldest) but Edwina was the one who held them together.

He timed his move so that he just brushed past their table as they both looked up. Timing, as with an actor, is a vital part of a detective's craft.

'Miss Fortune?'

There was a pause while Edwina looked at him, thinking what to do.

'This is Sergeant Crail,' she said.

Kit held out a hand. 'Kit Langley.' He sounded cautious, yet alert. I look after Edwina, his voice was saying, so watch it.

Crail sat down without being asked. No one expected a policeman to have good manners, so he never tried for any. He exploited this loophole in his mark's defences whenever it suited him.

'Mind if I ask you a question, Miss Fortune?'

'Depends on the question.'

'Do you think the telephone calls you have been getting are in any way connected with Mr Tory's death?'

'Isn't that for you to find out?'

'But what do you *think*?'

There was a pause.

'Feelings aren't evidence.'

He was a new-style detective. 'Ah, but they are.'

Kit obscurely felt that a battle was going on between the two of them of which he was not allowed to take cognisance. He took Edwina's hand. It felt warm and soft, not exactly responsive but not totally dead to him either.

'It's something I have to think about,' went on Sergeant Crail. 'We all know what's usually behind calls like you've had.'

'Sex.'

'Yes. Sex. You don't need me to go into it. But I have to take it into account.'

'Why?'

'Because what killed Luke Tory was agaric fly, cantharides. It has a common use as an aphrodisiac.' And it could have been sold to him by that dubious lady, Pickles Dover.

The skin whitened under Edwina's rouge. She was hearing a voice saying: You don't know how to love. I have the means to bring you up to scratch. She tried to blot the voice out but these were the words it was shouting now in her ear.

So you weren't going to be a victim, Edwina?

But supposing you were meant to be a victim and someone else got the dose that was meant for you and it killed him? Was that what had happened to Luke?

There was the other thought that she was repressing.

The idea that the poisoner had to be one of the three: Alice, Cassie or Edwina herself.

And if she was the victim, that left only Cassie as the poisoner. Cassie, in whose home the poison had been found, was the most likely poisoner.

CHAPTER FOUR

The red light was winking on Edwina's
telephone answering machine. She stared at it
balefully, unwilling to hear what it had to say.
Almost unconsciously she had made the
decision to start taking charge of her life again;
she had the feeling it had got out of hand lately.

An acid thought was floating round in her
mind like an onion in vinegar.

'An elderly primipara is well advised to have
an alphafetoprotein test too.' As well as all the
other tests, they meant.

The words echoed uneasily in her mind. I am
an elderly primipara, she told herself, trying to
see the joke. Primip, they call it. But she
couldn't laugh. We went wrong somewhere,
Cassie, Alice and I, and I'm beginning to see it.
We went to a marvellous party and we thought it
would go on for ever. But we were wrong. She
wondered if the other two had noticed yet or if
she would have to tell them.

Encapsulated in her memory was a little scene
earlier that day. She had lied to Kit. She had
been to the clinic in Ladybird Lane already.

She had returned home alone, after the drinks
in the Duke of York, refusing Kit's invitation to
a quiet dinner. He had insisted on seeing her
back to the gallery where she meant to finish

some work and then departed.

'If you have any more nonsense telephone calls, just summon me,' he had said as he strode away. 'I'll fix it.'

'Thanks.' She wondered how he would do it. Break the telephone probably; Kit believed in prompt strong action.

She could do what the police advised: have the number changed. But she did a lot of business over the telephone. It would be a nuisance. She would have to circulate all her customers and friends and the end might be the same as the beginning. If the caller wanted to find her number he would do so.

Besides, it was a kind of defeat and she was against that.

Be a brave girl, Eddie, she told herself, and listen to your messages.

The first one was Cassie sounding excited. 'That policeman, such a thug, but . . .'

Eddie turned her off and walked away.

She had taken a step out of their golden triangle, impelled by what had happened to her earlier that day at the clinic in Ladybird Lane.

If there had ever been any ladybirds it had been a long time ago and Victorian jerrybuilding had taken the place of the pleasure gardens where they might once have rested. The antenatal clinic was crowded but comfortable in an institutional kind of way and mercifully quiet. The line of gravid patients seemed glad to be still and to be silent.

Edwina, unexpectedly summoned by a postcard for an appointment that day, had agreed with them. She leaned back as far as she could in her upright chair, and closed her eyes, before suddenly hearing her name called.

'Mrs Fortune, please, Mrs Fortune.'

Edwina had accepted quickly that she would be an honorary married woman at this clinic; there was no moral judgement involved, they simply preferred to call her Mrs. She could have argued, some did, she had noticed, but it made no difference, you never saw the same person twice and they all went on the way they preferred. Mrs it was.

Edwina hauled herself up without resentment and went along the corridor. A welcome passivity had descended upon her as it sometimes did these days, alternating with periods of intense activity. A nurse had handed her a card and a loose white smock and made various straightforward suggestions about the lavatory. Edwina had decided at the beginning of her progression into childbirth that this was no time for false dignity. Or any dignity really, the word was better forgotten.

'We will read your scan today,' said the agreeable young doctor whom she had never seen before. 'Then I suggest as an elderly primipara you have an amniocentesis.'

'Elderly? Me?'

'Eighteen is the ideal age for childbirth,' said the doctor with the sincerity of the informed.

Damn her, thought Edwina, she too was informed.

At eighteen I was embarking on a degree, starting my career, no time for babies ... Nature and Edwina had been at odds, playing two different games but arriving at the same goal.

She went back to her answering machine and let it speak to her again. 'Such a thug,' said Cassie's voice, 'but he's got something. We are going to have a meeting. Says he knows a girl from our year at university ... don't believe that for a moment. He's got her name right, though, I'll say that for him ... Tina Andrews. Remember her? As if she'd be a friend of mine. Wonder what he really wants?'

Tina Andrews. The girl with no head, we called her. We were too exclusive, sometimes unkind. No wonder we've got enemies.

I've got an enemy. An enemy who loves me.

But all three of them had telephone calls to begin with, as if the emotion that provoked the calls was summoned up by them all.

Edwina considered this fact; that's how it *was*. But now the caller, this tall strange man, is preoccupied only with me. What's so special about me?

There was one thing that made her different.

'No, not that thing. Not the child. Nor being

pregnant,' she said aloud. 'That's sick. That's a terrible thought, somehow.' She got up and had a drink of water. Her throat felt dry. 'Besides, I hadn't told anyone. It was a secret.'

But was it? How many people did know, or could easily guess?

'Probably the whole Garden.'

Suddenly the world where her secret enemy moved, which had seemed enormous, had narrowed down into the Garden. He was there in the Garden among the people with whom she worked. Perhaps a face she knew. Perhaps even someone she counted a friend. She had only seen a tall, dark-coated figure who could be anyone.

She could almost hear Kit saying to her, in a steadying, reasonable way, 'You are only hypothesising that your telephone caller and the tall odd man are one and the same.'

'Seems likely to me,' she would say. 'I'm entitled to my feelings, like the detective said.'

'Nor do you know, nor can you know yet,' this imaginary Kit would say, 'that this person poisoned Luke. All this is speculation and idle fears.'

'I have some positive facts to go on. I have had the direct experiences,' she was answering. 'I have had the telephone calls, I have seen the man, or a flash of him, and I was there when Luke took the drink that killed him. We all were, all we three. The policeman, the man

Crail who is now making a play for Cassie with God knows what move in mind, thinks from our trio comes either the murderer or the chosen victim.'

Or perhaps both, said a yet deeper inner voice with the utter logic of despair.

I am afraid of my friends now, and perhaps they are afraid of me.

She switched on her answering machine again to take the next message it had recorded and right on cue Alice spoke.

'Hello, love, how are you? Haven't heard from you today. Give your Alice a ring when you feel like it.'

Her voice was gentle and sweet as ever. Hateful to wonder what she was up to, but she knew Alice so well that she knew something more was coming. There was always that little husky hesitancy in her voice, almost a stutter, when she was about to manoeuvre. No one knew how to play a hand better than Alice, but to Edwina it always showed. Usually her friend's diplomacy amused her, but not today.

'Do ring, Eddie. I'd like to talk. Or come round. A drink or a little late supper? Cassie telephoned to say she's had an invitation from the policeman.'

I know, Edwina said to herself.

'And I think she might go.'

I'm sure she will, thought Edwina. Cassie was never one to resist a dare. Especially if she fancied the man and in this instance Edwina believed she did.

'And who knows what she might say?'

'Does it matter?' And this time Edwina spoke aloud.

As if she'd heard, Alice's next sentence answered her: 'And say what you like, that man is out to get a conviction. On us if necessary. I think we ought to keep them apart. If she rings you up, tell her so.'

But here Cassie, as so often, had got in first.

Once again Edwina switched off the machine. She just had time to hear Alice suggesting once more that she come round before she was cut off in mid-voice.

In a little while Edwina would let Alice have her say out. No one silenced Alice for long. Besides, she needed to hear the messages that came after.

In case one was The Voice. Better know. Well, later, she said to herself.

But The Voice did not speak to her that evening. Instead, after a nasty pause which convinced her that it would be him because it was so reminiscent of the way he had of hanging on for a measured second before beginning to speak on a low note, it was Janine, politely informing her that the last batch of personal letters were ready for her to sign.

Not for the first time she rejoiced that Janine had come into her life through the agency of Bee

Linker. Bee worked through typists at some speed; they usually retired, hurt by the complexity of the tapes that Bee handed over to them with their many goings-back and revisions and alterations. Janine was the latest in a long line and seemingly the one to survive. A tall, soft, gentle woman, she took the author and her eccentricities easily while still having time and energy to spare for Edwina, Cassie and Alice. She had explained to Edwina that she was building up her own typing and secretarial agency for which end she was willing to work harder than seemed reasonable. Edwina found her an agreeable, reserved lady who let you so far into her life and no further. Bee had said once that she had the look of a woman nursing a broken love affair, but perhaps Bee *would* think that in her trade.

'Look, Bee?' Edwina had asked.

'Yes, look. I can remember how people look, you know, I have not been so long blind,' Bee had said with dignity. 'Besides, it's in her voice.'

There certainly was something in her voice, Edwina decided now as she listened. Perhaps one always gave oneself away with the voice. Perhaps that was what attracted the unknown telephone caller to her.

There were no other messages on her machine. For the moment she was off the hook. With a tremendous lift in her spirits she picked up the telephone and made arrangements with

Alice for a working lunch tomorrow: they were both involved in a scheme to start a women's cocktail club. Edwina thought they might get it to move.

Alice sounded pleased to hear from her but still had that note in her voice. She was worried about something. But when pressed she said there was nothing, just nothing at all.

'You got someone there with you?' demanded Edwina, suddenly wondering. She knew Alice.

'No one, no one at all.'

When she'd put the telephone down Alice turned to Kit. 'We ought to tell her. Really we ought.'

'I wish I knew what to do.' Not like Kit to be uncertain of himself.

'She'll find out. Bound to.'

'This would be the worst time possible.'

On her pad she wrote Tim, Luke, The Voice, as if they were one and the same problem.

Alice reflected, 'Why did you tell me and not Cassie?'

'Because you can keep your tongue quiet and I don't think she can.'

'I've trained myself. Cassie hasn't had to. In my world you have to bow and scrape a bit. Not in hers.'

The notion of Alice bowing and scraping was laughable, but Kit knew what she meant.

Kit had invited himself round for a drink with Alice that evening when the sun was heavy on the pavements and the air smelt of oil and of the heavy green leaves of plane trees. Alice was pleased to see him, he was an easy inhabitant of their world, moving in it as a welcome guest. She recognised he was interested in Edwina, but she was prepared to divert some of that attention to herself if possible. No disloyalty to Edwina was intended, but just occasionally Alice felt all was fair in love and war. She obeyed certain rules and was doing so now; one rule said that Edwina had to declare, tacitly or otherwise, an intent. To Alice, Edwina had declared one by becoming pregnant by another man. While the baby lasted (Alice didn't put it like that) Kit was hers if either of them wanted it.

She had put some white wine in the refrigerator, made some smoked salmon sandwiches and arranged some cigarettes. They were of an unusual Turkish brand that she imported from Paris and only allowed herself on special occasions, but were otherwise perfectly straightforward. Alice was all off about drugs. As she said herself: 'You can't sell baby clothes smelling of pot.' At college they had all tried everything they could lay hands on but their particular drug was success and they knew how to get it.

But she had known as soon as Kit arrived he wasn't thinking of Alice.

'In fashion you can't spit in the customer's eye. Cassie can hide behind her buildings . . . I think they even like it when she's rude to them . . . Not me, I have to be careful. So I can hold my tongue. But I shall have to tell Cass in the end.'

Loyalty held. Their friendship was under attack but the foundations were still strong.

'Not yet, please. And certainly not until I've told Edwina.'

'I don't know how you are going to tell her. What a thing to have to say: Eddie, the man you loved thought he might have killed a girl. There's the child too. I suppose she has to know. How did you find out?'

'I've always known. We were at school together. Our parents were friends and they kept up when Mrs Croft was widowed and went to live in Northumberland. Of course, she always maintained it was a complete accident Tim killing the girl, but of course it wasn't. Can't blame her for trying, though.'

Alice said with the sympathy of one who had made mistakes herself although not on such a grand scale: 'He must have been very young.' She was finding it hard to relate this story to the Tim she had known and Edwina had loved. But there had always been something withdrawn about him. 'I suppose it *wasn't* an accident?'

'It was real murder all right. In all the newspapers. "Teenage sweetheart strangled".'

'Poor things. And Tim went to prison?'

'For manslaughter; the judge sympathised

101

with him. He came out, completed his education, studied law, and buried the past. Told lies where necessary, I suppose. But I knew. He was always a bit older than he looked and he didn't lose that look but otherwise he was changed. You cannot expect otherwise. I don't know if it was for the better or not. Knocked all the stuffing out of him in one way but made him more sensitive, nicer, in another. He knew what suffering was.'

'I always knew there was something. Part of his appeal really, I could always see what Edwina went for. And do you know, darling Kit, I don't think it would have made any difference to Edwina if she *had* known. Rather the reverse, probably. She's very loyal, our Eddie ... But it's not the best of things to tell her with the baby coming.'

'I'd keep it from her for ever if I could.' Kit had his own brand of loyalty.

'Things have a way of coming out.' Alice had reason to know, but no need to go into that. She lit a cigarette. 'And with Luke's death the police will be prowling around. No, it's difficult.' She considered.

They smoked on in silence, then Alice said, 'Eddie makes a connection between Luke's death and some nasty telephone calls we've been having. You know about those, I suppose.' Kit nodded, happily ignorant that Edwina had put his name among possibles. 'She says she's not frightened, but she is.'

'And what do you think?'

'I think I saw a man following her and he fitted the description of someone who went into her shop and asked for her. She thought it was him; I think it was him. Tall, dark spectacles, dark grey clothes.'

Kit looked at her. He would never have called either Alice or Edwina overnervous or overimaginative. 'And have you told the police?'

'No. I thought about it, but I haven't. The trouble is I don't know how we stand with the police. They seem to think we might have poisoned the whisky Luke drank. They're working on that, I think. I don't know how they rate these telephone calls. Whether they even believe in them or not. So I thought I'd keep quiet. I haven't told Eddie herself, either.'

'Keep it to yourself for the time being.'

'I'm not keen to talk to that Sergeant Crail again. Nasty suspicious man. Pity Eddie ever reported those telephone calls. She could just have had her number changed. We all could.'

'She couldn't know that Luke was going to die.'

'No.'

Kit looked at her sharply, but Alice's face was empty of expression, except worry, and probably his own looked the same way.

Too many violent deaths clustered around Edwina.

'I don't trust that policeman.' Alice's face had that pinched look that at least one old acquaintance would have recognised. More than ever she wondered what Cassie might or could let out about Luke. Or whether, as she suspected, there was someone else in the wings who could blow the whole thing out of the ground.

★   ★   ★

Policemen have to learn how to manage people, it is part of their job. You can do it smoothly or roughly. Bill Crail did it smoothly, he chose to do it that way. Or almost all the time—he knew how to use his tough side when he had to. He actually liked people; that was something he usually kept hidden.

At the moment he had the advantage, or possibly the weakness, that he was attracted to Cassie. He could see a lot of things about her that not everyone would go for; she was tough, he suspected she could be devious when it suited her. But then so could he.

Two can play at that game, he thought, not admiring himself for the truth of it.

But behind Cassie's toughness, perhaps even a part of it, he sensed someone who, never mind all that apparent success and the ease of it, was a little vulnerable. He knew he could use that quality in her. He might use it now for his own ends but later on, if there was a later on, he would use it because he liked her.

He was being very nice. Not aggressive or sinister as policemen knew how to be if they chose. 'I'm telling you as a friend. I'm worried and you ought to be. If one of you three girls didn't put the poison in the old boy's grog, who did?'

Cassie flexed her hands in her lap in the way she often did at work when considering an important problem.

The two of them were sitting over a drink in her sparsely furnished room. Bill Crail seemed unconcerned so perhaps he was used to sitting on a cushion drinking cocktails like those Cassie had mixed. They were an experiment, pale green in colour from the chartreuse and oversweet. She could tell by the look on Bill Crail's face that he was not enjoying his and she took a silent pleasure in the sight. Serve him right.

'Isn't it your job to find out?'

'And I will. But you could be helpful.'

'No fingerprints?'

'No fingerprints,' he said grimly. 'And that's reserved police info that you should not know.'

Cassie was unimpressed. She did not believe he told her anything he did not mean her to know. But she did believe he found her attractive. She also knew he was a liar: he had not known her fellow student at college, he had not known anyone she knew.

'How well did you know your friend Luke Tory?'

'We employed him.'

'And?'

'That's about it.'

'Did you know he was a bit of a blackmailer?'

Cassie sipped her drink, it was nastier than she had intended. 'Let's throw these away, shall we? And are you taking me out to dinner?'

'My question.'

'I don't know how to answer. If I say No, I didn't have any idea, then you'll think I am a poor judge of character. If I say Yes, you'll wonder what he had on me.'

'Clever girl.'

'And who *was* he blackmailing?'

'The only one I know for sure was a young policeman called Miller. But where there's one there will be others.'

'Isn't there some regulation about taking a suspect out to dinner?'

'I won't tell if you won't.'

'Are you going to take us all out, one after the other? Edwina and Alice next? I know you're only doing it to get information.'

'Not quite the only reason,' he said, putting an arm around her. 'There is this.'

This was just for Cassie. Over Edwina hung a tremendous question mark, while Alice frankly terrified him.

Cassie kissed him back, in a leisurely, experimental kind of way: a new experience, a policeman, a new kind of taste. But a good one.

'Do I taste good back?'

'Mmm, splendid. Peaches and cream.' He did not really understand what she was saying, but was willing to try to play the ball back if he could. For him too it was a new kind of game. He extricated himself.

'Cass, girl, listen to me. You know more about Luke Tory than you're saying. You all three do. Must do. So try and tell me.

'Because until you do, you're doing what the murderer wants. Dancing to his tune. Letting him pull the strings.'

Cassie looked at him, and her gaze removed itself to an infinite distance. He thought he had never seen eyes go so blank.

'I'll think,' she said. 'Promise. Help if I can.'

Blank eyes, bland eyes, refusing eyes. Could tell, won't tell eyes.

★   ★   ★

On that same day, but somewhat earlier, another conversation had taken place in the Garden.

'I had thought,' said Bee Linker, 'of calling my new heroine Alice. The name takes my fancy and it suits her predicament in life, poor child . . . She is a dancer who discovers that she has a

107

mortal disease that will stop her dancing, but knowing Alice has rather put me off. I am not like Jane Austen in that respect.'

She waited for Janine Grandy to speak, to see what response she got. Very little. 'You call her Aline in the first chapter . . . I'll change it, shall I?'

Bee continued her thoughts aloud, ignoring Janine's question which she knew very well was meant as a sly brake on her rather than a real request. Thinking aloud was a luxury Bee Linker had allowed herself since going blind. Janine had developed her own way of dealing with it.

'Not that I think Alice Leather would really mind, do you? And after all, the girl in Chapter One has made a mistake . . . Or had it made for her. Wrong diagnosis . . . But I think Alice doesn't identify with bad luck in any case.'

'Do you think anyone does?' Janine was assembling the material just dictated to her as she prepared to go home.

'Oh yes. A lot of people do. It's a common affliction.'

'You wouldn't call it affection? Or even love?' For a person or race, Janine was thinking. Although in this case it would be a person. 'To be willing to share?'

'With some people, yes. But with others, no, it is definitely a disease, and one that grows upon them like a Cyclops eye. Dangerous, too.'

'Dangerous for them or for other people?'

'For both.'

'You do say strange things, Miss Linker.'

'Call me Bee, do please. I have asked.'

'Bee,' said Janine, politely if warily. 'You won't be putting that in your book, I suppose?'

'Gracious no, dear.'

'Bee, who do you think killed Mr Tory?'

It was not a totally unexpected question. Whenever you talked about one of them now, even obliquely as with Alice, you thought about the death of Luke Tory. Whether it *was* murder, or possibly a terrible accident. Whether, accepting that it was murder, the right person had been killed. There was endless room for speculation since facts were short and the police seemed disinclined to add to them.

But all the time the real question people were asking was: had it been one of them? Had Cassie, or Alice, or Edwina, been the poisoner?

In all the little bars, pubs and coffee houses around the Garden the same question was being put and it was those who envied the girls most who asked it most sharply.

Janine thought she had not envied the girls. In some ways she pitied them.

'I don't know, and I'm glad that I am not required to find the answer. But I can think of the sort of person who would do such a thing.'

'What sort of person?'

'A judging sort of person. A person with a

fixed scheme of values. A person who thought they could play God.' Perhaps all murderers except the very brutal, casual sort thought that, decided Bee.

'You didn't like Mr Tory, did you?'

'I didn't think about him a lot. He had an unpleasant voice so I didn't listen out for him,' said Bee, unconsciously revealing that the answer was No, I did not, and at the same time giving away her other game; that she listened for people, making their own character noise. 'You just off? I can hear you packing up.'

'If there's nothing more I can do?'

'Not a thing if you've got that last chapter safe.'

'Tucked away.' Janine patted the tape in her bag.

Reassured by the solid slap Bee said, 'Finished for the day here then?'

'More or less.' She paused, then asked: 'Will you use all this in your writing?'

'Good gracious no, dear.'

'Nothing about the murder?' They were all calling it that. 'I mean, it must creep into the way you are thinking and that will influence the way you write?'

'Not really.' Bee was amused by the idea, which confirmed her belief that Janine was not a reader.

'But it's a mystery and you often have a mystery in your books.'

'Not often a murder. There *was* a death in *The Golden Fountain*, but I like a mystery rather than a killing. The great mystery we have here, to my mind, is the telephone calls. Yes, the telephone calls are the puzzle.'

'Are they?'

'You had heard about them?'

'Oh yes. We all have.' The grapevine had been at work.

'I wish I'd heard one. I'd know the voice again. Wherever I heard it.'

'Disguised.'

'I'd know it.'

Janine said, 'I heard that Edwina thinks he called at the gallery; that he was actually *seen*.'

'Ah yes: the man in dark clothes. People who are seen mean to be seen. Don't you agree?'

'Do you think Edwina Fortune is like that?'

'No. Edwina certainly has an affliction but it is not that. Edwina's affliction is that she attracts love. It can be a great curse to a girl.'

'You do say strange things.'

Janine relinquished her smile. No doubt Bee was aware of this too. 'About a week today? I'll telephone to confirm I've got the two chapters ready.'

'And I'll have the next chapter ready.'

Janine nodded. 'I long to know the plot.' She gathered her papers together. 'I'm off then.' She had had an operation in the last year, and liked to get her rest; she had a strict regime of health.

111

'Could you do a little errand for me, dear?'

'Try to.' Janine had a natural caution. Life had taught her that she needed it.

'Go across to Miss Drury. Or Dover—I can never recall which is which. Anyway, the one who makes the bran bread, and tell her we would like to order a dozen rolls for Friday.'

'But I could do it on the telephone.'

'Well, it's on your way. You could just call in.' She felt for her purse. 'Just give them this, would you? I usually pay in advance. I don't fancy they do too well.'

'I want to get to the post office before it shuts.'

'Afterwards, perhaps? Could you?'

It was a windy, wet day and Ginger and Pickles were huddled behind their stall, wrapped in waterproofs and drinking something which might have been herbal tea but was, in fact, good strong mocha laced with whiskey. Everyone had their moments of weakness.

They saw Janine Grandy walking towards the post office; they knew who she was, of course, but since she was not a regular customer they took only a marginal interest in her movements.

'Not coming our way,' Pickles passed a judgement, as she sipped her drink.

'No,' said Ginger as she considered pouring in some more whiskey. There are days when you need it; this was one. Whisky had had a slightly bad name in their circle since Luke's death, but

112

not with Ginger and Pickles; they had simply (silently but unanimously) switched to Irish.

'Those poor girls,' Ginger sipped her brew. 'Wonder how they feel.'

Cassie, Alice and Edwina were now 'poor girls'. Had they known, they would have been angry. Everyone, certainly Ginger and Pickles, knew about the telephone calls and the man who had followed Edwina. Also that they were suspected of the death of Luke. They did not know all the details but they could put together a good picture.

'Terrible,' said Ginger. 'Like me.'

'Got some news?'

'I'm worried about Edwina. I saw her going into the antenatal clinic today. Hope there's nothing wrong with her or the baby.'

'Trust you to be there.'

'The public library is opposite,' Miss Drury reminded her friend. She changed her library book every day.

'And is that the news?'

'No.' Miss Drury's face changed. She was no longer Ginger, laughing and quarrelling with her friend, nothing serious, but had become an anxious, middle-aged lady who was really worried. 'Something I saw.'

'Come on now, don't blather. What is it?' Then Pickles groaned. 'I sense trouble.'

'Now don't go telepathic on me, dear.' But it was a mechanical blow in their usual shadowboxing, without heart in it. Ginger's mind was elsewhere.

She put down her mug, considered refilling it, and decided not.

'You know that instant-photography booth that stands in the Happy-Hour Market? They sell tourist junk now but it used to be bananas.'

'I know. I had my own phiz done there last year for my passport when we were going to Bayreuth.' Miss Drury and Miss Dover were ardent Wagner lovers and last year had made their long-saved-up-for visit to the English *Ring*. They had liked it, but then they greatly admired Sir Peter Hall too; they had once sold him some Bulgarian yoghurt.

'That's the place. I went past it yesterday, and I saw a man sitting in there photographing himself. Didn't have the curtain drawn—or not to the full. I could see, anyway.' She paused.

'What did you see?'

'It was *him*. Grey suit, dark kind of cloak thing, dark spectacles, dark hat. Imagine taking a passport photograph in dark spectacles. He sat there, taking himself again and again. And I thought: that's him, the one that called on Edwina in the gallery, the one that made the telephone calls.'

'That's just guessing.' Miss Dover was lofty.

'No, I'm sure I'm right. Must be. Too much of a coincidence for there to be two of them. So, not guessing. Call it intelligent deduction.'

'So what did you do?'

'Nothing; I couldn't. I was frightened. I could feel myself shivering inside. He's not *nice*, my old dear, not nice at all.' Then she added, with apparent inconsequence but as if it had been the worst thing of all, 'I could see tiny, thin ankles in black socks under the edge of his trousers. And he had such red lips.'

After a pause Pickles said, 'So that's your news? I don't call that good news.'

'No.'

'You frighten me, Ginger old thing.' And Miss Drury knew that she had done.

'Not wanting to.' She had frightened herself. 'Now if it was—is—the man who's been pestering Edwina and to a lesser extent Alice and Cassie, if it really was him and not me being imaginative, then why was he taking the photographs?'

She shook her head. It was as if a stench of nastiness, of a rotting something, had floated across from the photograph booth and settled all over her.

'You know, she's coming here.'

They watched the tall, elegant figure of the part-time secretary pick her way delicately across the Piazza, avoiding both puddles and litter, placing her narrow feet in their high-heeled shoes as delicately as a pony.

Janine delivered her message about the bread in a polite voice.

Miss Drury received the order cheerfully, writing it down on a pad she kept hanging from her wrist on a chain like an old-fashioned Victorian chatelaine. 'I'm the bread queen. Dover here specialises in the oddities.' Pickles made a grumbling sound at the back of her throat like an angry cat. 'Doesn't like me saying that. I tell her she's got no conscience but it's not true, her conscience comes and goes. She's working up for an attack now.'

'And what happens then?' Janine sounded mildly interested.

'Depends: either a priest or the police.'

'Shut up,' said Miss Dover.

'Joke, dear. Whoops—customers.'

The stall had suddenly filled with a small crowd, an actor from the Cardboard-Cut-Out Theatre collecting his supper, a member of the chorus from the Garden, and a cellist carrying his big case.

Miss Dover and Miss Drury ceased to quarrel and fell to work while Janine was glad to leave.

Across the road, the Cardboard-Cut-Out Theatre was packing itself up to move on to Woolwich for its later performance. They were a fluctuating group whose members came and went as other work offered. The murder of Luke had shaken them too; after all, two of the actors had been present at Lily's wedding. The police had questioned the two kings but they had not been able to help much. They had been

116

in and out, choreographing their act. Space was what they used, they explained, so they had to know what they had in order to shape their act, but in the end no one had looked at them, their act had fallen away into nothing so they had joined the party. No, they had not noticed. As a matter of fact, dressed up as they were with masks and crowns they had what you might call tunnel vision. The first king acted as the spokesman, the second king nodded assent.

But, as they packed away their scenery, their most pressing worry was financial. Rent was due, and not a penny in the bank for it. 'A sub all round,' said the actor who had been the first king. 'Same as usual.' He added, 'I'm broke myself but Albie ought to be good for a bit as he's got a voice-over, and Nina will come forward as usual.' Albert and Nina were stand-bys.

From her desk in the gallery window Edwina watched the activity; she always felt a little sad when the Cardboard-Cut-Out Theatre packed up. Perhaps they would never come back.

Cassie appeared on her doorstep; she had Sergeant William Crail with her. She waved at Edwina who gave a token little nod of the head back.

And there was Janine. Cassie waved at Janine who strode across the pavement, seeing no one; she did not wave.

Janine had seen Cassie as she had seen

Edwina, but she did not feel like waving at a policeman. There were times when Janine found employers hard to understand.

That evening Edwina cleared her desk of all important papers, left some work ready for Dougie to do in the morning, then reset her answering machine.

There had been no messages from 'him' after all. Maybe that was at an end.

She returned to her flat in Packet's Place and let herself in. The telephone was ringing, and full of her new-found confidence in her power to take charge again, she picked it up.

'Edwina? I know it's you. I know the sound of your breathing.'

The voice with its message; the voice that once again was, inescapably, the message.

If it had said nothing more she would have understood the threat.

'I want to teach you what love is about . . . I want to teach you the pain and the grief.

'You don't know what it is all about, you three. You attract men and then you put them down. I call you the three witches.

'But you are the worst. I loathe your guts.'

Once again, she had the tantalising feeling that she knew the voice, that if she tried harder she could say, Yes, that is the person.

CHAPTER FIVE

The murderer had a way of going walkabout, looking out of a window at the world of Covent Garden with a silent, secret satisfaction.

In this state of mental fluidity the world as seen from the window had a strange air to it. To begin with it was almost empty, being sparsely peopled only by those whom the murderer was emotionally involved with. There were quite a few of *them*, to be true, but hardly a stageful. Two of the principal actors walking around on this scene were already dead, as was at least one of those with only a non-speaking part: a cough and a spit as actors say. One character walked there who had not yet done so in real life, and perhaps never would.

But filtered out were the entire staff of Tuttons, of the Duke of York, the tourists, and all the passing crowd of the area around Covent Garden. For the murderer they did not exist, not on the stage where the puppets moved as their strings were pulled.

Absent also was the entire detective arm of the Metropolitan Police, with the exception of the despised Sergeant William Crail, known by face, unknown by name, a man of no account, who had been seen with Cassie Ross. As a tracker-down he could be disregarded, as could

119

the whole police force; to the murderer they had disappeared.

But prominent on the scene were all those whose lives touched Edwina Fortune. Edwina was the centre, the image at which all blows were aimed. Hatred extended outwards from her like a fan, with each ray of the fan one of her friends.

First in this group were Cassie and Alice. This trio seemed larger than average, more than man-sized so that they seemed subtly but decisively out of proportion with the rest of the scene. This was how the murderer saw them. Tagging along behind came Canon Linker and Bee in company with Ginger and Pickles. Kit Langley also walked the scene; he was growing in size lately, a bad magnification. But he would never grow bigger than Edwina.

Edwina's gallery was a principal object of fascination, for all the faces portrayed were of women; the murderer called it the Witch Gallery, occasionally altering the consonant to Bitch according to mood. One day, with luck, it would burn down. When it went up it might meet Cassie's workroom coming down. One explosion would do for both. Possibly. You could always think about it. An interesting thought for a sleepless night. Or when work became mechanical, so that the mind floated free.

After such a free flight the spirit seemed

stronger in itself, more resolved in its purpose. Or so the murderer felt.

From similar excursions in a private landscape the mind usually returns with an enhanced sense of life.

Or, in this case, death seemed to gain strength as if fertility was added to it. Or so the murderer thought.

CHAPTER SIX

After the voice had ceased talking Edwina stood still, trying to be calm; she poured herself a glass of brandy and stood there sipping it.

Deep inside herself she felt a movement, a kind of inner tremble; for a moment she thought it was the child moving and put her hand protectively on the flutter to calm and soothe it.

But no, she knew this was too soon; she wasn't supposed to feel this yet. Life was lurking within her but it was smaller than a mouse and not so mobile.

She knew how she felt about it: positive.

I am going to protect this creature, it is my creature, my responsibility, and bring it through. It was hope stirring inside me as well as life; I reject the idea you are just a uterine murmur.

In the morning she called the number that the

police had given her earlier to ask for her own telephone number to be altered. An efficient voice promised a return call to tell her what action had been taken.

One decisive move made; Edwina's mood this morning was strong and aggressive. She was already dressed, ready for the day ahead. She must be ready; she had an instinctive feeling that her time was limited.

In one way, very nearly six months.

But that was the long-term view. In another way she guessed she had days, possibly just hours.

Someone was out there trying to break into her citadel; she thought of herself now as a kind of fortress, no longer impregnable, far from it, more of a sandcastle than a stronghold, but still ready to resist a siege.

In this private, protected place was just her and the baby, no one else was going to get in. Cassie and Alice were on the outside, Cassie just that bit further away.

Because she now slightly distrusted her friend Cassie's relationship with the policeman, she telephoned Alice first to propose a meeting. 'Things to talk over.'

'Oh, meet here. In my place—the shop,' Alice suggested at once, as Edwina had known she would. Alice always did; she liked her own territory. Alice was a very territorial animal, like a little cat.

'No, here.' Edwina was firm, almost abrupt; she knew what she wanted. 'Tell Cassie, will you?'

Alice was interested. 'Aren't you talking to her?'

'Things to do here first. And you know what Cassie is like on the phone.' But it was true, she was edging away from Cassie Ross. 'In my gallery; lunch-time, if you can set it up. We'll have a glass of wine. Dougie will be there.' She had a part for Dougie to play.

The Cardboard-Cut-Out Theatre was trundling into its chosen position; she could see Hal Everett, one of the two kings at Lily's wedding, and Lynette Parsons, co-founders of the troupe. She had handed over her cheque for their services at the reception and hoped it had relieved the pressure on them, she had heard the rumours of financial extinction. She gave them a wave as she passed.

Hal waved back. 'And Nin's cheque came through today; she dropped it in herself, so we're afloat again, Lynnie.'

'Nina herself again?'

'She seemed fine. She'll be coming to Woolwich as from Wednesday. No daytime work till she's finished with the new voice-over: Dog-meat special: she's the cat.'

They were slightly envious. Nina could do any voice, Nina always had money.

At the Help-Yourself-to-Health stall, Miss

123

Dover was alone dealing with an elderly customer. 'No, I haven't taken the primrose-oil capsules myself but we sell lots of them. Yes, they come expensive. No, I don't know why; I suppose primroses haven't got a lot of oil. Yes, I should think it would do you a lot of good. Why not take a month's supply and see how you feel at the end of it?' She packaged up the capsules of oil, received a satisfyingly large sum of money and turned to greet another customer, a regular this time who came for the usual supply of wheatgerm and iron. Separate, not mixed. Pickles handed them over without much chat: she was longing to nip out behind the staff for a quick puff of Virginia; sinful, but with Ginger out she could do it. And after days of healthful food and talk, the system longed for something sinful like tobacco. She did not allow herself to think of alcohol, although she and Ginger kept a bottle of gin and one of whisky in the kitchen cupboard to fortify them in their lower moments. Last night had been such a one, at least for Ginger, and, her mood rubbing off, they had both overdone the drinking a bit. No wonder Ginger had not been herself this morning.

Pickles looked at her watch: Ginger ought to be here soon.

She waved to Edwina who was looking so nice this morning, fresh and pretty.

'Honey, dear? In the comb or a jar?'

'Comb, please. All on your own? Where's Miss Drury?'

'Ginger's gone to the doctor, soon set her to rights.'

'Sorry she's not well.' You never thought of either of the two at the health food stall being ill. Seemed unprofessional somehow.

'Terrible nightmares, wakes up screaming, wolves or witches. I tell her it's that red hat she wears. So she's gone to see Dr Fisher. He'll soon set her to rights.'

'Oh yes, he's my doctor too. GP, that is.' Of course, her obstetrician was someone else again. She had left Dr Fisher when she became pregnant; somehow it had seemed safer so to do.

Edwina took the honey and sped away, pursued by Miss Dover urging her to take care of herself and to remember her to her friends.

Oh, my friends, my friends, echoed Edwina, who knows about them? A swirl of antique, archaic suspicions, that arise in women when they are pregnant, was moving inside her, asking age-old questions about loyalties and love and sex. It's all rubbish, unfounded, unbelievable, she told herself, you're just being irrational. Yet she could not stop herself; did not even want to do so very much, because she thought this might be where her newfound strength was.

She wondered what sickness or what wound Miss Drury was revealing to the doctor, and what he was saying in return. He was a pleasant, easy man, Dr Fisher, although it might have been Fischer once. Or perhaps it had been his father who made the change, for this one was still quite a young man, barely of middle age. He was reputed to have the largest list of patients with hysterectomies in the district, as if he was saying: 'Don't worry about the loss of the womb. Most women would be the better without it,' and adding to himself: 'And most men the safer for it, too.'

An uneasy echo went through her mind. She seemed to see Ginger Drury facing Dr Fisher across the table, looking as frightened as Little Red Riding Hood and murmuring that she was afraid of wolves or witches, she was not sure which. What would the doctor say? What was the remedy against nocturnal wolves and witches? He would probably ask her where she was getting them from. Or would he?

Something else stirred in Edwina's mind: she had a strange notion she had caught a clue as to why she was being pursued, and the idea of Little Red Riding Hood Drury no longer seemed quite so mad.

Tim was dead: I ought to have been allowed to see him dead. He won't rest, otherwise. Echoes of him seemed to come through the description Dougie and Cassie had given of the man, the follower. Surely not? Not the voice, oh, she would have known the voice, wouldn't she?

Every so often she thought it would help if she could read Tim's diaries. She knew they were still among his possessions left with Kit. She had asked for them once.

Tim had not been a happy person. Looking back, she saw that now. Gay, impulsive, lively, but not really happy. She wanted to know why. Now she had started asking questions, she saw there was a puzzle.

It is true, Edwina thought to herself, what the writer said: most women do not know how much men hate them.

Gravid and alarmed, she sped on to the gallery. There was a fresh early morning smell to the Garden. She caught the whiff of coffee brewing from one of the coffee shops on her left, mixed with the scent of fresh-baked croissants from the *boulangerie* close by.

She collected a beaker of coffee and a bag of croissants on her way. Without knowing it, she was running. Dougie looked up from his desk. 'Hungry? I could have made you coffee.'

'I fancied their mocha.' She had fancied it ferociously, her mouth watering for it.

'It's your condition.'

'Thanks, Dougie. You've got a great sense of humour.'

'Probably when you've drunk it, you'll never want to taste it again.'

'What a lot you know, Dougie.'

'All down to my sister.'

Edwina spread honey thickly on the croissant; there were thick bits of waxy comb embedded in it, and her stomach gave a gentle roll. Resolutely she took a bite, swallowed it, then pushed it away. 'Damn you, Dougie.' She drank the coffee thirstily and by the time she had finished she knew Dougie was right. She would never drink mocha again. Or not for approximately six months.

'Never mind.' Dougie had been watching sympathetically. 'There are at least six varieties of coffee: Costa Rica, Brazilian, Kenya . . .'

'Shut up, Dougie.' Already she began to hate the thought of coffee.

'Do you know you came running in here? Absolutely running. What were you running from?' Then he added, 'Or to?'

Edwina considered. 'From, I think, Dougie.' Then: 'Tell you what, Dougie dear, the way I feel I don't know if it's more dangerous running away or running towards because I don't know whom I'm running from. Could be you, could be any man.'

'Except you know it's not me.'

Edwina gave him a smile: 'I trust you, Dougie. I don't think you hate me.'

'I know which side my bread is buttered . . . And you are the very best butter.'

Edwina's stomach gave a twitch and she stood up. 'Don't ever mention butter again.'

Or coffee. Or honey on croissant—soon there would be nothing left to eat.

'I suppose it's the telephone calls that are really getting to you.'

'That and several other things.' Like the murder of Luke and the sober realisation of what it meant to be alone with a child coming. She had never felt so alone. Cassie and Alice were receding into the remote distance. 'Events that seem to have no connection except through me. Me. That frightens me.'

Further back in time there was yet another connection, another person, and behind that person yet another person and even another further removed still.

A chain of people of whom Edwina was only one, and not necessarily the last. She perceived this in a vague way without realising it yet. Tim was there somewhere.

'I've got a job you could do for me, Dougie, if you will.'

Dougie said, 'You don't take me seriously. You think I'm just a niminy-piminy young man who happens to have a good eye for a picture. I care for you, Edwina.'

'You're a good lad.'

'I'm more than that, a whole lot more.'

'And five years younger,' went on Edwina steadily.

'What's the job?' said Dougie sulkily.

'Hide me.'

Dougie looked behind him as if seeking how to do it, then he stepped forward and threw his arms out protectively.

'No, no, it won't be like that,' said Edwina.

From the door Alice said, 'Like what?'

Cassie and Alice had arrived together.

'She's going to hide,' said Dougie.

Cassie stared. 'You can't do that.'

'I am simply going away.'

'But you can't.'

'Watch me.'

'The police won't let you.'

'I'm not going to tell them. And if your loyalty to the sergeant is stronger than your loyalty to me then I won't tell you either. I was going to, but I won't.' It was the nearest she had ever come to quarrelling with Cassie: a bit more of their relationship had come apart.

Alice interposed: 'We'll look after you, Eddie. You'll be better with us. I promise you will. You're upset now, but leave it to us.' She looked at Cassie. 'We've made plans, haven't we, Cass? You're to move in with me. Just for a bit, until things sort themselves out. Say till the baby is born.'

'Yes,' Cassie nodded. 'And Kit agrees.'

'You've told him?' Edwina went white with anger.

'Yes, of course. And he's coming here. We sent a message.'

In a quiet voice, measuring out every word,

130

Edwina said, 'I did not want any man here. Don't you understand: no man. It's a man, some man, I'm running away from.'

'Not Kit,' said Alice; she was a bit in love with Kit, she admitted, and could see no wrong in him. They had not met since Kit had turned to her for advice on what to tell Edwina about Tim, and although they had not come to an agreement, she had enjoyed the encounter. It was a start, and Edwina did not seem to want him.

'What about me?' asked Dougie.

'I don't count you.'

'Thanks. This is where I came in.'

'We feel protective towards you, Eddie, don't you see that? We're tender.' Cassie was in earnest, her hair spikier than ever. This week her hairdresser had introduced her to a blue metallic wash so that her fair crest glinted like a battleship in the sun.

'The worst of women,' Edwina was brisk, 'is that they always think they know best.'

From the door Kit Langley said, 'I've often thought that, but I never expected to hear you say it.'

All three women turned round, taking up without hesitation their characteristic grouping: outsiders need not attack us, they were saying mutely, this we sort out for ourselves.

'Sorry I spoke,' said Kit.

The triple alliance might be under strain but

131

it was still strong enough to rebuff him: 'Men Keep Out' was the slogan.

He held up his hands in mock supplication.

'Tact, diplomacy, all are needed, I admit.' His eyes met Alice's alert blue gaze, saying silently: You and I have failed Edwina there, we have shirked telling her what she ought to know about Tim.

Dougie grinned. 'You'll get no help from me.' He knew what Edwina expected from him now: he was to be on her side totally. In spite of his air of privileged youth, he had come from a poor background so he always identified with women, because he saw that his mother had had all his own troubles and those of her sex as well. Edwina's upper-class self-confidence had attracted him to her in the beginning: he was not going to dent it now. He and his sister Laura had dragged themselves upward, hand in hand; he would not betray a woman. Unconsciously, Edwina had chosen well when she elected him her ally.

Edwina sat down at her desk, facing them all. Usually her eyes rested upon it with pleasure, since it had been her own find, as a student, a desk by Ruhlmann, picked up in an auction in Bristol where no one had recognised it for what it was; her first venture into taste of her own. Today she hardly saw it; just something she would leave behind. 'I'm off,' she said. 'You won't see me around for a bit. I've had enough.

I'm frightened. Get in touch with me through the gallery. Only Dougie will know my address. He'll pass on a message. But I shall get my letters.' She was selecting keys from the rack behind her.

'You're running away,' said Kit.

'You can put it like that. And well advised to, in my opinion. I shall feel safer if no one knows where I am. I shall *be* safer.'

'The police—' began Cassie.

'They will be able to find me. If they want to.'

'You're running away from your friends.'

Edwina shook her head. 'You will be better without me. Safer, too. The hate is rubbing off on you.'

'I won't let you go off.'

'You'll have to, Kit.'

He nodded without animosity. 'You know where to find me.' There was warmth and love in his eyes. He wasn't going to turn away from her. He was apprehensive for her, but his instinct was to hang on.

'I know now what divides women.' Alice fixed her eyes on Edwina. 'It's not men, but children. The great open space between those who have and those who have not. It's coming on us, Cass,' she said sadly. 'Eddie has started it. We're breaking up.'

Kit said protectively, 'There's been a death, remember. Don't forget Luke.' He put his arm around Edwina.

Died a death, she thought. Luke died; I am pursued; where is there a connection? Or is there one? If there is, I could find it. Connections work and exist through people. Dead or alive there had to be such a person.

Perhaps she should look for that person. Not leave it to the police but go at it herself. You had to learn to ask the right questions, she had not learnt yet.

Cassie said, 'I am totally against this.' She did not look at Dougie but she was conscious of him; inside she was saying: I'll get the truth of where Eddie is out of him. 'You're mad.'

'Leave her alone.' Alice was still protective. 'She can't help it—it's her form of morning sickness.' She thought she had the measure of Dougie: he'll tell me where Eddie is hiding, I'll find out, was her thought.

Kit turned towards the door. 'I'm off. I'll see you, Dougie.' I'll get the truth of where she is out of you if I have to kill you. But these words he did not say aloud.

'Kit?'

He turned, eager, hopeful.

'You have the box with all Tim's books and papers from his room in chambers, haven't you?' Unconsciously she had come to the point of asking one of the right questions.

He nodded; he had collected them and kept them at a time when Edwina could not face doing so. Tim's mother seemed not to know of

134

them or care. He'd also had his clothes and other possessions. He had Tim's diaries, but perhaps he should hold them back?

'What did you do with Tim's things?'

'Sent them to the Sally Army. Or Jim Linker did; I gave them to the secretary woman to give to him.'

'Everything?'

Cautiously he said, 'Think so. Except his books and papers.'

'Can I have them?'

He said he would see to it. He was tense, not pleased, but it did not matter. The vague immensity of their relationship was like a stone building, something you could walk around in. There was comfort in it.

One by one they left, each determined they would find out where Edwina was.

Edwina watched them go. Not by a flicker did she reveal that even Dougie would not know, for long, where she really was, and what she was doing.

*　　　*　　　*

A day later Edwina let herself into Lily's flat where her belongings were already distributed in a homely fashion. A photograph of Tim on a small table by the bed; a pile of books and her typewriter on the table in the kitchen, and the bunch of flowers which Dougie had pressed on her as she left the gallery in a bowl in the window.

'And can't I have your telephone number?'

'No, Dougie, not even you.'

'But if something urgent comes up ... There is the Barlow picture. Now supposing Alan Yorking made an offer? He was hovering over it yesterday and breathing heavily.'

'I shall ring every day. And you have an address for letters.'

Dougie noticed she did not say 'my' address; I'm not fooled, he thought. You've got something up your sleeve.

'And I'll be working, Dougie. Don't think I'll be idle. I'll complete the catalogue. And do other things.' She was not specific about the 'other things'. Better he had no notion.

'But won't you need the libraries—the BM and the London Library for the catalogue?'

'I'll manage. Don't fuss.'

Now she came into the room to put down her shopping. Already she felt at home. Lily had remained faithful to her roots and her flat was in a renovated building with new pretensions to smartness overlooking Deptford Broadway.

The place was full of Lily's character, full of her love of bright colours and eccentric furniture—there was her solid Edwardian washstand with the green-tiled back turned into a sideboard, and here her Victorian brass birdcage, which she used to keep her make-up

136

in—all of which even smelt of her.

It might be thought strange of Lily to have a flat in Deptford, but she had affection for the area; Lily was loyal. Once she loved you, she always loved you. Also, the house was early nineteenth century and of great charm. Every window had a little curving iron balcony, still intact, having survived bombs and property developers.

Lily's own, personal scent, that everything she touched seemed to pick up, was a mixture of roses and amber, sharpened with a hint of lavender and a touch of verbena. Or so one of her lovers had analysed it, although Lily claimed it was just from good soap used often.

Lettuce in the refrigerator, bread in Lily's stone crock, and layers of frozen food in the freezer; she could stand a siege.

On the shelf stood the bottles of vitamin tablets and iron pills that she was taking for the good of both parties concerned. Her food love-hate was in abeyance; she actually liked coffee again: it was a good sign.

Lily's telephone was silent, as it was likely to be since Lily was known to be away on her honeymoon, and, anyway, she had not been at the end of any threatening calls. Perhaps no one could threaten Lily, who rose like a balloon above everything. In any case, she would not answer its ring.

Then it rang. Shrilling through the rooms.

Let it ring. She went out of the flat again, closing the front door firmly behind her.

Lily, with her famous face, had not been anonymous in her neighbourhood but Edwina passed unnoticed. Lily had chosen the flat well for its privacy. She was the sole inhabitant on the top floor. The flat below was lived in by a person who never appeared; he or she was simply never seen, although noises suggested someone was about. Lily claimed he was a local gangster in bad with the Mafia who dared not show his face. The ground floor was occupied by a baker who worked all night then slept all day.

Edwina walked down the quiet stairs, turned into the busy main road, then a quick left turn into a side street when she went into the newsagent.

'Morning, miss.' The proprietor was a young Londoner, busy shaping himself into an old-style Cockney using his grandfather as a model. His own father was in prison, had been there for the last eight years and had another four to do. He was wearing a black-and-white checked waistcoat, a dark flannel shirt and a spotted muffler tied at the neck, cravatwise. His hair was pomaded down and he was cleanshaven. He was a clever copy but not quite genuine.

He shuffled forward on his carpet slippers, handing her a copy of *The Guardian*. 'Got it in special, as ordered. Not much call for it here.

Like *The Sun* as well?'

He knew she would not take it, and as a matter of fact he read *The Guardian* himself, but he was just playing his part.

'Give over, Sid,' said his wife from her corner by the cigarettes and chocolates. She would not play her part and remained adamantly unreconstructed. A punk she had been when he married her and a punk she still was, but one dressed and coiffed with considerable skill and expense. She had been at school with Lily.

Edwina took the papers. 'I'll have *The Times* tomorrow as well, please.' Must keep an eye on current exhibitions, couldn't opt out of her career altogether. Her future demanded she be a good earner.

'Give you one now if you like.' He produced a copy from beneath the counter. He and his wife knew Edwina was Lily's friend but did not connect her with a gallery in Covent Garden or a murder which was getting some publicity now. Least of all did they know she was Lily's stepdaugher. Edwina, for her part, did not know that they knew she was living in Lily's flat.

But they knew she was a Woman of Mystery. Sandra had called her that the minute Edwina's back had been turned, after her initial visit, when she had asked them to receive her letters.

'I always wanted to be a poste restante for someone. Staying in Lily's pad, isn't she?'

Edwina had not told them but Sandra always knew that sort of thing. Sid said she was a natural spy. 'She's a strange lady, our Lily, but you can usually trust her friends. We'll trust this one.' Sid set great store by his wife's judgement.

Sid had carefully recreated a newspaper shop of pre-war London, even to buying some old tins of Mackintosh toffee and Clarnico confectionery to put on the shelves. From the Caledonian market had come a large mirror with 'Cadbury's Drinking Chocolate' written across it in large letters. Sid's favourite purchase was a newspaper placard which he displayed on the wall behind him, annoucing: *Hitler marches into the Saar*.

It was a popular shop with the customers, who enjoyed a walk backwards in time although frequently pointing out that Sid's prices were 1987. Locally he was ironically called Granddad.

Edwina departed with the two newspapers, having paid cash; somehow she knew prompt payment and no weekly accounts were the way to Sid's heart. In addition she was paying for his receiving her letters.

Edwina, nameless now (except to Sid and Sandra who knew both her name and where she lived), walked through the street back to Lily's flat. She spent a peaceful afternoon and evening finishing off her catalogue. She had not been quite truthful with Dougie because there was

140

hardly any work left to do and she had never intended to do much.

The first day was recuperative; the atmosphere of the flat worked upon her so that she felt gentle and calm like the owner herself, only not so pretty. A few large freckles were appearing on her face, like blotches. Tiresome. Not true, she thought, that pregnancy improved your looks, rather the reverse. At night she stayed up in bed reading some of her own letters to Tim that she had extracted from Kit. But so far, nothng else. There were other letters, books and his diaries; she knew he had kept a diary; she meant to go through them all. They were part of her past and it was her past she wanted to study because in it must be the reason, somewhere, that she was hunted. But first she had to get hold of them.

Her letters were happy, hopeful letters; she hardly felt herself to be the Edwina who had written them. She remembered fondly that Tim had a little habit of writing notes to himself, and leaving them around. 'Remember laundry; Tim you are a fool to send your best shirts. They get pinched', or 'Flowers for Mamma's birthday. *Not* white carrations.' Once she had gathered them all up and destroyed them as ephemera. Now she wished she had them still. She felt irritated.

On the second day she put her work on the catalogue in an envelope which she addressed to

Janine at the gallery; Dougie would hand it over.

Then she went round to Sid's shop to collect her papers and any post there might be.

'Morning, Granddad.'

'Oh, you know that name then?' He was opening a drawer. 'How'd you pick it up?'

'A friend told me.' Lily, of course. 'You don't mind?'

'Made it happen, didn't I?'

There were no letters for her, so she was satisfactorily cut off. She felt liberated, neither mother-to-be, nor grieving lover, not even woman. Just a completely free creature off on her own. Like a dog on an afternoon ramble.

She took a bus to Lewisham where she entered a large, busy post office to despatch the catalogue to Dougie. Thus she avoided the Deptford postmark in case prying eyes were about. She might telephone Dougie tonight to advise destroying the envelope.

Two days passed peacefully for her; not so peacefully for others.

* * *

Leaning lightly on Janine Grandy's arm, Bee Linker toured the Garden. It was a trip she liked to take at least once a week; 'Gathering strength' she called it. Creative strength, she meant. Somehow the area fed her imagination. 'I've

142

been much more creative since I came here to live,' she had said. She could not see the place but she could remember it as it used to be and she could smell and hear it as it was now. The two made a stimulating mix to her.

She never let on to Janine how much she could hear, how much finer and more sensitive was her hearing than that of the fully-sighted. To overhear was a little luxury she allowed herself. It was a small compensation for what she had lost. And invaluable for her work, since she picked up hints and undertones that she might not have heard if her eyes had been busy.

On Janine's arm she prattled.

'You're talking your head off.' Janine spoke without malice.

'I know, but I'm enjoying it.' Canon Linker was a quiet man; he did his best but he usually seemed abstracted and talked to her with the air of one anxious to get back to his book or the letter he was writing. Even his sermons were quiet affairs: his parishioners loved him for other reasons.

On their walk they passed the site where the Carboard-Cut-Out Theatre used to set itself up. Today there was nothing but rain on the cobbles.

Bee knew at once. 'Where are they?'

'I don't know.' There was a notice stuck to a lamp post. Janine looked at it for a moment, then walked across to read. '"Performances

143

temporarily suspended", it says.'

'I knew they were short of money.' All gossip filtered quickly around the community of the Garden.

'I heard they were a bit pushed,' agreed Janine reluctantly.

'Does it cost much, I wonder, putting a show on here?'

'Well, something, I suppose. More than they had.'

'I should have made a contribution. One art should support another ... There's another vacant space, isn't there? Where Ginger and Pickles usually put their stall?'

The rain had washed away at another patch of bare ground, cleaning it up, taking off some of the surface dirt and sediment left behind by the stall. Ginger and Pickles were tidy women, but still you cannot live and work in a place without leaving traces behind. They had left a stain where Ginger had broken a bottle of walnut oil, and a long mark caused by an accident with a sack of cardamom: Pickles had been responsible for that. The rain had partly dealt with it all.

Bee knew, though. 'No. They aren't here? Their space is empty. I wonder why?'

Janine shifted her weight from one foot to another; Bee was leaning on her heavily, too heavily for her comfort. 'How do you know? How can you tell?'

Bee considered. 'I suppose I smell it. And feel

144

it, too. Emptiness vibrates.'

Janine did not laugh. For all she knew it might be true.

They walked on. Emptiness is not peace and can sometimes be a worry.

Two empty places must reflect two sets of people with problems. Bee meditated upon it.

She heard a car start, then stop. 'That's a police car, isn't it?' The police car had been about enough lately for her to have no difficulty in recognising its engine. 'Calling on Cassie Ross again, I suspect?'

'He is.'

'It's one way of pursuing an investigation. If that is what he is doing.' He was pursuing something certainly, and probably not only Cassie Ross. 'You know, I believe I should make a good detective. There have been precedents for a blind detective. Ernest Bramah invented one.'

Janine kept silent, she found Bee Linker alarming sometimes.

'He's seeing a lot of Cassie Ross, but not much of our Edwina who has temporarily disappeared. At least, I have not heard her around lately.'

Sergeant William Crail was an anxious man, too, but he was not worrying about Edwina. 'Don't waste time telling me about Miss Fortune,' he had said to Cassie. 'I know she's gone and I know how to get hold of her if I want

145

to. I'm a copper, remember, it's my job. That's not what's on my mind at the moment.'

Cassie was on his mind, in her own particular corner of it, but she was not his worry, either. Another woman was, and she was missing. Or if not missing, absent from her usual haunts. Not a woman much noticed, but one who interested him.

The police were slowly putting together a picture of the killer of Luke Tory. Or, at least, they were placing his movements and some of his characteristics as discerned through his behaviour. One striking characteristic was his power to disappear: he was here, then nowhere. It was as if he had evacuated the district.

Still, it was their belief, from forensic evidence, that the murderer had placed the poison which killed Luke in the decanter of whisky which only he drank. This suggested a good knowledge of Luke, and also access to the kitchen.

From this, a list of names had suggested itself. Among these names, those of Cassie, Alice and Edwina had come first. Sergeant William Crail had submitted personality profiles of each girl (successfully filtering out his personal interest in one of them). Yes, they were capable of killing; yes, it was his belief that two of them, Cassie and Alice, had been blackmailed by Luke Tory: they had tacitly let him know it. Largely by not denying it to him with any energy.

So there was motive and, since it was their milieu, evidence of their passage—fingerprints and clothing traces—was everywhere. Otherwise, this was where the murderer first disappeared. He, or she, had been here, but so had half smart and theatrical London. If he came from that world he had gone back into it leaving no discernible trace. (There might be one: they were hopeful but secretive on this clue.)

So at least they knew that if the murderer was not one of the three he could move in their world as a familiar figure. Although it was possible he changed his clothes. Was he a servant who could take off his apron and join his employers as their equal?

The extra dimension, the frill on the cake— the telephone caller whom Edwina Fortune complained of—was dismissed by Sergeant Crail's superiors as irrelevant.

Bill Crail now thought differently and believed the telephone caller and the murderer had one thing in common: how to come and go.

Edwina was central to it all, he thought; nothing that happened to her was irrelevant. Because, after all, it did look as though Luke had blackmailed Tim Croft over something. And Tim Croft, like Luke himself, led straight to Edwina.

'See you this evening,' Bill Crail had said to

Cassie; they had already worked out an arrangement for meeting.

He drove briskly past the empty spaces where the Carboard-Cut-Out Theatre and the health food stall usually stood. Gone.

*   *   *

Miss Drury looked down on their van which was parked beneath her sitting-room window. A group of local children were larking about it, as they often did when it was there. For some reason it amused them. Young devils, she thought, and banged on the window.

The room was square with a wide bay window, identical to the one immediately above belonging to Miss Dover. The two ladies lived similar but different lives, and Miss Dover's was the more way out. She had a wider, rougher circle of friends than her colleague, including some to whom Ginger closed her eyes, while there were one or two from whom even Pickles averted her gaze. But Pickles knew that from out of this circle of friends, and sometimes unhappy people, came profits.

Not hard drugs, nothing illegal, but there were products that Pickles could provide that might or might not help with certain urges. You could always hope, and Pickles' ragbag of clients were, whatever their sad lacks, hopeful people.

Ginger hated these people, but knew that

148

Pickles had to have them, needed them somehow, and profited from them. They both did. In fact, from people who wanted sexual stimulants, love potions or hate potions, their health food stall greatly prospered. Indeed, they needed it to.

This awkward fact was not exactly a secret between Ginger and Pickles, but it was unexpressed between them. A lot of things were left unsaid by them; life was like that, they felt. It was one of the points they had in common. Ginger now paced up and down her sitting room using the narrow passageway between sofa and table as a marching ground. The worn patches on the carpet showed how often before she had taken this walk. Pickles had gone absent without leave many a time before: Ginger always worried; she felt so alone. Alone except for a horde of fears with faces like devils. Ginger was not a great believer in the Devil as such but from experience she had come to believe in evil.

She thought she heard a noise in the room above; she went to the head of the stairs.

'Pickles, old love, is that you?'

Pickles had left the house yesterday evening on some unspecified errand of her own. She usually took the van on these occasions so Ginger presumed she had done so last night. She had not checked. The van was parked as a rule in the yard behind, where you could see it from the bathroom window if you leaned out and

149

twisted your neck. Ginger had done this once and badly ricked her neck. The proprietor of a health food stall with her head at an angle was a bad advertisement.

Yet the van had been outside the house when Ginger drank her early-morning tea. The old girl's back, she had thought, but her friend had not appeared.

The noise from the children below grew even louder. Vandals, she thought, I'd better go down and send them packing. She knew from experience that they only went if threatened with chastisement, so she took a walking stick with her.

She sped down the stairs, stick in hand. I could murder a cup of tea, she thought.

The word murder reminded her of Luke, then it produced her secret fear that someone would do in Pickles one day. She seemed so eminently murderable, somehow. Perhaps she was dead now, sitting propped up in their van. Or else bundled up, eyes staring, ready to roll out the back.

Halfway down the stairs, the stick dropped from her hand and rolled down the steps.

Very shortly afterwards Pickles returned from her night out. Feeling somewhat repentant after her gallivanting and anxious to make amends, she had gone to the bakers to buy some iced buns which were Ginger's favourite.

There she had fallen into conversation with

her friend the baker about the day's big race. Pickles was a punter of great enthusiasm yet little skill. The chat went on longer than she had intended; Pickles was always a little jolly after one of her escapades. Eventually she picked up the buns and started for home. 'Back Suzie's Joy,' she advised. 'Ten to one winner.'

'Armourer's Apprentice,' came the countercry. 'That'll do for me.'

Pickles rolled home. The first door was unlocked but they were casual about that, so she was unsurprised. At the bottom of the stairs she tripped.

A walking stick. Ginger's walking stick.

'Silly cow,' said Pickles. 'Leaving it there. I might have hurt myself.'

She moved forward, half wondering what that shadow was on the stairs.

Blackness moved, a shadow flowed forward, darkness came to life.

Canon Linker had seen darkness move, now Pickles saw it for herself.

CHAPTER SEVEN

Edwina had made what she considered satisfactory arrangements about her post, but the absent Lily had done nothing of the sort. There was already a pile of letters on the floor when Edwina arrived and then more were delivered every day. Lily appeared to have a whole horde of friends, all of whom delighted to write to her but none of whom seemed to know she was married. Neither close friends nor newspaper readers, then. Edwina, as she dealt with the letters, sorting them into neat piles and putting them on Lily's desk wondered about them. Some must be circulars, of course, while others were certainly bills. The evidence suggested that Lily paid her bills once a year, and that time of year had not yet arrived.

Edwina stacked the bills separately. Lily had a simplistic attitude to money; she squirrelled away large quantities of her earnings into what she called 'portable cash' and parted with it for bills only when she had to. But her creditors appeared to accept this, and to be making no serious complaint.

This morning the baby was beginning to make himself felt. Edwina did not mind. In a way she welcomed it as justifying her present hiding away from her usual world. Thus she was protecting the future. Her future and his.

She had given the child an identity: he was a boy and would resemble a neat amalgam between her and his father. The features of her own father might be indicated somewhere. She had created the child she wanted to have. Not all first mothers personalise their child as highly. Edwina was unusual in this as in her other circumstances.

Lily's flat was a curiously calming haven, where Edwina felt rested and at home in a way she had not noticed when its lively mistress was in residence. But then she had only been there when that lovely and volatile creature was entertaining. Lily's parties were not rowdy, but they were famous for their liveliness.

Now what Edwina noticed was the comfort of the chairs and the bed, the blue and white china in the kitchen, the way the light through the windows fell upon the furniture, and the unpretentious ease with which Lily had invested everything. It said something peaceful about Lily that was unexpected but which Edwina was glad to hear.

This flat was giving her something and she was taking it with open hands. I'll be able to manage the child now, she thought. I am beginning to feel my way forward to a way of life for the two of us that will work. I can be alone with this creature and still survive as a person. How strange that the murder of Luke, coupled with the telephone calls, should bring about such an end. It would move her one step further away from her friends, and out of that tight triangle. You could compensate, of course. I'll let Cassie and Alice help. Then, instantly: No, I won't. This is me. Alone, I'll do it. The step away was for ever then?

The day was going to be truly hot. Edwina

had all the windows open so that the noises from the street below floated up to her. She heard a woman shouting something about the price of lettuces and a man answering with a complaint about the late delivery of his newspaper. A third voice joined in with a message from someone called Eenie (so it sounded) who had gone off with someone called Scilla and who might never be coming back. This provoked an explosion from the first woman who seemed to be closely related to Scilla, if not to Eenie as well.

A dog began to bark, while from another open window pop music suddenly burst into sad sound with the beat banging away underneath like a cross voice with only one thing to say.

I'll buy some flowers, she decided. Roses, if I can get them, but anyway something sweet-smelling, then some salad stuff. The woman's voice shouting about lettuce had made her hungry for something crisp and green; food fancies were plentiful with her at the moment. And I will see if Dougie has sent on any post.

She did her shopping first, rather delaying going for her letters, reluctant that anything should break this happy mood she found herself in.

At a street stall she chose her flowers, not roses after all but white lilac, heavy and sweet. In the end she did not fancy lettuce, the smell seemed to choke her, but bought asparagus instead.

154

Then she strolled on to Sid's shop, where Sid was behind the counter smoking a herbal cigarette; the smell reminded her of Ginger and Pickles.

'Morning, miss. Come for your post?' He opened a drawer and handed over a packet of letters. 'Nice little pile for you today.' He looked curious but did not ask any questions, as Edwina had guessed he would not when she set up her arrangements. He was well paid for his service; silence was built into the bargain.

'Thank you.' She put the letters in her shopping basket, one borrowed from Lily's kitchen. 'Any news?'

'Nothing local except our dentist has eloped with his nurse; knowing his wife I don't blame him. In the world outside, the usual couple of wars.' He pushed a newspaper across for her to read the headlines. 'Have it on the house . . . Had someone in here just now asking after you.' He watched her face, eyes interested, mouth half smiling.

'What?' Instantly she was alert. 'Who?'

He relented at once. 'Don't worry. Only Mrs Waters who lives next door to us. "Who's that lovely lady?" she asked. She loves to know who her neighbours are. She thinks you're an American.'

Edwina relaxed; he was aware of it. So she did mind enquiries after her. He had been testing her out. 'Oh yes, so she's Mrs Waters, the one with the hats? Why does she think I am an American?' Mrs Waters was the proprietor now of a small café, from whose window she watched the world, always wearing a brightly coloured hat.

'Because of your clothes . . . They're not the sort we usually see around here.'

Edwina took note of that; in future she would watch what she wore. It was her first intimation that out of your own habitat you stood out like a banana on an apple tree; you did not notice the other inhabitants but they recognised you for a stranger. London was made up of lots of villages and now she was in a new one.

'Thanks.' In his way Sid had been helpful, had perhaps meant to be, perhaps not. 'Well, what did you tell her?'

'Nothing. Don't talk about customers too much. Rule number one in my business. Any business.' Then he added tolerantly, 'But she's not a bad old thing. Used to be a milliner up west and that's where the hats come from. She's using up old stock.'

Impossible to know if he was telling the truth or just building up a story.

His wife came from the room behind and gave him an alert, affectionate look. 'I heard that. But why was she asking? A nosy old thing she may be but old Mother Waters never does anything unless she's got a reason for it.' She gave a brisk nod towards Edwina. 'I'm only just saying. I mean, she sits over there at her window watching us all but I wouldn't call her a detached observer. If she asked questions, then someone asked her. Money might even have passed hands.'

'Take no notice of my dear wife,' said Sid. 'She fancies herself as a spinner of yarns.'

'Thanks anyway,' said Edwina. She took her letters and went out into the street. She had a quick look at the letters, identifying most of them easily enough as business of one sort or another. There was a picture postcard from Alice, nothing from Cassie. There was a small manilla envelope of which she could make nothing, while somehow feeling she should. She would have to take it back to the flat and open it.

As she walked back she glanced towards Mrs Waters sitting at her cash desk by the window; her gaily turbaned head was bent over the accounts but she seemed to be keeping a weather eye on the street because her head moved slightly as Edwina paused across the road.

Edwina watched, her mood nicely poised between amusement and annoyance. You old witch, no one knows I'm here, so you can only have been asking questions for your own amusement. But I'll bear in mind what you are like.

She ran up the stairs to Lily's place, her feet moving lightly although she already felt heavier in the body, for today she was charged with energy.

The postman had called on Lily too. There was a letter on the mat, the smallest post since Edwina arrived. Lily's friends were sporadic correspondents.

She picked it up, thinking: I won't send it on, Lily won't want it. Anyway, they're travelling. Lily and Edwina's father were touring France and might push on to Italy.

But this letter was not for Lily. She stared down at it, not wanting to believe what she saw.

The letter was addressed to her in clear typewritten characters. Her name and the full address. No mistake about it.

'No one knows I am here,' she said aloud to the empty flat. 'Not even Dougie knows.'

But in front of her was clear evidence that this was not true. Someone did know, knew precisely where she was and had addressed the envelope accurately.

She opened it. A photograph fell out and fluttered on to the table in front of her. It was the small sort of snapshot picture you used for passports.

You sat in a booth, paid your money and waited for the flash. And this was what you got.

A face was staring up at her. If you could call it a face, hidden as it was behind dark spectacles and with a soft-brimmed dark hat pulled down over the brow. A greyish coat, a raincoat possibly, dragged towards the throat.

Oh, she knew who he was all right. *Him*. The telephone caller, the follower.

She did not even have to ask herself what was the meaning of the photograph, so crudely taken and cruelly despatched. This, too, she knew.

It meant no more telephone calls, that stage was over. Now he would be coming in person. She was meant to know his face...

That man, whoever he is, she said to herself, both desires and hates me.

But there was a strange, still archaic smile on the lips, as if the face wanted to say: I am a Fury.

She felt quite sick. She stood for a moment, letting the wave of sickness pass over her, her forehead began to feel wet. As a child she had had a terrier dog who, when about to vomit (and this happened to him often, he was a thief and a hunter), had stood still with his eyes rolling, waiting for the worst to happen. She could feel her own eyes doing this now. With an effort she held them still, focusing them on a photograph of Lily. The sickness began to ebb away; she sat down and closed her eyes. Her head steadied and the panic subsided. Keep calm, she told herself, and start to think.

So running away wasn't such a good idea after all. She had been tracked down without too much trouble. It hadn't even taken very long.

I'm not good at running away, she told

herself. But I could learn, I could go further and run harder. Only where to?

There were places, she could think of several without any trouble; her family had more than one house. But she had this other traveller coming with her now: the child who would be her constant companion for the coming months. Perhaps she ought to take his opinion into account. Just because he could not voice it, was not to mean he did not have one. He had called her to a halt just now by the sickness.

At the moment this fellow traveller was telling her to sit down and take it easy. Since he had ways of enforcing his advice, she took it.

She had some unpleasant thoughts to handle. First was the fact that she had been found so easily. But behind this alarming thought was one even more alarming. Only her closest friends had known she was in hiding at all. Dougie was meant to have covered up with everyone else that she wasn't in her own place.

So one of them, somewhere, somehow, had let it all out. Accidentally or on purpose, one of her friends had betrayed her. It was terrible to think that she could no longer rely on their loyalty or, at least, their discretion.

Who were the candidates? She was still inclined to rely on Dougie. He was clever enough to know that she could ruin his career in the art world if he let her down. Besides, there was a tough, resolute quality to Dougie, apart from his gentleness, that she respected. He held true, she thought.

Cassie then? It was fearful to her to think of Cassie other than in terms of total trust, but she was coming to it. Cassie's tongue had always been suspect: she said too much, too freely. And now she had the policeman to talk to. Edwina had always thought that Cassie's sexual wanderings could be dangerous, but she had thought of the dangers in terms of Cassie herself without thinking it might brush off on her.

Better withdraw a bit further from Cassie. Just to be on the safe side. The child's side. Not that the child had uttered on this point, it had remained silent, might even have wanted to remain close to Cassie, but Edwina was doing the thinking now, for the moment in control.

Then what about Alice? Well, as to Alice, who knew what went on behind that pretty mask? Edwina who loved her had caught Alice out in one or two tricks that had made her raise an eyebrow. Alice could fight dirty if she had to. Sometimes she loved Alice without liking her.

What Alice had felt about Tim she had never been quite sure, but how Alice felt about Kit she had no doubt. Alice had betrayed herself in all sorts of little ways. Alice was very serious about Kit, and probably Kit knew it.

She would not let herself think about Kit Langley as a possible betrayer, but of one thing she was sure; of all the people concerned he was

161

the one clever enough to have tracked her down if he had so wished.

But she wanted to trust Kit, he was something to hang on to. She put the lid down firmly on any analysis of her feelings for Kit. She felt she owed something to that silent other occupant of her body. Tim was not only part of her past life, he had entered into her present in a very vital and lively way. At the moment he was part of her, and even when that conjunction had its term he would have his representative with her for the rest of their lives. In time one might put certain things behind one, but they had a claim.

The burden of her past and her future sat on her shoulders heavily at that moment. Somewhere, somehow, she had got something wrong. Misunderstood, a person sent out the wrong signals so that what she was getting now in return was hatred.

She felt the hatred without knowing where it came from or why. She had to pray it was not emanating from her tight circle of close friends but she no longer knew whom to trust.

She took another look at the photograph. The glance yielded her nothing. Impossible to recognise anyone in that rig. It might be someone she knew, someone she saw often, but she couldn't tell. It could be Dougie or Kit or the postman. All you could see was a longish nose and eyes that looked dark behind their glasses. It could even be Cassie. God knows her friends had often complained that her nose was long enough. Only not physically, it was her curiosity that was legendary. Perhaps the policeman Crail knew what he was about in chatting her up.

Or perhaps he just suspected her of killing Luke and wanted a close look. The figure of Luke moved out of the background at that moment and reminded Edwina that death had stood close to her. She had pushed Luke behind her these last few days but he was moving forward with a vengeance now to recall to her what could happen. What might have been meant to happen to her and not to Luke.

I was right to run, she told herself. That wasn't a mistake, but I didn't run far enough.

Or fast enough, or secretly enough. The welcome and security, the feeling of comfort that Lily's flat had seemed to offer had been a delusion, like hiding under a table when the roof is blown in.

I can go further. Shift myself out of reach. There are places to go: that was one thought.

Then almost at once she heard Sid's voice saying, 'Someone was asking after you,' and his wife adding, 'old Mother Waters never does anything for nothing.'

Had that been what she said? It did not matter. Edwina had stood in the street and studied Mrs Waters through the café window and been unable to make up her mind about the woman. She looked harmless enough, but she had been asking questions. She might just be a harmless eccentric or she might not. When Edwina had stared through the windows, Mrs Waters had not stared back. If anything, she had avoided looking at Edwina. Almost as if she preferred not, a pleasant thought.

Edwina decided: I'm going to take another look at that lady. Some quiet questions if she could phrase them right might not come amiss either.

Picking up the photograph she threw the rest of her post on the table, gathered up her bag, and hurried out of the flat and down the stairs.

The staircase was as empty as always, the whole house of flats quiet and still. So far she had never seen any of her neighbours and had hardly heard them. Just the baker going out late at night. He had a terrible cough. But she knew he smoked too much, that was one thing she did know about him, the cigarette smoke drifted up the stairs and through her door.

When she walked into the café it was to find two other customers standing at the counter and a third installed at the table by the window.

She asked for a cup of tea. It was not the sort of place she usually ate in, but she knew without being told that you could rely on the tea but not coffee.

She carried her cup over to a corner seat next

to the window, well aware that Mrs Waters was looking at her with interest, and that one of the customers had turned round to give her an open stare. The other two drifted out.

Mrs Waters, having put the money for the tea in the till, had moved to adjust her red turban in a mirror while giving Edwina a covert survey.

Edwina gave her a minute then moved over to the counter. Mrs Waters turned round.

'Tea all right, love?'

'A bit stewed.'

Mrs Waters glanced at Edwina's cup, she could see the girl had scarcely tasted it. 'I'll make you a fresh pot.'

'Don't bother.'

'Can't have my tea impugned.'

'I want a word with you, Mrs Waters. You are Mrs Waters?'

Mrs Waters gave a little adjusting tug at her red turban. 'My name is Mignon.'

The customer leaning against the counter gave a melancholy little hoot as if he had now heard everything.

Edwina ignored all this. 'You were asking after me? Asking who I was?'

Mrs Waters poured out another cup of tea. 'Take this, dear, and with my compliments. On the house. You'll find this cup nice and hot. Mustn't drink the other if it's not quite right. Soon have you down the collywobble shop, wouldn't we?'

Edwina persisted. 'Why did you ask?'

'Oh I don't think so, dear,' said Mignon Waters in a soothing voice. 'Why should I do that?'

'Sid said you did.'

'Oh Sid. I should drink your tea, dear, and forget it.'

Edwina said nothing but she made it clear that she was not going to go away. The other customer finished his drink and moved out of the café. Not his quarrel and he didn't want to get involved. But he remained outside, pretending to read his newspaper but really keeping an eye on what was going on inside. He was a spectator of life and he had hopes of drama.

Edwina pushed the new cup of tea away from her slowly and carefully while keeping her eyes on Mignon's well-made-up face. It was a long time since she had seen such impudently false eyelashes on a human face.

She made her point. Mignon moved the cup infinitesimally towards herself, signalling defeat. 'Well, I'm a nosy old thing,' she said cheerfully. 'And there you are such a beautiful young thing, and I've never seen you before. And your clothes are really something special. Bond Street, at least, the good end of it, too. I'd say that jacket was Valentino. Now aren't I right? Admit it. I know about clothes. Hats, more.' She put a hand to her turban. 'I trained

166

with Madame Mirman in the *big* days, when before Ascot or a big society wedding we'd work till we dropped ...' She paused to get her breath.

'You asked,' said Edwina. 'Why? Not just because of my clothes, and the jacket is Ferragamo.'

Mignon Waters stretched out a hand and touched a sleeve, stroked it. 'Well, I knew it was Italian. You can always tell.' As if the touch of the excellent Italian silk tweed had made up her mind for her, she said, 'All right. A customer saw you out of the window, asked if you lived in Lirriper Street and how long had you been here. I didn't know but I said I'd find out. Anyway, I wanted to know. He never came back to ask.'

Because he knows. Somehow he knew. He was just checking for the hell of it. Enjoying it probably.

'What shall I say if he does?'

'Do you always do what people ask you to do? Or how much did he pay you? What did he look like?'

'Now who's asking questions?' The disciple of haute couture abandoned elegance, got her arms akimbo, and looked remarkably like her grandmother who had sold clothes from a stall in Woolwich market. 'I didn't notice him specially. Just an ordinary man. It was a wet day and he was all done up in togs.'

'Wearing dark spectacles?'

167

'Can't say. Might have, might not.'

Her tone was defiant. Not an ordinary man, thought Edwina, and you know it. Your voice gives you away.

Edwina left Mrs Waters looking at the still cooling cup of tea. Presently she would drink it. Nothing went to waste with her.

★   ★   ★

The man who had been enquiring after Edwina sat in the back room of Mignon Waters' shop drinking his coffee while considering what to do.

Now he knew where Edwina was. That was one thing. What to do was another.

He had heard Edwina's voice, not really heard what she said. Seen her through a crack in the door.

It was his second visit to Deptford but well worth while; except, of course, he had to decide how to act.

Mignon came back into the room. 'Well, you heard that then?'

'More or less.'

'I hope it's given you what you want.' She sounded uneasy. Money had changed hands, but she did not want to feel a Judas. My name is Mignon, she told herself, not Iscariot.

'It's given me what I want.' The exact place where Edwina had taken refuge. 'Thank you.'

The polite response soothed Mignon's nerves. He must, after all, be a nice man.

'She's gone off now. I'm afraid she was rather angry with me. I don't mind.' Mignon was respectful; anyone who wore clothes like Edwina's was someone to regard.

Now she hoped that he would go away so she could put the episode behind her. Forget it. She had forgotten many worse things.

He had left his umbrella behind, a good one. She picked it up, recognising it as an expensive one made by Swaine, Adeney, Brigg of Piccadilly. On a small gold plate was engraved a name:

Timothy Croft 19 October 1982

'What a shame.' She stroked the beautifully polished handle with an appreciative finger. 'He's lost it.'

Mignon put the umbrella away in a cupboard gratefully. Later, she would pawn it.

★　　★　　★

Edwina walked slowly down the street, thinking: I'll pack this in, it's not working out, living in Lily's flat. I like it here, but it won't do. I'll put my things together and move out. Go to Scotland maybe. It's peaceful up there. Stay there for a bit and pull myself together. That's how it could be. I won't even tell Dougie ... Tell the bank, I suppose; he can send letters there. If they matter.

She crossed the road, neatly avoiding the traffic without looking at it, causing one driver to shout, 'You want to die, miss?'

She stood for a moment looking in Sid's shop window. The evening newspapers were being delivered from a small van.

No, he was no ordinary man who pursued her with sickness and desire.

She caught sight of her reflection in the shop window; she looked normal, ordinary enough, but she was not. She had not been since she fell in love with Tim (or whatever that turbulent emotion had been) and ceased to be whatever it was she had been before—tough, cool, professional—and became what she was now, a one-person problem family on the run.

Tim would hardly know her. But would she know Tim any longer? His figure had been receding into the distance more and more, and the further he went the more of a puzzle he seemed. He *hadn't* been straightforward; she could see that clearly now, although she had not seen it then. For the first time she faced up to the fact that there had been a dark area in Tim's character that she had sensed without admitting.

From somewhere in that dark area could have walked the person stalking her now.

Luke's face joined hers and Tim's as she stood staring in Sid's window. She had to give

Luke a place too.

As she turned to walk away, Sid waved to her as he bent forward to pick up the heavy pile of evening papers. His wife was already reading one. Then they had a cup of tea and studied the paper together.

Several interesting stories were running, but it was the death by strangling of a woman in South London and the attempted murder of her friend that caught their eye.

A few minutes later Mrs Waters came across to collect her evening paper; she too read the story.

Across London Cassie and Alice already knew that there had been a new killing.

Canon Linker had told Bee and her secretary Janine as they sat at work. He felt obliged to tell them, a moral duty to speak. For him darkness was over everything then.

No one felt obliged to tell Dougie but he heard anyway, and was now running around distracted, wondering if he ought to get in touch with Edwina.

Only Edwina did not, as yet, know. She ran up the stairs to Lily's flat, her hideaway, no longer so welcoming.

On the table was the photograph, still lying face up. She put it in her handbag. If she got brave enough she might show it to the police.

Her eyes rested on the pile of letters also on the table. The letter in the brown envelope was

171

on top, still unopened.

Belatedly taking in the significance she stretched out a hand, her heart beginning to beat fast. No news in the medical sphere was good news; if the clinic was writing to her, then there had to be a reason, and it was probably not good.

The letter opened itself, spreading out on the table in front of her.

But the message was short and to the point: Dr Michaels wanted to make some more tests. An appointment had been set up for her. Would she confirm it?

There was to be no running away; she had to stay.

The silent traveller inside her was asserting his rights and would stop her running.

CHAPTER EIGHT

The scene was breaking up. As Edwina, all unaware of the new murder, travelled back across London to her own flat by bus and tube (Sid said it was safer with her in her present state, she could collect her own car later), the Cardboard-Cut-Out Theatre was packing itself up and trundling away. Perhaps for ever. The area where the health food stall usually stood had been empty all morning.

Canon Linker was talking about death to his Aunt Bee, who in turn was composing sentences in her head to be transmitted to Janine who sat, pad in hand, patiently waiting. Bee Linker was having a difficult time with composition. She had got her heroine to the bedchamber door but was undecided what to do with her. Events had got in the way of the bedding of her heroine. If only Jim would stop talking she might be able to get on with it. But she recognised his need to talk and reached out a hand to him. They were all wretched about Ginger and Pickles. Somehow those silly nicknames were still how you thought of them even in death.

Jim was telling them how the two women had been discovered by the postman on the stairs of the house where they lived and the police had been called in. 'It was clearly murder, you see. Strangulation.' She could tell by the black bass note in his voice that he was both sad and angry.

Cassie Ross was talking to the policeman, Bill Crail. He had had a fractious scene with his colleague, Elsie Lewis, who thought Cassie too clever by half, which she was, and a snob, which she was not. Also a hindrance to the police investigation of Luke Tory's death and a bloody nuisance, both of which she might have been. His relationship with Cassie had settled into a form they both recognised: they might not stay together for ever, nor perhaps even for long, but for the moment it was good. She had established that he had been lying when he claimed friendship with her old college chum, and he had established that she did not mind and had never believed it anyway. Honour was satisfied on both sides.

He had just given Cassie his version of the finding of the bodies of Misses Drury and Dover, a version substantially the same as Jim Linker's but containing a few details of his own. Such as that Ginger had been whacked on the head, while Pickles had been strangled. Ginger was not yet dead; she might pull through. But she could not yet talk. There was some doubt if she would ever talk again. She'd have the throat and the voice-box all right, but not the mind. Brain damage.

'I know where your friend Edwina is, so you don't need to worry over her.' In which he was wrong; Cassie was quite right to be worried.

'I could make a fairly good guess myself,' said Cassie thoughtfully. 'Eddie can be pretty transparent sometimes and so can Dougie.' She had worked out where Edwina had gone and so had Dougie. They had both known that Edwina was looking after the key to Lily's flat and both had seen that it was gone. It did not take much working out. Others might do it.

'Perhaps her state of mind needs watching over.'

'There's nothing wrong with Eddie's mind. She's one of the sanest, cleverest people I know.'

'Normally, no doubt.' He gave Cassie a hard stare. 'But she's not in her normal state at the moment, is she?'

'She has good reason.'

'The man she claims is after her. And *that*'s a funny business.'

'A typical male, police reaction,' said Cassie angrily.

They were drinking in the Duke of York in the hour before noon when it was less crowded. The Duke produced a reasonable cup of coffee as well as a good sherry; they were combining the two. 'Oh, I believe it, in a way. And she's pregnant.'

'Oh, you know about that?'

'Of course.'

'I don't know about "of course". I thought medical matters were confidential.'

'I didn't have to go to a doctor to find out she was pregnant. I'm a detective, remember?' He was not prepared to admit how he had found out, but the means had been somewhat unethical, involving a policewoman and a medical student. 'I guessed.' That was partly true, anyway, he had guessed before finding out. She was beginning to show.

'It hasn't touched her mind.'

'But what about her emotions? These telephone calls . . .' He shrugged.

'We all had them,' Cassie said sharply.

'But she took them to heart; she responded. That's where she went wrong. She should have taken a tough line. Instead she runs away. Not far but far enough to be a nuisance.' He drank his coffee which was too strong and bitter for his taste; he had recently given up sugar and not managed to achieve a relationship with a substitute. He pulled a face. 'We will be out of your place soon.'

The police investigation team had kept control of Cassie's Garden premises since Luke Tory's death. Cassie had been locked out of her offices, but not her living rooms.

'Sorry if it's been an inconvenience to you.'

'Oh well, I hadn't really moved into the office and drawing room; my staff have been operating from the Baker Street office. I hadn't planned to make a total move till the autumn so it hasn't mattered.'

'You've been living there, though.'

Cassie grinned. 'And well you know it.' He had spent two out of the last seven nights there, departing discreetly with the dawn. Elsie Lewis knew, of course, and this partly explained her fractious moods. Bill Crail decided that although he loved women he did not always like them. 'But I don't mind living in a muddle.'

'I had noticed.' He was an orderly man himself and would have tidied Cassie up if he had thought of a long-term relationship, but that was not how he saw it and he doubted

176

Cassie did either, and he was too wise to probe. If you probed in that area you frequently dug up things better left hidden. He had done it once, when younger, and been rapidly married then unmarried as a consequence. 'How well do you know Edwina Fortune? And I don't mean that bit about all being born on the same day and sharing horoscopes, I mean how well?'

'I love her,' said Cassie. 'And that's well enough.'

'In a way.' He had picked up the story about the three of them being a unit, friends indissoluble, examined it carefully and found that it held true, but it wasn't the answer he wanted. 'But you loved other people too.'

'Well, we had relationships, yes. Alice got married.'

'And Edwina Fortune loved a man called Tim who got killed. So did Luke Tory. And now another death. There's a lot of death around you three.'

'Yes, I'm shattered about Miss Dover. But there's no connection, is there?'

Bill Crail started his sherry, which was sour to his taste too. 'I don't know. Not my case. Not even in my patch.' He sipped his sherry. 'We agreed when we started that you wouldn't ask questions and I wouldn't answer them.' This was what stuck in Elsie Lewis's throat: she couldn't believe it.

They stared at each other.

'I can't help thinking, and you can't help telling,' said Cassie. 'Yes, tell.'

He stared at her indignantly.

Cassie began to laugh. 'Oh yes, you do. All the time, and more than you know.'

Bill Crail opened his mouth to speak, then shut it again. Sometimes she made him speechless.

'For instance, I know you still hold the belief that one of us three killed Luke. Poisoned him with agaric powder. One of us.'

'Cass—'

'And you'll choose your time to tell me which it is. In bed, probably. A bit like a detective story. A Raymond Chandler? "Baby, I hate to tell you—it's you. You're a murderer."'

'I still have feelings, Cass.'

'But you're the detective.'

'I'll tell you what I am: I am like a small electronic eye moving over the ground, seeing, reporting what I see. Or think of me as a little insect grubbing up facts. There's a lot of other people at work, forensic scientists, other policemen, a lot senior to me. It doesn't matter too much what I think, Cass.'

He did not usually take such a low view of himself; previously he had felt that he had given colour to an investigation, materially aided its turnout, even if as a junior detective, but the company of Cassie seemed to demand honesty. Beside her he felt a nothing. For the first time

178

he asked himself if there might be something enduring in this relationship. After all, marriage might be right some time; he was a man with unconsciously conventional moral standards.

'What I want to know,' said Cassie, 'this other murder, poor Pickles', is it connected with Luke?'

Bill Crail was careful; with women like Elsie Lewis and Cassie Ross around in his life, he had to be. 'As I said, it's not in my patch . . . I am not privy to anything,'—Cassie started to giggle, she found his turns of speech endearingly formal—'but there does not, as yet, seem to be a connection.' Then he added carefully, 'Other than that they sited their stall in the Garden and that they knew both you three and Luke Tory.'

There might be another connection; he had been holding it back, but he could afford to let it out now. It was hardly a secret, being well passed around in police circles. He himself had caught a smell of the truth the very first day of the investigation into Luke Tory's death, when he had picked up the newspaper that Tory had been reading in the taxi. You could call it coincidence if you liked, but he did not believe in that sort of a coincidence; when you were working and thinking at a certain level, things stood out so that you saw them large and clear. He did not know how Luke Tory had reacted when he read the name of the corrupt constable Edward Miller, but Crail knew how he had felt himself. Poor bloody fool, he had thought.

'I don't want to go into details,' he said. 'But we think that Luke Tory used the special insight he got into people's lives to blackmail them, small sums, but enough. One of his victims, a young policeman, has confessed ... His name plus notes of money received was in the notebook that Tory kept in his desk. Tim Croft's name was there, sums of money mentioned, again. Likewise Miss Drury's name ... no sum mentioned there.' Was he blackmailing her? He could have been, they knew she had peddled strange odds and ends of drugs. Perhaps they were blackmailing each other.

'Tim!' Cassie seized on the name at once. 'Edwina's not going to like that much.'

He shrugged.

'I suppose she has to know?'

'She may know already.'

Cassie digested what he had said; when she spoke her voice was cold. 'Edwina is not a murderer.'

If anything she was a victim, but Cassie did not say this aloud either. She had only just seen it as part of Edwina's character and she did not like it.

'Nor is there any direct connection between Tim's accident, Luke's death and the murder of Pickles Dover.'

'Nothing clear,' agreed Bill Crail. 'All

circumstantial. But wouldn't it be interesting if there was?' He was hoping; he had heard there was one interesting possible forensic link. A strange, and biting one.

Cassie finished her drink and stood up. I covered up well there, she told herself. I think, I hope . . . but Tim. Well, that explains a lot. The toad beneath the harrow knows. I wonder? And she thought about another name that might be added to Luke's blackmail list. The trouble with blackmail was that it was like a crawling disease that never stayed still. 'I'm off.' She hitched her bag over one shoulder so that it hung like a school satchel and marched out. He stayed where he was.

Things were breaking up in the Garden and good might come out of it.

For the police, anyway.

★   ★   ★

Edwina was almost home when Alice finished trying on the winter clothes of her most distinguished customer. The child had been easy, mother and nanny difficult. Across the room her eyes met those of the child, a boy of about six, small for his age, and a cool measured glance passed between them. They had come to an arrangement, tacit but negotiated: he would behave with quiet dignity when fitted and she would do what was expected of her. Children of his age, he especially, were supposed not to need money. But whether he needed it or not, he liked it, and the small secret golden coin was a sweetener. She wondered what he did with them, possibly stock-piling them against the deluge. They had always been a far-sighted family and not foolish about money.

Alice looked at her assistant who was holding the pins and suppressed a yawn. Her most important engagement of the day and the last. She was tired. They were going now. Moving out of her showroom in a dignified procession.

When they had gone Alice retired into her small office and closed the door on the world outside. The elation and sense of triumph that would once have followed such an encounter no longer bubbled up. She'd done it, succeeded in her own particular way in her own special world, but was it worth it?

She would like to have talked it over with Edwina and Cassie. Part of her present trouble was that she was missing their old closeness. She had a shrewd idea where Edwina was hiding away, but she wasn't going to do anything about it. Alice guessed that Edwina would soon be back; she wasn't a girl to hide away for long. And anyway, life forced you back as a rule. Nature did not seem to favour evasion.

The news about Ginger and Pickles had reached her that morning from two sources, first Dougie and then Canon Linker who was on his way to talk to the Cardboard-Cut-Out Theatre.

She was miserable and unhappy. Not frightened exactly, for Alice had the deep feeling that nothing could touch her, but coming close to it.

She felt very much alone. Cassie had struck up a relationship with the detective and Edwina had fled, only Alice was left on her own. She had tried telephoning Kit Langley, but there was no reply from his flat and his chambers in the Temple would not answer questions about where he was to be found. Perhaps they did not know, either. But of course they did and were only protecting him from Alice. She sighed: she really loved Kit, wherever he was.

He might be with Edwina.

Alice was, in the end, a cynic about human behaviour, and thought anything was possible.

There had always been something about those telephone calls (of which she had had, initially, her share) which had aroused her scepticism. Something not quite right, she told herself. How did a man behave who was, obscenely, pursuing a woman? Not so, she thought.

Even to question the truth of what her friend was undergoing seemed a heresy, one did not think of Edwina like that, but the natural sceptic inside Alice stirred and would ask questions. What was behind it all, and wasn't Edwina's reaction too extreme, too hysterical? She was pregnant, that had to be true, the hospital said so. Otherwise ... No, Alice, repress the thought, she told herself.

Oh Edwina, Edwina, she thought, we were all so close once. What has gone wrong at the heart of us that we have fallen into this trouble? No answer there, either.

They were three separate entities now, drifting apart like continents, pulled by subterranean forces beyond their control.

As Edwina travelled back to the news of the death of Pickles Dover, carrying with her in her baggage, together with letters and memories, that photograph she passionately studied while desiring not to recognise, things were breaking up in the Garden. Cassie, Alice, Bee and Jim Linker, even Janine Grandy, were drawing into themselves and apart from each other.

And the Cardboard-Cut-Out Theatre, worst hit of all as they trundled back to base in Woolwich, had mislaid a patron and a fellow performer. 'Nina's away,' was their sad refrain. She'd be back, of course, she always was, but meanwhile they were in need of a paymaster and a friend.

.

CHAPTER NINE

'Whatever happened to us?' said Alice sadly. It was a rhetorical question, not demanding an answer. They were all together again, the three, fallen without thought into their old position in Edwina's flat with Alice on the floor, Edwina elegantly on the sofa, and Cassie upright in an armchair, spectacles on her nose, looking formidable. But it felt different, no disguising it. They knew now that Edwina had been at Lily's place in Deptford, and even in the short space away they could see how she had changed. Or perhaps the change had been coming on slowly all this time and the absence made it show. Her very shape was different.

'Apart from murder and sudden death?' Cassie took off her spectacles, revealing eyes that looked as though she might have been crying.

'I know what happened to me,' said Edwina with feeling. She was no longer wearing the clothes that Mignon Waters had admired, but had put on a loose dark cotton house-gown made by a famous Japanese designer in a low mood. It was very chic, high-fashion, lost-person clothing, as if a refugee had managed to get to a good couturier to have her rags made up. Only someone with a lot of money to spend and a lot of self-confidence could afford to dress like that. The effect was both vulnerable and highly sexed, and ought to have had a danger label on it. Cassie, looking at Edwina, wondered if she knew what the effect was and decided she did not, but that it explained a lot about Edwina that she had chosen to wear it. Asking for trouble. Open to violence.

As if reading this thought, Edwina drew her bare feet in under her frayed hem. A curve of breast white against the dark curtain could just be seen beneath a well-placed tear in the fabric. Cassie turned her eyes away.

Alice reached out a hand and patted Edwina's. 'Sorry, love, we do forget. Was it lousy at the pre-mums clinic?'

It was the day after Edwina's return to her own flat in Packet's Place.

'Not too bad, really,' said Edwina. 'They've even got a new coffee machine that makes stuff you can drink with some pleasure so I could quaff while I waited.' She was being brave and they knew it. There had not been good news for her at the clinic. 'And would you believe it, they now hand out paper robes cut like this when you undress.' She held up one arm, letting the dark cotton fall away from the wide armhole.

'Not that colour, though,' said Alice.

'No, love, a sort of dirty white. Not bad all the same.'

Alice examined the idea. 'Be nice pleated.'

'Yes, it would ... I was pretty miserable about Pickles, of course, so my blood pressure was up. If that was why.'

'Oh yes, I expect so, nerves.' Alice was soothing. She was good at this sort of conversation, she got so much practice with her own customers.

'It certainly wasn't the baby, poor thing.'

'Don't worry about it.'

'But it's too small, you see.'

'Babies are small.' She gave a quick glance at Edwina who was, in fact, filling out. 'Minute.'

'Small for dates, they call it. And that's bad.' She got off the sofa and started to pad barefoot up and down the room. She had given them no real reason for her return. Certainly no account of what had happened in Deptford. She had just remarked that she had 'felt like coming home'. But she thought they had both given her a long, thoughtful look while welcoming her back. And the news about Ginger and Pickles had been what they talked about. 'I can see the doctors are alarmed and so am I. So would you be.' The other two made sympathetic noises. 'I could do with a drink, couldn't you?' Her hand hovered over a decanter. 'Small for dates,' she added reflectively. 'Whisky? Sherry?'

'Make it coffee,' said Cassie, 'and I'm with you. I've got to work tonight when I get back.'

'Alice?'

'Coffee too,' Alice stood up as well. 'Shall I make it for you?'

'No.' Edwina moved away. 'Prefer to potter round my own kitchen.'

When she had gone Alice said, 'You sent her off to make that coffee on purpose, didn't you?'

'Yes. Wanted a word with you. I'm worried

about her. She looks terrible.'

This was true; there were rings around Edwina's eyes, and although her waist looked thicker, her face was pinched.

'Yes, she does look bad ... I'm worried about this baby.'

'Everyone is.'

'Puzzled ... I suppose there really is ...'

Cassie broke in. 'We've had this conversation before ... They've made strides since Mary Tudor. Science is wonderful. They can *tell*.'

'But the mind ... It can do strange things.' Alice shook her head. 'I just feel there's something terribly wrong with the whole picture ... Edwina, the telephone calls that drove her away ... The man she says pursued her.'

'She looks shocked,' said Cassie, following her own thoughts.

'We're all shocked ... With her, it's that and something more.'

'Such as?'

'Supposing there isn't anyone following her, supposing it's all her imagination?'

'Well, we know that's not true.'

'We don't, do we? We know the beginning phone calls happened, I saw a man, or so I *thought*, but how much of the rest has been a kind of hyperimagination?'

Cassie said nothing and Alice swept on:

'And don't tell me the police don't think so as well.'

Cassie still said nothing but that was enough for Alice. 'So it *is* what your pet policeman thinks, I'm right.'

'He doesn't quite tell me what he thinks.' That was true enough, he kept a lot back and you couldn't expect otherwise, but he had ways of letting her see beneath the surface, and what she had seen had been disconcerting. The police were so hard.

The smell of coffee was floating in from the kitchen and they heard the chink of china. 'Won't be a minute,' called Edwina.

'There's something you and I have got to talk about,' said Cassie quickly to Alice.

Alice raised her eyebrows. 'Just me? Is Edwina not included?'

'Not at the moment. Later perhaps.'

'You are being mysterious. Something you know and I don't?'

'I'm sure,' said Cassie grimly.

'Does your policeman still think one of us three killed Luke?'

Cassie gave a short laugh. 'I believe he would if he was pushed to it, but at the moment he hasn't quite got the evidence.'

'And you don't mind?'

'I don't think about it.'

'I'd mind,' said Alice.

'Of course I mind, you fool, I didn't say I didn't mind, I said I didn't think about it.'

'So it's serious with him?'

'I don't know.'

One more step in their break-up as a group had been taken. They had always been open with each other about love affairs. More or less. Even if they had told little lies (as Alice always had), the others had always known the truth. Now Alice did not know what to think, not about Edwina nor about Cassie and not about herself. She knew better than anyone the trouble she could be in if too much digging around was done. She gave Cassie an assessing look; trouble there too. Alice was a shrewd observer and had known for some time that Cassie had a problem.

Mustn't be heavy, she thought. Might all work out.

But their three-way relationship would never be the same. The virus had eaten away at it in vital places, weakening what could never be rebuilt. Alice knew this, she suspected Cassie did, and whether Edwina did, or even cared any more, was part of the problem.

'I wish Lily was here,' she said aloud.

'Why?' asked Edwina from the door as she backed in, carrying a tray set with her best gold and white china. A bad sign, she only used that when her morale needed a lift, otherwise it would have got chipped. Edwina's family had believed in hanging on to things for generations. They valued chattels, and respected property, anyone's, but especially their own. 'Why Lily?

Though I miss her myself.'

'She's so honest.'

Cassie poured herself some coffee. 'Sometimes Alice says the weirdest things. It must be mixing with her clients so much. Take no notice of her.'

'Lily is honest. So honest she doesn't even have a decent lock on her flat.'

'Is that the reason you left? Have you told Kit you are back, by the way? You'd better. He's prowling around like a hungry lion.'

'Certainly Lily's locks was one of the reasons.' Edwina poured herself some coffee, then put it down undrunk. It was no good, she was right off coffee. 'Rather a nasty thing happened to me while I was there.'

'Ah,' Alice looked at Cassie, who dropped her eyes. 'That man? The one who's been bothering you on the telephone.'

'More than that ... You saw him once. Following me.'

'I thought I did.' Then, Alice said to herself; now I'm not so sure.

'It was worse out in Deptford. He came there, asking questions, then he sent me his photographs, through Lily's door. It was frightening. He's sick. Very sick. That's why I ran away.'

'Show me the picture, Eddie.' Cassie put down her coffeecup and waited.

'I can't do that. I threw it away.'

'That was a silly thing to do, Eddie.'

'It made me feel dirty.'

'It was evidence.'

'I didn't keep it,' repeated Edwina.

Her friends both knew she was lying. Whatever had happened, Edwina had not destroyed or mislaid the photograph. But she might never have received it.

Of course, she thought she had, they could see that, but where was the truth?

'But Eddie, how did he know where to find you, where to look?' said Alice.

There was a pause, and Edwina stood up, defensive, angry. 'You don't believe me, do you?'

'No one knew where to find you, no one knew where you'd gone.'

'You knew,' said Edwina. 'You knew, both of you. You knew.'

There was another pause.

'Damn,' said Alice quietly. 'Damn and damn.'

There had been such a tight, warm bond between them, making a wall with 'World Keep Out' written on it. Now the wall was coming down brick by brick, that was how it seemed to Alice. She was surprised that she appeared to be the one who minded most.

Cassie thought: we're splitting up. Inevitable, I suppose. Adolescent of us to have clung together so long. Still, it was a trademark almost, to be Us Three. Sad. I wonder whose fault it is? Mine mostly, I suppose. And her mind sped to the conversation she meant to have with Alice. Nothing was going to be the same after they had had that matter out.

Edwina tried to drink her cooling coffee, failed to enjoy it once again, and put down the cup. Her friends both frightened and irritated her today. They were children, not fully grown up. She herself had taken a frightening step into maturity. She had a great responsibility now. The silent traveller within her was once again asserting himself.

In an even quieter voice than Alice's, Cassie said, 'That's a rotten thing to say, Eddie. You know Alice and I would do anyting to protect you. I didn't tell anyone where you were.' And she looked at Alice who silently shook her head. 'So you see.'

'But you both knew.'

'Well, it wasn't hard to guess. Just guess. I didn't check, though, or try to find out for sure. It wasn't my business.'

'We're quarrelling, aren't we?'

'We've done that often enough in the past.'

'But this is different.'

Alice said, 'We'll never leave you alone, Edwina.'

'Perhaps I'd be better on my own.'

'Ouch,' said Alice. 'This is where I exit.'

Hurt and perplexed, the two walking

wounded, Cassie and Alice, left together, walking round to the Garden; Alice to collect her car and drive home, Cassie to work.

Alice said, 'What was all that about?'

'Oh, she's in a state. She'll come round. We were right to leave her. You always leave Eddie alone when she flies off the handle. Remember? Our rule? Let Eddie simmer.'

Cassie was busy trying to paper over the cracks, rebuild the wall, but Alice would not let her.

'You're living in the past. That was long ago.'

'Think so?'

'Yes. And so do you . . . But that isn't what I meant. I meant: what is it you and I have to talk about?'

They were standing by Alice's car, that gleaming testimony to her success. She was still proud of it, it was a moving, shining proof of what she had achieved, a potent symbol of success in male and female worlds. Buying it had been a high point in her life. Absently, Alice reached out and gave the car a pat.

'Come in,' said Cassie. 'We'll talk upstairs.'

Alice hesitated and looked up at the big window where Cassie had left a light shining.

'It's all right, the police have all gone.'

'*All* the police?'

'He doesn't live here, you know.'

'Pretty well has the last few days.' Alice still hung back. 'It's not that . . . I think about

Luke. Don't you think about him?'

'He didn't die here, thank goodness.'

'No,' Alice acknowledged.

'No, poor old Luke.' In spite of what she had said, Alice was following Cassie through the front door and up the straight wooden stairs, polished and pale, which led to the floor where she lived.

Over her shoulder, Cassie said, 'Do you mean that? Poor Luke?'

'Of course, why?'

'Just asking.'

They were facing each other at the head of the stairs. To the left was the big living room and beyond it the kitchen, to the right, the entrance to the great room where the wedding reception had been held. Ghosts ought to walk there, Alice thought suddenly.

'What is this?' Alice's voice had suddenly gone hard, the woman who had created her own business in a tough world was showing. 'What are we really talking about?'

'Blackmail ... Luke was blackmailing me, and I have a pretty good idea that he was also blackmailing you.'

The second accusation of the day had been brought out and laid on the table.

*   *   *

Edwina, left alone at last, was accusing herself.

195

She had attacked her two closest friends, practically accusing them of ... Of what? Of being a party to the process of persecution being inflicted upon her? That must be rubbish. She *trusted* them.

After Lily's flat, her own place seemed overfull of carefully chosen, beautiful objects. Too careful. She looked round it with a critical eye. She should have a clear-out. It was not the sort of home in which to bring up a child.

At the thought of the child, her lips and throat went dry. The doctor and nurse at the clinic had been reassuring and kind, but in that manner which convinces you that something is wrong. Perhaps not badly wrong, she couldn't be sure, but wrong.

The trouble was, she had lost confidence in herself and in almost everyone else as well. It was almost like a disease. Perhaps it was a disease, a sickness from the unborn striking outwards to her.

As a matter of fact, she would not let that happen. Of one thing she was sure, she would bring this enterprise through to a good conclusion. She would survive, the child would survive.

Irrationally anxious, even terrified as she was, she was convinced of this. She was two persons in one and somehow she would drag them both through.

But it might be a struggle.

If the child grew. She looked at herself in the looking glass on the wall; she seemed to be expanding but the child not. Perhaps she would eventually give birth to a fish-sized infant.

But even tiny children, ounces in size, survived now in special units. She did not feel tender to the child, simply determined, feeling would come later. She might get to love it, but at the moment she was simply concerned to bring it to life.

Life and death were hanging around her at the moment. She felt like a beast of burden; a donkey, say, with panniers on either side, and in one basket was death and in the other life. She was carrying both.

Or, if you looked at it a different way, geometrically placed all the dead people in space, marked each spot with an X, and then drew lines to join them, where they crossed was where Edwina stood.

She was a mark on all three death lines. They might be joined nowhere else, but they joined at her.

The telephone rang, she ignored it. That was rule one in her life at the moment: only do what you really wish to do.

She carried the coffee tray back into the kitchen over which several weeks' dust and disorder seemed to have settled in at a short absence. This was not to her fastidious taste and she set about cleaning it. Last night, after arriving back and almost simultaneously hearing the news about Miss Dover and her neighbour downstairs, she had been too tired and dejected even to unpack.

Then today had been the antenatal clinic. You went in there early and emerged exhausted and late, that was her experience, and today had been no exception. She had no real appointment and had been 'slotted in' (that this had been done without protest was a mark of the doctor's disquiet about her, she judged) but it had meant more hanging about than usual.

When she got back she had telephoned Dougie, Cassie and Alice in that order. The evening's visit had been the result. Dougie she would see tomorrow.

The telephone did not ring while she cleaned so she felt triumphant. Silenced that, she thought.

Tomorow Dougie, and then *he* had to be faced: Kit. By now, he probably knew she was home. There was, although neither of them would admit to it, a flow of communication between him and Dougie where she was concerned. She knew it, but had never been able to prove it. Just one of those masculine secrets hard to lay hands on. It could have been Kit who had just telephoned.

She went into her bedroom to finish her unpacking.

Edwina's bedroom had been furnished by her

with pieces from her old home, as one of her economies at a time when all her money was going into the gallery. So her problem was how to live with a selection of white-painted and cane furniture she had chosen when she was twelve. Her solution, now some years old, had been to paint abstract designs on the plain panels; these she now regretted, her taste had moved on, and she fancied something more figurative when she had time.

She moved around the room, her mood having taken one of those rapid switches she was getting accustomed to, so that she felt almost cheerful. In a little while she might be happy again.

A flutter of silk over one arm, she opened the drawer set aside for nightgowns. Edwina, product of a stern Scottish nanny, kept an orderly house. Her drawers and cupboards were pleasant to see, a neat harmony of colour and shape.

But today something was wrong. The drawer was stirred up.

Edwina closed it quietly, then went round her room. Now she looked carefully, she could see a lot wrong. All her clothes and small possessions had been touched.

'I've been turned over; I've been done.'

But she knew she was wrong even as she hurried round the other, untouched rooms. She had not been burgled. Entered, invaded, yes, but not robbed.

Only her bedroom appeared to have been touched. Inside it all her clothes had been fingered, her make-up opened and inspected by unknown eyes, and a pearl necklace dipped in her own scent. Or it smelt like it.

She held it to her nose as her stomach gave a heave. She closed her eyes while it steadied, hanging on to the cool marble top of the dressing table.

She had had a spoiler in the place; she felt ashamed, dirty.

★   ★   ★

'Cassie? Are you awake?' Edwina kept her voice cool.

'Of course. I'm working.' Not quite true. She was pacing up and down, thinking, arguing with herself. She had confessed to Alice some of the truth about Luke's reason for blackmailing her, but hung on to the crucial information. She imagined Alice had taken the same precaution, she'd have been a fool not to. There had, at any rate, been an interesting vagueness about both mutual confessions.

'I want to ask you something. How did you know where I was?'

'Ah well—you always keep a rack of keys above your desk in the gallery. I knew you were looking after Lily's keys. I saw her key had gone.'

200

'Simple.'

'Yes. I don't suppose I was the only one.'

'When you know the answer.'

'What does that mean?'

'Not everyone knows where I keep my keys. Or has a chance to see them.'

'Plenty do in the gallery. Besides ...' She hesitated.

'Well?'

'You wrote to Dougie—sent him something.'

'My work on the catalogue.'

'I saw the envelope, guessed from the postmark. You aren't very good at hiding, love.' Cassie asked anxiously. 'Are you all right? Has anything happened? Shall I come round?'

'No, nothing. See you tomorrow.' Edwina put the receiver down on a still protesting Cassie.

No, nothing was wrong. Only that someone close enough to me to read my habits and see my mail has been in my home.

'I excuse you, Cassie,' she said aloud. 'And you, Alice. You are my friends; I have to believe in you. But otherwise, nobody.'

Someone is after me, someone who knows me well, perhaps very well. A friend, a lover, an ex-lover, because there had been some. But whose face fitted?

'There is one thing that comforts me: there cannot be any real connection between the deaths of Luke and Pickles Dover. It must be coincidence.'

★   ★   ★

Within a few days the link between the death of Luke and the murder of Miss Dover had become established.

On that day Ginger Drury became fully conscious and able to talk. She wanted to talk.

Her eyes opened, and she muttered something. The nurse bent over her. Ginger had been stirring, opening her eyes and muttering at intervals all day. They were anxious to establish how lucid she was; from the X-rays they expected brain damage.

But Ginger's eyes, although bloodshot and bruised, were focused on the nurse.

She can see me anyway, the nurse decided. She was a little creature with auburn hair who might have merited Ginger's nickname herself.

'You don't mind, dear, do you?' continued Ginger.

'No, of course not.'

The woman police officer sitting on a chair in a corner of the cubicle stirred. She too had an interest.

'I need to talk.'

The policewoman came nearer the bed but Ginger took no notice. Only the nurse seemed within her range of vision—or, perhaps, caring.

'I've been thinking ... Hold my hand, will you?' The little nurse did so, she had been on special duty with Miss Drury for some days now and had come to like her patient who remained as polite and co-operative as was possible while being exceedingly ill. 'There is something I want to tell you.'

The policewoman rustled her notebook; the nurse gave her a warning glance.

'I've forgotten for the moment.' Ginger Drury closed her eyes. 'I've been thinking about it. I shall remember in a moment.'

The nurse waited a while, then she turned to the other woman. 'She's gone again ... You'll have to wait.'

With a small resigned sigh, hardly audible, the policewoman went back to her corner.

They returned to this scenario every so often over the next few days. Of the actors, only the patient remained the same, the others came and went as duty times changed. Finally, the original pair at the first wakening were reunited.

'She does *mean* it?' murmured the policewoman.

'Oh, yes. But don't count on anything.'

'As if I would,' muttered the policewoman as they took up their usual appointed places.

When Ginger opened her eyes this time, she smiled. 'Have I been asleep long?'

'Some time,' agreed the nurse kindly.

'But I've remembered what I wanted to say

. . . I've been thinking about it all the time . . .'
Her eyelids fluttered.

'Don't go off again, dear.' The nurse put a hand softly on her patient's wrist. 'Who am I? Do you know who I am?'

This was a question that Ginger had hitherto been unwilling or unable to answer. Today was different.

'Nurse,' she said. 'A nurse. Must be. Don't know your name.'

'Good *girl*.'

'Old lady,' corrected Ginger with a faint smile.

'You are better.'

'I could do with a drink.'

'I'll get you one.'

A faint squeak of protest came from the policewoman's corner. She wanted talking first.

But the nurse had been well trained, she got not only a drink but the doctor.

The doctor examined Miss Drury and afterwards said that a few minutes' conversation could be allowed.

There was something faintly ridiculous about this permission as Ginger had been talking all the time.

As the policewoman struggled to keep up with the flow, some of it repetitive, she wished vainly now that Ginger had waited for the arrival of her senior officer.

She got one word clear, though, because it

came out often, and that was Black.

Blackmail. Or black-coated?

Ginger, who was struggling gamely, sometimes got the words confused.

★   ★   ★

The police put in quite a lot of time, listening to Ginger, because what she had to say came only in snatches. They had questions to ask as well, for which opportunities had to be sought. It all needed patience. They used only one questioner because, as they soon discovered, Ginger did not like, nor the medical staff welcome, a constant flow of new faces. So stamina was required as well.

Alpha Morris had both qualities and to spare; she had come back into the Force after raising her own family where bringing up two sons and a daughter had taught her to go without sleep and still be alert. Tolerant and gentle, she was also patient and persistent. Alpha was well-known to the hospital staff even before the days with Ginger began.

'So you were on the stairs when you were struck? And from behind?'

But about this Ginger was not sure, sometimes she thought one thing and sometimes another. This was understandable, the doctors said, because more than one blow had been struck and the first blow of all had probably been delivered from the front. Then as she fell she had been struck at the base of the skull . . . This was the blow that alarmed them, a miracle she had not died on the spot.

'So you saw someone?' Alpha pursued gently.

Ginger assented to this and added a murmur of her own.

'Black was he? A black man?'

Ginger corrected this.

'Blackish? What does this mean, dear?'

Another low murmur, Ginger gripped Alpha's hand tight.

'Black-dressed? Wearing black clothes?'

'All dressed up and nowhere to go,' said Ginger clearly.

Alpha sighed. 'Here we go again.'

Miss Drury had a way of drifting off into nonsense talk before losing her grip altogether and going silent. Whether she was asleep or unconscious when she was silent Alpha had not established, but she thought neither. Ginger was just trying to get the words sorted out, that was her belief; she had real speech problems.

She was nearly always worth listening to, though; the essential sharpness and chirpiness of Ginger came through even these short bursts. She had seen something that she meant to get across.

'Blackness,' she said clearly the next time she felt like having a conversation.

'Yes, I got that dear,' said Alpha.

The black bit she had certainly got down in her notes, whatever Miss Drury meant by it. Black, blackness and variants of it kept being tried out.

Every so often a blackmailer would creep into the text and then be edited out of it by Alpha Morris who was convinced that this was not what her friend (Ginger counted as a friend by now) meant. But the blackmailer crept back in; he was Ginger's King Charles's head and every so often she *would* have him in.

So conscientiously Alpha went back and inserted the blackmailer back into her notes.

There he was encountered by her superior officer who had sources of information she was not privy to. He was investigating the death of Miss Dover with his usual thoroughness.

He found himself believing in both the black figure and the blackmailer, although he had reason to believe they were not the same man.

He had a question he needed to put to Ginger himself if she could answer it. By this time she was somewhat steadier in her witness. There was even a faint suggestion that she was beginning to enjoy the court around her.

'Are you there, love?' he asked.

Ginger heard that and was able to answer with great clarity that she was not his love. The spontaneous cry of pleasure with which the nurse greeted this did not quite please the inspector, even though he knew that it was happiness at Ginger's returning speech that was being expressed and no criticism of him.

'I shouldn't have said that,' he decided. 'She's younger than I thought and a good looking woman beneath all those bruises and swellings.' Ginger had two swollen yellow-and-blue rings round her eyes where most of the blood had congregated, but was now ebbing away.

'Sorry. Here I am, let's start again.' He let a pause take place, he knew you had to take things slowly. 'Now, there was someone on the stairs; we won't go into the question of colour, I think I've got it clear ... And, of course, it was dark on the stairs—' Like Canon Linker he had caught the essential darkness of the scene. Picked it up somehow and felt it creeping into his own mind. It really had been a rotten business, that attack on the two women on the stairs of their own home. 'You were struck on the head and fell.' She had fallen down the stairs and into a corner where the staircase twisted. Part of her injuries had been due to this fall. Deep trauma, the surgeons called it. 'Now, although your consciousness came and went and you felt unable to move, you did take in certain things ... Your assailant stayed on the stairs ... ?'

It seemed to be what Ginger was saying, and was, anyway, confirmed by forensic evidence. The attacker had crouched on the stairs waiting for Pickles. It looked as though Pickles was the real victim. Ginger had just got in the way. Perhaps she had even been attacked by mistake. There was an indication of this in the way she had been attacked: there were bruises on her neck where it looked as if the murderer had started to strangle her and then thought better of it when he saw her face.

Little by little he drew all this out of Ginger. 'And did you know this person who attacked you? Recognise him in any way?'

Ginger was flagging by now, it had been a long session for her, even though her physical resources had been carefully monitored by the nurse. Alpha too, still sitting there, knew the signs of fatigue.

'All dressed up and nowhere to go,' said Ginger decisively. She closed her eyes.

But the inspector wasn't having this; he had superiors on his tail and thought he detected more reserves of energy in Ginger than Alpha (he could see her fussing) allowed.

'Did you know your attacker?'

'Not known . . . Saw.' Ginger started to talk.

This was what Ginger had wished to confess: the killer had been a customer. One of those customers of whom Ginger did not approve because they came with the wrong motives. Not looking for health but stimulants. This man had wanted an aphrodisiac and Pickles had supplied a potent preparation of cantharides procured (never say how) from Hong Kong. Taken in small doses, it was a diuretic; taken in larger doses, it might be sexually helpful but it was certainly poisonous.

The inspector took this in with some relish; he was not concerned with the death of Luke Tory but he knew what had killed him: cantharides.

He gave Ginger's hand a little pat. 'Just a bit more. Important, Miss Drury, or I wouldn't bother you.'

Ginger opened her eyes as widely as she could manage to show willing.

'Did you eat anything on the stairs?'

'What I want to tell you,' said Ginger as clearly as she could, which was not so very clear, 'is that the black figure ate a cake. Iced. It was not me.'

'That's it,' said the inspector. 'Imagine you seeing that. Eat he did. Killed Miss Dover and then ate an iced bun.'

On her way home on the day of her murder, Pickles had bought four hard iced buns. The icing was thick, rich and firm, a speciality of the baker, and one of which Ginger was particularly fond. They had been a peace-offering from the errant Pickles.

The buns had spilled out of the bag on to the stairs as she fell. After killing Pickles, the killer had sat on the stairs eating his way through the buns.

Yes, said the medical experts when consulted,

a stress reaction: the body would be crying out for sugar. He probably couldn't stop himself.

Pickles had bought four buns. Two had been eaten, a third, half-eaten, had been left behind, and the fourth had been untouched.

In the icing were the clearly defined marks of the killer's teeth: he had a rather individual bite with separated front teeth. Teeth prints can be as individual as fingerprints.

In another case, another killing, but across London, there had been a piece of cake with teeth marks on it. At Lily's wedding reception where Luke Tory had downed his dose of poison, someone had left a piece of wedding cake in Cassie's kitchen with the teeth marks clearly visible. This piece of cake had been collected and preserved by the police team when it went over Cassie's premises. It hadn't looked important, but you could never tell, so it had been duly placed in a plastic bag and the teeth marks noted and measured. All that could be done with those teeth marks had been done.

* * *

There was one last question that the inspector got in before Miss Drury fell into a natural sleep.

'Did you know the identity of your attacker?'

'Not me. No. But I think Pickles did.'

This answer was, in some short time, passed

on to the teams investigating the death of Luke Tory. It confirmed what the teeth marks were telling them.

In spite of the conclusion Edwina had come to, the two deaths were now firmly linked together. Not two cases but one, not two murderers but only one.

CHAPTER TEN

Between the murderer and his victim there has, at some point, to be a common fantasy land through which they walk. It is when their paths cross that murder can take place. Luke Tory had had a fantasy that he could enter into other people's lives, pilfering their secrets and taking money for keeping them; he used the money to surround himself with the kind of possessions he liked, beautiful, desirable objects. He was running into troubles with his blackmailing of the policeman Edward Miller (because Miller was going to tell in the end) when his path crossed that of his murderer. The murderer's fantasy was also one of entering other people's lives; in this case not for profit but to wound and control. It was because the murderer's fantasy had a stronger hold that it ended with a killing. Luke's fantasy that he could extract money from one killer for not exposing the acts (which Luke had discovered) had been countered by the killer's stronger need to get on with what he was doing. His dream world was the more active and the more hostile: he killed to keep it going.

The murderer's fantasy had to be like this, because it was a creative dream, working towards a definite end.

Pickles' fantasy was at once more innocent and more dangerous. If she had not been killed now, she would have been damaged badly at some other time. She was operating on the margin of too many disturbed persons' dream worlds. She was probably destined to die violently and might easily have taken Ginger with her. Underneath, Ginger had always been aware of this chance.

Pickles' fantasy was that she was in charge, could hand out benefits and punishments as she thought fit. In short, that she could use the rules of life as suited *her*: she was the judge and, just before her death, had given notice that she meant to hand out a judgement of guilty. The murderer also thought you could use the rules as suited you, was also determined to be in charge, and was nastier and quicker about it than was Pickles. In other words, they were a threat to each other.

Edwina crossed paths with the murderer because she was a love object and the murderer was in love; magnificently, religiously, and more than somewhat madly, in love.

The possible identification of the murderer of Luke Tory with the killer of Miss Dover was not known to Alice or Cassie or Edwina. Canon Linker and Bee were equally in the dark. But everyone was questioned about the piece of cake and the news about the half-eaten iced bun soon spread among those most interested, in the form of a half-believed rumour.

It had a strange effect on the three women. Almost with a click there was a circuit going between them again. The telephone lines were kept busy.

A telephone call to Edwina was preceded by a short one between Alice and Cassie.

'We've got to tell her.'

'Yes.' Alice was thoughtful about it. 'I don't want to.' Her voice dropped away as it always did when she was doubtful; Cassie could hardly hear it. 'Alice going Mouse' was what she called it.

'Oh come on.'

'I'm thinking.'

'You told me, remember?'

'Only because you knew.' Alice could not keep the note of surprised indignation out of her voice, it still rankled.

'You'd been sending out signals for quite a time,' said Cassie. 'I could read them.'

'Perhaps Edwina could too, then.' The thought appalled Alice. Edwina represented standards and a way of life that she respected without aspiring to. She knew that beside Edwina she was shoddy stuff, but just knowing Edwina had raised her quality. One of her strongest reasons for paying Luke to keep quiet was so that Edwina would not know what she had done.

Cassie's motives she could only guess at, but since Cassie was hard to bully, they had to be powerful indeed. Even in the extremity of her own discomfort Alice found time to wonder what Cassie had been up to.

But Cassie was not saying, not to her anyway, any more than she was herself. They had agreed not to swap tales.

'No, not Eddie,' said Cassie in a decided voice. 'She's been too sunk in her own troubles to notice anyone else. Besides, she had Lily and the wedding on her mind.'

'We did most of that ... You did the reception and I did the clothes.' Even when agitated, Alice did not forget what was due to her.

'So we have to tell her. Clear your mind of confusions, love, and dwell on this fact: we are right back in the frame as murderers. Have you got an alibi for the night in question?'

'Now you're talking like a detective.'

'It's rubbed off on me. But have you?'

No, Alice had not got an alibi for the night of Miss Dover's murder. Neither had Cassie. Both of them had been at home and alone. This was the state with them more often than they chose to admit: they knew what loneliness was. Successful women had their own brand of solitariness to experience. Because they had achieved prominence each in their sphere, everyone took it for granted that they had a glittering social life. Alice (and she suspected Cassie too) knew better. She remembered how in her very early days of starting out, when she had thought that the mark of a successful woman was to have a London club, she'd encountered in the cloakroom of Groucho's one of the most prominent women barristers of a generation older than hers, a byword for beauty, charm and success. This woman was in tears: she was crying, as she let Alice know, because she hadn't been asked to a dinner party, because she was lonely and afraid. She had dried her eyes, implying: forget it, just hormones. 'You're new,' she'd said bitterly. 'You'll find out.'

★   ★   ★

Perhaps it was this sense of outer darkness that made their group's adhesion so strong. Alice knew it was why she submitted to blackmail rather than be thrown outside.

'All right,' she said reluctantly. 'Set it up then if you must. But let it be in the open air. If I've got to bare my soul then I shall need to breathe deeply.' Or get up and run, she told herself.

'We'll make it the Terrazza in the Garden then. I'll get hold of Eddie.' The Terrazza had a large open terrace where you could eat a light meal. 'I'll book a table.'

'Where I can breathe, mind.'

'Don't build up the drama,' said Cassie crisply.

'Sorry.'

Sorry; the word seemed to dissolve a temporary block inside her and she was able to put down the telephone and even contemplate getting on with her own life. She wasn't sorry, that was hardly the word, what she felt was immeasurably stronger than that, like rage or despair.

Vindictiveness came into it too: she really hated having her life dug up. It was almost a pity, she thought, that Eddie had come back. She stood up, her figure tall and thin. People were apt to think of Alice as small because she had a small, delicately boned face, but in fact she was tall for a woman.

Cassie gave herself a pause for thought before she got in touch with Edwina. She knew she was pushing Alice, perhaps dangerously so. Alice could be so stupid sometimes. She had a couple of little blind spots which Cassie had found useful before.

Her hand caressed the telephone; it had always been her preferred instrument of communication.

Her hand dropped away from the telephone. Leave it, let it be for the time being. Her own feelings of guilt were stronger and more hideous than any Alice could know because at the base lay love like a golden egg at the bottom of a dirty basket.

She had to telephone Edwina several times before she got an answer. Dougie had told her this was how it would be. 'We've set up a system now,' he said, 'a secret, but I'll tell you. Initiate three calls, one after the other with no time gap. She'll answer on the fourth. It's a pattern, see.'

On the fourth call Edwina duly answered. She sounded all right but vague, as if she was not really listening. Cassie wondered if the clinic had prescribed her any drugs, but after listening to Edwina's dreamy tones, decided that pregnancy was its own drug.

'I just feel quiet today, sleepy,' said Edwina as if answering this thought. 'Yes, the story that the killer of Luke might be one and the same as the killer of poor old Pickles, yes, I've heard. Did you think I wouldn't have done?' Her tone was mildly ironic. 'News like that gets about, you know. Dougie told me, as a matter of fact. He said Janine told him. I don't know who told *her* but it was probably Bee Linker, that woman knows everything.'

'You're waking up.'

'I believe I am.'

'Meet us at the Terrazza in the Garden.

Twelvish. I'll give you lunch. Alice and I have something to tell you.'

'About cake?'

'Not about cake.'

A piece of iced bun on the stairs was changing all their lives, would go on changing them until there was nothing left of what they had been, and everyone's life was different.

★   ★   ★

Janine and Bee Linker had been working together all the morning. Not in total harmony because Bee was in one of her irritable moods. She was reluctant to admit she had them, preferring to think of herself as the gentle-tempered invalid around the house, but all those about her recognised her bad days when they came along. As far as Janine was concerned, it was like going for a row in an open boat on a day when the wind was against you. She felt ruffled and tired. So, presumably, did Bee or she wouldn't have carried on so.

'Janine, did you eat cake at the wedding?' demanded Bee.

'No, I did not. I wasn't there, remember?'

'Oh, I'd forgotten.'

No, you hadn't, thought Janine irritably. You remember very well, you just felt like asking.

'It worried me. Doesn't it you?'

'No,' said Janine.

'Oh I think you like a bit of drama in your life.'

'Not at all.'

'Ah well, if you say so. Let's get down to work again, shall we?' They had just completed the first draft of Bee's book. 'I think I've got all the pieces, don't you? Not perhaps in the right order yet, but I shall achieve that. I like fitting them together.'

Janine wondered if Bee was saying this to get a response; she did not answer.

'That's one of the things I do with my days now: put all the pieces of the jigsaw into order and make a picture . . . I think I'd make a good detective, don't you?'

'Well . . .' began Janine doubtfully.

'Oh you mean because I can't see? People would have to tell me things, of course. But then they do, much much more than they know, my dear. Jim does, the postman does, so does the milkman for that matter. Those nice young actors and actresses . . . just talk, of course, but I pick things up. And Cassie and Alice are always popping in with the news.'

'But not Edwina Fortune.'

Bee said, almost sadly, 'Ah, but then Edwina had already told me all she knows and perhaps more than she knew herself.'

'My word, you're a dangerous lady.' Or you would be if I believed half of what you said, Janine added to herself. She knew her employer

220

for a prize romancer. Probably she was trying out her next book for size on her secretary.

Bee got to her feet; she was soft and nimble in her movements, and able to guide herself round very well, but she liked company and the touch and sound of people.

'Let's go for a walk.'

'Are you sure?' Janine was doubtful.

Her employer knew what she meant. What pleasure is there in it for you? she was saying.

'I have *some* sight. I can see outlines. Besides, I like the air on my face.' She always wore a beautiful Italian silk and tweed cloak for summer walking. 'I do hear things too,' she said as she arranged herself on her secretary's arm.

And want to hear more, no doubt, thought Janine who was beginning to entertain considerable doubts about her employer.

'Someone ought to keep an eye on that girl Edwina. Not me, of course. I couldn't quite do that. But you, Janine, what about you?'

'You think I should watch Edwina?' said Janine in a serious, quiet, incredulous voice. She did not know what to make of Bee Linker today; she did not trust her employer.

*　　*　　*

After she had finished talking to Edwina, Cassie stood by her upstairs window, still holding the telephone and looking out. She got a good view

221

of the Garden with its shops and restaurants. Today the area seemed more crowded than ever. Two women, one heavily pregnant, the other older and possibly a mother or an aunt, were stepping out of an olive green Rolls and going into Alice's shop. Even as they arrived another woman holding a toddler by the hand and carrying one of Alice's famous carrier bags left by taxi. Trade was clearly good. Two buskers were playing a lively tune on flute and cello. Cassie, a keen opera-goer, recognised the unmistakable music of Richard Strauss. Not *Rosenkavalier* as so often; indeed from no opera, but the lively, bitter sweetness of *Til Eulenspiegel*. Almost immediately underneath her own window Cassie could see that a flower-seller carefully got up to look like Eliza Doolittle had set up her basket in the gutter and was already making a steady sale of buttonholes to a group of young men in jeans and jazzy blazers, also wearing boaters. One young man tucked a rose in his boater.

She turned her head, looking leftwards to where the Cardboard-Cut-Out Theatre had its place. They were all set up and ready to go, a placard said 'Harlequin', but no one was playing.

Instead, a police car was parked outside. More investigation. The Cardboard-Cut-Out team were getting their share. Having their teeth and bite checked, no doubt.

Cassie wondered very much what was being said. There was a hole in the canvas structure through which you could overhear what was going on inside if you placed yourself right.

But she turned away from the window, deciding she could not go and listen. Bill Crail might tell her something.

Or might not.

*　　*　　*

Edwina, still bemused, walking slowly to her appointment with Alice and Cassie, saw the police car parked near the canvas structure of the tiny theatre. Like Cassie she knew that if you lingered in a certain spot you could catch snatches of what went on inside.

She was walking so slowly it was hardly necessary to linger. In the shade behind the theatre the air seemed to have collected into itself the concentrated essence of several old oranges, a hint of onions, and a smell of wine. There was an empty wine bottle in the gutter.

She could hear a voice which she recognised as that of Joly French, the oldest of the team and the one she knew best. 'Yes, I was one of the kings at the wedding but I didn't eat any cake. I took a bit, but lost it . . .' His voice faded away. Either he moved or another solid body came between him and the aperture.

Edwina went on, she knew what they must be

223

talking about. Yes, two of them had been at the wedding reception, not guests, but paid performers. Part of the fun, should have got the whole outfit in one of the glossy mags, but it hadn't quite done that. Plenty of publicity of a sort, although it didn't happen to have helped the theatre troupe, they were on their uppers.

Edwina filled in the conversation for herself; she knew Joly so well, she could almost hear the begging bowl rattling. It was Joly's expertise in this line that kept the troupe going. It was because of this skill of his that Luke and Edwina had booked him to perform at the wedding. He had magicked the idea out of them or into them. Probably he regretted it now. Joly had been the king in a paper crown and Fergus Frame had been booked for the other; they matched in height. But Fergus had got a part in a TV serial and left for Birmingham, so some other luckless chap must have filled in, and was no doubt equally regretting it. The theatre had a floating group of actors and actresses to call upon, they came and went. It was considered quite a cachet to work with the CCs, as they were called, and people boasted about it. It didn't get you an Equity Card but it got you noticed. People might be less keen now; actors were a superstitious lot.

In the distance Edwina saw Bee Linker on Janine's arm going in the direction of the theatre. Bee seemed to be moving with her usual purposeful dignity, Janine looked the perfect secretary, with her hair in a neat, pale chignon as always, and wearing a dark, loose linen dress.

She ought to lose some weight, thought Edwina absently, she's too heavy for her bones, somehow. And she could dress better.

Edwina wanted to be first at their meeting place but she could see Cassie approaching and Alice was already sitting at a table in the corner looking quiet and pensive.

Edwina sat down. 'Has anyone seen poor old Ginger?'

'I tried.' Cassie had arrived. 'But they wouldn't let me.'

'I sent flowers,' said Alice.

'I've done nothing.' Except think, endlessly think. There was a constant rumble at the back of her mind, like a train going through in the distance, not always heard clearly, but not forgotten and never stopping.

'You're meant to be looking after yourself,' said Alice protectively.

'Doing the best I can.' Sometimes I am full of confidence in myself, sometimes full of nervous apprehension, but always I know that I shall bring the child to life. Only what child? I am beginning to be worried about its parentage. I know that genetically my family is all right, but what about Tim? Perhaps there is something on Tim's side I ought to know more about.

Looking at her as if she could read these

225

thoughts, Alice said: 'I've ordered coffee,' and made it sound as though she had ordered her own execution.

'Oh come on, love.' Cassie was brisk. 'This is business. Treat it as such. Let's get it over with.'

'So what is it?' Edwina could see a tray of coffee coming their way, carried by a minute and fragile waitress whom she knew to be an actress sometimes to be seen performing at the Cardboard-Cut-Out. 'What was it all about?'

'Let's drink our coffee first,' said Alice nervously.

'We have a confession to make.' Cassie put her hand on Alice's, she could be protective also. 'We have been paying blackmail.'

'Doesn't sound like my idea of business. Unless, of course, you were blackmailing each other.'

Cassie ignored the attempt at a joke. 'We were paying Luke, had been for quite a few months. In my case at least, I can't answer for Alice.'

Alice muttered something inaudible.

Edwina drank her coffee, her eyes fixed on a distant view of rooftops across the open square of the Garden. Not particularly beautiful, but a good everyday view which belonged to real life. She didn't feel that she did herself at the moment. This was not real life, it was a bit from a soap opera. She took a deep breath and turned to gaze at her friends.

Alice looked sick, Cassie had on that air of tough insouciance that usually masked an inner turmoil. Her eyes met Edwina's then dropped; she had engineered this meeting, would go through with it as 'business' but she did not enjoy it.

'I won't ask what you were both paying blackmail for.'

'I shall tell,' said Alice, looking down at the table. 'Rather get it off my mind . . . I stole a set of designs—they launched my first solo show. Got me noticed . . . The girl who did them was a friend . . . She was ill at the time and on drugs . . . She died later. I don't know if she ever knew what I had done. She was pretty far gone. But we'd worked together a lot, and I had them in my possession when I wanted them . . . I had a chance of a backer but suddenly couldn't do it. I'd gone dead. Didn't have an idea. So I took hers.' Even now she found it hard to say the name aloud.

Edwina wanted to help her. 'But after that, it was your own,' she reminded her. 'All your hard work all the grind, all the risks.'

'Oh yes, once started I was all right. Even better. But there you are.'

'How did Luke find out?'

'Oh—I kept the original sketches signed and dated, there they were. They were in my office. He was poking round and found them.'

'He did poke,' said Edwina, remembering.

227

'That was a part of him I never liked.' Her gaze fell on Cassie and she was unable to keep the speculation out.

'A love affair,' said Cassie shortly. 'I'd rather not talk about it.'

Edwina found it hard to speak for a moment. Alice said nothing, and all three sat silent. Edwina broke the silence.

'You've shocked me.'

'Ah.' Cassie gave a wry smile.

'No, not you. Luke. How could he do it? And how could you let him do it?'

'It wasn't hard, we all have our dirty secrets we want to cover up. And he didn't ask much.'

Edwina said, 'What did he ask?'

'A bit of money, an object he fancied, little favours.'

Edwina gave her a quick look: 'What sort of favours?'

Cassie laughed. 'Oh, nothing like that. Nothing sexual. That wasn't Luke's scene at all. No, just help him get the invitation he wanted, that sort of thing. This job, for a start.'

'Yes. It *was* you that recommended him,' said Edwina thoughtfully. 'So—well, you two have told me. Thanks. I'd rather not have known. Sorry I had to. But why?'

Not for the first time recently Cassie thought that Edwina's mind was not working as sharply as usual. The baby again, no doubt, all the wrong, mind-deluding, comforting, protective hormones flooding in.

'Murder, love. It brings a lot of things out. Alice and I think this might be one of them. The police will find out about Luke. Probably have done so already.'

Bill Crail has told her they know, decided Alice, whose mind was not dulled by motherhood; she *knows*.

Cassie confirmed this.

'They will find out about us. We shall be under suspicion. They are bound to think that someone whom Luke was blackmailing killed him.'

'And poor Pickles?'

'She must have known who the killer was. He may have got the poison that killed Luke from her.'

'Sergeant Crail—' began Edwina.

'Yes. I got the idea from him. Oh, not directly—he's too canny for that. More by what he didn't say.'

'Does he know?' Edwina hesitated. About your love affair, she meant. Cassie understood.

'He knows.'

She didn't mind telling Bill Crail, although perhaps it ha been a shock to him. She had the idea he was still thinking it over, but Edwina she would not tell. Someone might, some time, but she'd face that when it came.

'Let's have some wine, shall we?' Edwina signalled the waiter. 'I should think we could all

229

do with a drink. Thanks for telling me all this. If it's of any interest, Luke was not blackmailing me.'

'You wouldn't have stood for it, anyway,' said Alice. 'Publish and be damned, that would be your line.'

'I might have said that once. Not so sure now ... Anyway, I'm in there with you, don't forget. The police are looking at me with interest on account of the phone calls. Something funny there, I expect they think.' The wine arrived and Edwina watched it set down before she said, 'And so there is.'

'Well, we know what happened in Deptford, we know what's been happening to you. It's horrid. A mystery. But can it have any connection with the murders? Do you really think so?'

'Do you believe in coincidence? I don't. Logically and intellectually, I might be hard put to it to maintain connection, but emotionally, I know there is.'

'I think I believe you,' said Alice in a low voice. 'I'm quite frightened myself. After all, I had a phone call or two to begin with. So did you, Cassie. And I saw him. Or sort of saw him. Could have been. It's scary.'

'I don't think I'm scared,' said Cassie. 'But I don't like it. All right, so let's admit, it's all one scene, so what have we got? We've got a murderer who is pursuing our Eddie from rather mixed-up sexual motives. He loves and hates you, Eddie.'

'Perhaps all women.' Edwina was thinking of what had been said: *I want to teach you what love is about.*

Alice shivered. 'That's why I'm frightened.'

'And there is something that ties the deaths together with what's been happening to me. Luke was killed with an aphrodisiac. And the telephone caller said: "I'have means to bring you up to scratch." That's what he meant.'

'You mean Luke was killed by mistake?'

'Yes, perhaps.'

'And Pickles was killed because she sold the poison and knew to whom she'd sold it?'

'Yes.'

'Then we have Luke the blackmailer as the coincidence,' said Alice despairingly.

Any way they looked at it the picture would not come clear.

They had a murderer who was a poisoner and also a strangler. They had an obscene telephone caller who was turning into a sexual pursuer of Edwina, yet expressed his love for her.

'Come on now, Cassie, you know more than you're saying. What do the police think?'

'They think they've got a chancer.'

'What's that?'

'I suppose it's the police equivalent of what doctors call an opportunist infection.'

In other words, a killer who saw his chance

and stepped in and took it without a lot of preplanning. A hard kind of killer to catch, the worst.

'And they still think it could be one of us?' said Alice incredulously.

'Oh yes, one of us could be the chancer.' Cassie was matter-of-fact. 'Why rule us out?'

Alice turned to Edwina.

'Have the police asked you for your bite?'

'No. Not yet.'

'They will.'

'What about you?'

'Oh yes, I obliged. On a lovely piece of clean laboratory wax.'

'I don't think I ate any cake at all that day, I was off cake.'

'I don't remember,' said Alice, almost despairingly.

The sounds of the Piazza swelled all over them. Voices chattering, laughter, the sound of a rock track from the shop selling smart trash next door. Not far away someone was smoking hemp, no missing the smell even though it had been lavishly mixed with a sickly scent.

Something in the sounds got through to Edwina. They reminded her of the noises heard on one of the telephone calls. Not a bar, she thought, with conviction, not a pub. I was wrong, it was from here, from the Terrazza. That brought it right home. She could hardly bear to look at her friends, in case they could

232

read her thoughts.

'How are things with you, Eddie?' asked Alice, as if she had picked up something. 'Are you still having trouble?'

'Nothing much since I came back from Deptford, but I don't feel safe. Silly, I suppose, but there it is.' She took a long drink of wine and failed to feel any better. There were too many worrying thoughts now.

'And I can't run away again, you see, because of the child. He needs help. I need help with him. I have to stay around. I'm hobbled.'

Hobbled by her sex and her fertility so that her pursuer could draw closer.

She knew he would.

How much was she being overimaginative, creating things that were not there? You had to ask this question, and it was hard to answer.

'It seems so real,' she said aloud. Some things had an objective reality, the photograph, her disturbed possessions, the caller on Mignon Waters, asking after Edwina by name. If this man is real, would the police ask to see *his* teeth?

'You ought not to stay on your own,' said Cassie.

'Come to me,' said Alice at once.

'She needs a man.' Cassie was brisk. 'Move in with Kit Langley. He's got plenty of room.' He had the room where Tim had lived, but she did not say this aloud.

'Did he put you up to this?' Alice asked.

'Well—' Cassie turned to Edwina. 'He suggested it.'

Edwina laughed. 'I trust Kit, but it hasn't come to that yet.'

What she could not, would not, admit to them, was that her latest impression was that she was being watched.

Continually, obsessively, perhaps with love, perhaps with hate, observed.

CHAPTER ELEVEN

To the police, what they had now was a murder hunt with a double killer. In their eyes it was a kind of family killing, only the family was the community that used the Garden, either working or living there. From past experience they were convinced that the killer and his victims knew each other well. How well, of course, was something they could only guess at, but they had to try to do more.

If they could characterise the relationship between killer and killed, then it would set some limits to their search for an identity. They knew they were dealing with a crowd. The 'family' of the Garden was made up of a floating population, some of whom lived there, others of whom owned businesses there or worked in them while others might do nothing more than be regular visitors, who ate in the restaurants, drank in the busy bars or bought in the shops.

Or might even, as Bill Crail said in morose speculation, be a worshipper in Canon Linker's church, 'I believe he does a good line in sermons. And they have lunch-time concerts or organ music.'

He did not make this remark quite without reason. He had interviewed Canon Linker several times and had noticed that the cleric had a trick of pulling a face as if the questioning was provoking dark thoughts he was not prepared to pass on. Crail had prodded, trying to purge him of these black thoughts, but he had not succeeded.

Neither Canon Linker not his aunt, both of whom had been at the wedding reception, ate sweet cake with icing. This was well-attested by all independent observers.

'Never eat sweetmeats, my dear fellow, now,' said Canon Linker, showing his neat white teeth in a smile. Crail found himself looking at people's teeth with interest these days, although the odontologist had told him that he would get nothing by looking at people's teeth. Apparently it was the shape of the murderer's incisors that were so individual: he had eye-teeth like a cat. Very, very pointed. Not everyone showed their teeth much, anyway, Bill Crail had noticed, especially women, who sometimes guarded their smiles like their purses; he knew now what a 'tight' smile meant.

In the 'family' of the Garden, then, the police were looking for someone who moved around as a regular, without being noticed because he was always there. A person who could get into the wedding reception, either as a guest, or a worker, or simply as a person who could be accepted as having some right to be there. That was one important part of the character established. This person had been at the reception and been given (or taken) a bit of wedding cake. The murderer had not finished the cake, though, and so perhaps did not like the cake, if they could ever find out. But by the time they got close enough to know they would probably know his name as well.

Another and important part of the profile was the relationships with Miss Dover and Miss Drury. The killer had bought poison from Miss Dover with which he had (one could only guess) poisoned Luke Tory. Thus his face was known to Miss Dover. But Miss Drury had, in her own words, just 'seen him'. Not known, just seen.

There was a suspicion that he might also have a relationship with Edwina. Was he, or was he not, the telephone caller? The accepted police theory was that Edwina Fortune was imagining a lot. They did not rate what was happening to her as important. But there were certain details of her description of the man that matched what Miss Drury had to say.

Darkness and blackness came into it.

It all made an interesting profile of the killer. Bumpy. As if the killer had a big nose which might sometimes not be there.

He was an oddity, that was clear. And oddities did, in the end, get caught.

That was Bill Crail's private hope. He could almost, only not quite, see his oddity walking around the Garden. However, his were not the only eyes watching, he was only one of a team, and a junior one at that, so there might be information and opinions he was not privy to. Privately, he was convinced that his eyes were the sharpest.

He thought about Cassie; he would have to go away. It was getting too serious on both sides. He didn't know if he wanted a long-term commitment to such a high-powered lady, she might be too much for him. On the other hand, he considered himself pretty high-powered too.

He'd be seeing Cassie later tonight; they were meeting for a drink in the Duke. Afterwards— well, they'd see. What she had told him earlier had been a surprise, a shock even. You never could tell with women and Cassie was the last he'd expected to come out with that particular confession. But it was over now, she swore.

Brave of her to tell him, he thought fondly.

He knew one other person she'd be talking about: Edwina Fortune. When Cassie was not talking about herself and her plans, she was

237

talking about Edwina. The subject seemed to obsess her at the moment, and the girl certainly had problems.

In a quiet way he was keeping an eye on Edwina. But, of course, she would never notice.

It was very odd, but as he had done this, he had had the strange feeling that other people were on the job too. He seemed to keep seeing familiar faces. Or they were getting familiar. Kit Langley—understandable that, Cassie had enlightened him on how Kit felt about Edwina, but still . . . Then there was Janine Grandy, she was around sometimes, and then there was someone else whose face seemed familiar, as if he might have known it once. A man? And yesterday there had been a woman wearing a red hat.

Crail knew very well that he was one little bit in a jigsaw, joggled around by other pieces that didn't quite fit into the picture. It was an unsettling state of mind for a young policeman who had believed himself to be a competent observer. He was inclined to blame it on Cassie.

★   ★   ★

Meanwhile, across London, Mignon Waters had come to a decision. It had taken her some days to decide what to do; she was never a quick thinker or mover, but she was a trier.

She had taken a great fancy to the handsome

umbrella left behind by the man who had asked after Edwina. She recognised it for an object of quality. She would have liked to keep it for ever, and had addressed the cat Tabitha who lived with her on and off (Tabitha was a cat of great appetite and many homes) about it.

'I do like excellence, Tab. I miss the old days when I had it around me all the time at Madame's. Not much here, puss.'

She would have liked to keep the umbrella, but it was very saleable, and money was tight with her. She took it round her circuit of buyers, the curio shop down Deptford High Street, the Almost New Outfit in Greenwich Church Street and old Lew's stall down by the bridge. At all of them she was well known. She was often a seller, sometimes a buyer, she was a middleman in a disorderly market.

To her surprise she could find no buyer. No one wanted her treasure. It was examined, fingered, admired, but no one wanted to buy.

'It's no good,' said old Lew. 'I don't fancy to buy it. Sorry, love.' He ran his fingers over the engraved gold plate with Tim's name on it. 'Don't think it'd go somehow. Not for much, anyway. Forget it, that's my advice.'

Mignon bore her trophy away, she had her superstitions. 'It's unlucky, that's what. Something's touched it. Better get rid of it.'

In her book, the only way to get rid of it correctly was to get it back whence it had come.

Easier said than done. She looked up Tim's Croft's name in the telephone book, but he was not listed. But he had been interested in Edwina and Edwina she might lay hands on. She had no reason to like Edwina, so she was not averse to dumping bad luck on her. Besides which, she looked like a girl who had bad luck coming to her.

She tackled Sid who, at first, refused help. 'Don't know any address, Mignon. She didn't leave one. Can't help you, I'm afraid.'

His wife stood behind him, giving Mrs Waters a hostile stare: they were not friends.

But Sid on his own with Sandra out of the way was easier. He was an agreeable man, anxious to please. Pushed by Mignon he gave ground.

'I don't know an address but she had several letters sent here with the name Gallery Ariadne and an address in Covent Garden. That's the best I can do for you.'

Mignon Waters put on her red hat, took a bus to the tube and then, with a change at Charing Cross, went to Covent Garden where she added her eyes to the ring of eyes watching for Edwina. She identified the gallery, saw Edwina in the back talking to a young man, and got her name from the portrait in the window. Stupid girl, she decided, if you make it all female like that you're throwing a challenge and some man's going to pick it up and throw it back. *We* knew better in my day.

240

No trouble; she would know how to find Edwina now. She had enjoyed the trip; she scented drama.

She adjusted her red hat in the gallery window, not caring whether Edwina saw her or not. It was nice to be back in Town, not that Covent Garden was Piccadilly exactly or even Knightsbridge. On the way past she looked in the window of Alice's shop, recognising the quality even if not liking the style. Not exactly haute couture, she observed critically, but not rubbish, either.

★　　★　　★

Edwina had seen Mignon Waters; she went on talking to Dougie without showing emotion. When she looked again, Mignon had gone. If she had ever been there. It might have been some perfectly innocent woman in a red hat. Or no one at all, just her imagination. Either way it was alarming.

'Are you all right?'

'Fine, Dougie.' She turned back to the work in hand. In a year's time they would be launching an exhibition of 'portraits of English actresses': *Mrs Siddons to Gladys Cooper* was the provisional title although Dougie thought this too unscholarly. She might have to let him have his say; if she didn't watch out, she might lose him to the Mellon Collection or some such.

Young men like Dougie, acknowledged experts in English painting, had their market.

'Glad you came in. Lonely working on my own, miss you.'

'You're doing splendidly.' Yes, definite signs of complaint: she would have to look after him. 'And yes, you'll be seeing more of me.' In every sense, she was begining to look quite maternal. She met his eyes, and giggled; her first laugh for days. 'You don't mind?'

'*No*. I told you—my sister. And I like children, not babies at first, perhaps, because they are rather frightening, but I always feel I could cherish them.'

'You are nice, Dougie.'

'Well, look after yourself.'

The two of them spent a quiet afternoon at work. A steady stream of people came into the gallery, having heard that Edwina was back. She was popular. One picture was sold, and another sent off 'on approval' to see if it could be lived with. Edwina allowed this liberty to those she knew. 'You ought to start up a picture library,' said Dougie idly. Edwina thought she might do it. Certainly it would move around her stock which sometimes clogged the gallery, her women artists being a prolific bunch.

They closed the gallery together, Edwina pocketing the key. Then she walked cross to eat at the fish restaurant which had just opened; you could eat vegetarian or fish there, but no meat. Edwina ordered sole.

In a few minutes Cassie appeared and sat down with her; in another few minutes Alice appeared. No communication had taken place between them, but Cassie had seen Edwina, and Alice, from her shop window, had watched them both.

It was good to be together again: the self-confident, successful trio, but beyond the familiarity of pleasure perhaps a little unnatural. Suspicion and a degree of mutual distrust had bored in like worms into wood.

They shared a bottle of Sancerre, then Edwina walked home, refusing a lift from Alice.

It was early, there were plenty of people about, she had no reason to feel alarmed. But she began to believe someone was following her.

There were footsteps that seemed to echo her own. She quickened her pace, they seemed to follow; she went slower, the feet did the same.

She turned to look in a shop window full of pale furniture. The plate glass reflected nothing back, not even her own face.

Out of the corner of her eye she saw a young couple, arms round waists, pass by. Two elderly women carrying theatre programmes and talking with animation about Verdi. A man on his own followed, but he passed on without a look at her. None of these.

Just the echo of my own feet, she told herself. Strung out in a line behind her were three solitary pedestrians: a boy in jeans, a man in a grey summer suit, and behind him a policeman.

For a moment she hesitated, a memory dragging at her, then she walked on.

She walked quicker and quicker, not wanting any feet to follow her, dreading that they should catch her up. Tim had had a grey summer suit like that. He'd been wearing it when she had last seen him; might even have been wearing it when he was killed.

She pushed the thought back to the bottom of her mind, and hurried. She could no longer hear anyone behind her.

She ran up the stairs to her front door, there was no one following, she knew that, but she got the door open quickly.

She knew at once he was in there with her.

Not following behind after all, but walking ahead, the footsteps in her mind.

It was not dark in the flat, there was still the light from the long summer evening filtering through. Nevertheless Edwina felt the need for brightness. Quietly she reached out for the light switch. She flicked it down: no light came on.

She stood there, breathing quickly, hanging on to self-control. She had the very strong sense that the person who had been persecuting her was there, with her. Hidden but present. It was *that* person.

Better to run, out of the door and back down the stairs to safety in the street. She had time to

think: how did he get in? Swift as the thought
came the answer: the keys hung in the gallery
again.

She edged backwards, still keeping her eyes
on the sitting-room door. The light from the
window beyond seemed to change, as if a figure
had moved into position between it and the
door.

Edwina turned quickly; a wave of dizziness
and nausea hit her. She closed her eyes, and
threw out a hand to steady herself.

To her horror another hand took hers in a
firm, warm grip. The hand held hers, and she
felt the little finger stretch out and stroke her
gently.

Then the dizziness rose up uncontrollably and
she fell forward into darkness.

But even as she fell she retained enough
perception to think: Is this love or hate that's
being directed at me?

CHAPTER TWELVE

Kit said: 'You can't live like this.' He too had
been keeping an eye on Edwina.

He was standing in her own sitting room,
looking down at her. Janine Grandy was there,
with a glass of brandy in her hand. Clever of her
to have found the brandy, thought Edwina,

dismissing the thought that she might have had it with her. Even people as well organised as Janine did not come supplied with flasks of brandy. Kit knew where it was, of course. How long had she been unconscious? She put up a hand to the back of her head where a bump was to be felt.

'Not too long,' said Janine, as if she had read her thoughts. 'At least I don't think so. I came in with a chapter that Bee Linker wanted you to read and found you lying here with the door open.' She did not add the bottom line that Bee Linker, who appeared to have some prescient idea of what would happen, had told her to keep an eye on Edwina, because she was deeply distrustful of Bee's intentions. Who wanted to be a creature in one of Bee's dramas? But she and Edwina might have been chosen to be. 'I think you'd just fainted and you must have hit your head on the door as you fell. No concussion, I don't think, but perhaps we should get you to hospital?' She looked at Kit.

'Probably. But anyway, out of here.'

'How did you get here?'

'I came in a few minutes after Janine and found her with the door wide open trying to revive you.'

'Did you see anyone leave?'

'No.'

Janine shook her head. 'No one passed me on the stairs . . . I think you'd been out quite a few minutes. You were very cold.'

'There was someone here. In my flat. That's why I fainted.'

'Then we ought to tell the police,' said Kit decisively; he turned towards the telephone.

Janine stopped him. 'I think we ought to make Edwina comfortable first.'

'I'm taking her out of here.'

Edwina sat up. 'Wait a minute.'

'I'm not leaving you here alone. Either you come with me or I stay here.'

'Or I could stay?' suggested Janine. She wondered what Bee Linker would make of that—her characters acting out of turn?

Edwina stood up, she felt less dizzy, quite well suddenly. What a strange business this child-bearing was. 'The thing is, I felt as though I knew him ... When his hands touched me, I felt: I know this person.'

'Then we'd better get you out of here.'

'Then you don't think it imagination?' She was comforted to think Kit took her idea seriously.

Kit shook his head. 'If you had that feeling strongly, then there's probably something in it.'

'Much more likely to be a common break-in,' protested Janine.

'There was no break-in,' corrected Edwina. 'This person had a key.'

This person held my hand, this person stroked my hand, this person is not a stranger.

247

'I'll phone the police from my place. Get your things together and we'll be off.'

'Can I help? No, then I'll leave you to it.' Janine picked up her handbag. 'I've left that stuff from Bee on the table. You were going to check it for historical accuracy.'

'I'll do it.'

It was death of a sort those hands had been seeking, Edwina was sure of it, but it would have been a loving death; somehow, that came through the fingers.

Whatever love meant in that context.

Janine departed, leaving them alone. Kit looked at Edwina then turned away.

'I'll ring the police while you pack.'

'Won't they want to talk to me?'

'They can do that later. I'll say you're not up to it now. The main thing is to get you out of here, and with me.'

Edwina hesitated, just for a moment. 'Yes, of course. I'll put my things together.'

'Take your time. Don't hurry.'

'I won't need much.'

Kit did not answer, but he helped her with the small case and locked the door behind her. 'Tomorrow we'll get the locks changed.'

'And then I can move back.'

'If you want to.' He sounded patient but, for the first time, tired.

'And you don't want me to?'

'Of course I don't want you to: I don't think

it's safe.'

'I've run away once already; it was no good. Moving in with you will be running away, but I have a life to lead. People, like the doctors, I have to see. An appointment at the end of my nine months that I can't run away from. It's all there, ahead of me; I've got to accept it. Live through whatever is waiting for me.'

'Come on,' said Kit with good humour, picking up her case. 'My fatalistic lady.'

He did not know the story of the blackmail (although rumours were getting about), he did not know exactly what had happened to Edwina in Deptford, nor was he privy to as much of the police investigation as Bill Crail. He knew that Luke Tory had been poisoned. That Miss Dover had been strangled, and he was prepared to guess that the murderer was one and the same. He did not believe in coincidence, either. But he could draw upon another source of information. He knew a lawyer who worked with the Department of Public Prosecutions where he had many police contacts. One top-flight policeman had told the lawyer, who told Kit, that the killer was a 'clever bastard' who had planned the poisoning carefully, but 'grabbed a chance' to kill Miss Dover. This policeman had also added that the physical force used to kill Miss Dover had been the minimum necessary. 'Not a bruiser, this one, but a nervous, highly-strung bugger.' Hence the need for sugar, and the eating of the cake.

And something else, too. This senior policeman reported that the murderer of Miss Dover might be under average height for a man, since the strangler had had to stand on the stair above to get a good grip on Miss Dover who was tall for a woman; from the marks on the stair-paint, the killer might have worn built-up shoes.

Another wart on the killer's nose was becoming visible.

One day someone would see all the warts and recognise the face.

All this time, the police were continuing an orthodox investigation, which meant considering all the forensic evidence, and studying the movements and backgrounds of all possible contacts. In their way of business, one thing led to another. It would pay off in the end because this killer had a past and a history which was waiting to be uncovered.

Meanwhile, the murderer was up and walking away. But not unwounded. The encounter with Edwina, although planned, had proved bruising. Edwina, somehow, had to be loved.

Perhaps naturally, Edwina slipped into a state of drowsy sleep for the next few days. Her head felt small and her body large, it was better to sleep it away. The episode of her intruder had drained her of some vital force that she now had to make up. She had tucked herself away in the spare room of Kit's flat and turned into a sleeping princess.

To the anxious enquiries of Alice, Cassie and Dougie, not to mention the police, Kit had said that it was natural in pregnant women to have periods approaching hibernation. No, he was not calling the doctor, and he was feeding her on fruit juices, milk and honey, and he felt sure she would live. Would wake up, as well, when it suited her.

Edwina had stirred herself sufficiently to tell the police all she could remember. She was not alert enough to take in the sceptical smile with which WDC Lewis received it, but Kit did, and resented it.

He had to leave Edwina alone a lot; she had slipped into his life as a resident just when two important cases were coming to the boil. He was in court or involved in consultations for most of the day. But he was worldly wise enough to guess that it was probably the best way for it to be. Hang around Edwina and she'd clear out the sooner.

Three days passed like this in tranquillity, during which time the police investigation into the deaths was continuing and Ginger Drury was making her bid for recovery. She was putting up a good fight.

The whole circle of people whom this case touched was vibrating now, some strongly, others gently, to the central event, which was a death, as if they were part of some delicate metal construction like a piece of mobile sculpture where, if you touched one part, the rest moved.

The death to which they moved had taken place some time ago, longer than some of them realised; the movement initiated then had taken a while to pass through the frame, but now it was reaching out to agitate everyone, including those who had not guessed they would be touched.

Such as Lily, the new Lady Bulkley.

It was during this period that Alice rang Cassie. 'She doesn't trust us. Wouldn't stay with us. Gone to Kit.'

'Do you blame her?' Cassie was forthright. 'But do we trust her?'

'What do you mean?'

'I don't mean she's causing all this, but my God, it all hangs around her.'

On the fourth day, Edwina woke up feeling refreshed and lively. She was alone in the flat, Kit had already departed, but he had left a Thermos of coffee and a note.

'Mrs Vicars comes in today to clean. She has a key and won't bother you.'

Edwina lay back on her pillows and drank a mug of coffee. She decided she wanted to be bothered. Today she felt like company. Presently she became aware that Mrs Vicars had arrived, and was at work in the next room.

A head wearing a duster tied on like a surgeon's cap was poked round the door. 'Care for a bit of toast? Nicely buttered?'

'Love a bit.' Several bits. Edwina suddenly felt very hungry, and blissfully normal and well. It was marvellous to be alive again.

Mrs Vicars brought in two golden slices of toast on a thick white plate. 'I knew you'd fancy a bit. Mr Langley said not to bother you but I've been pregnant myself and I knew you'd fancy a bit of toast if I asked.'

'You know about the baby,' said Edwina biting into the toast.

'Bless you, dear, the messages we've had while you were laid out. You're quite a famous lady ... Anyway, I always keep an eye on Kit's young ladies.'

'Do you now?'

'I was at the wedding, you know. At the church. Oh, she's a lovely young lady, your step. I knew her aunt ... We went to school together. Funny how things turn out, isn't it? *She* was beautiful-looking too, but, of course she didn't have Lily's opportunities. Dead now. Died young. But Lily won't die young. Takes after her father. Strong bones there.'

Edwina ate her toast, and let Mrs Vicars talk herself gently round the room dusting as she went. It was quite obvious to her that Kit had asked her to look after Edwina and had probably ordered the toast. She had a quick picture of him in court, addressing the judge, raising some delicate point of law and all the time thinking

253

about her eating the toast that he had ordered. Dear Kit.

Mrs Vicars did not stay long. 'Not one of my long days,' she explained, departing.

Edwina dressed, studied her diary, noted that she had an engagement at the clinic in the afternoon of tomorrow for another scan, but was otherwise free.

Kit's living room was full of sunlight which showed up where Mrs Vicars' dusting had missed and a certain happy disorder which, apparently, it was not Mrs Vicars' purpose to destroy. Books, papers, letters and shoes were left as they had been put down. A man's room. Kit's specifically: it had all the imprint of his busy, eager personality.

In the window was a big table, and under the table not hidden by the red plush cloth, was a big box with the initials T.C. stamped in gold.

Here at last was the box of Tim's papers to which she had often felt she was coming close, only to have it drawn away again.

She knelt down on the floor before it. Locked, of course. She looked about her. Kit did not follow her useful habit of leaving all keys labelled and hung on a rack for all to view; where he kept keys was his secret. She opened a few likely-looking drawers, but except for neat piles of writing paper with envelopes in one and socks and shirts in another there was nothing to see.

'Prudent fellow.' But this she knew already. He would always look after his keys, not leave them around. Pity about Tim's box.

Wait a minute, she told herself. You know Tim better than that: he never locked a box in his life. If he had, then he'd have lost the keys. This box of his looked locked, you think it's locked, but I bet it isn't really.

She pushed at the tongue of the lock, trying to force it upwards. It held. Perhaps she had been wrong after all and it was locked.

She went into the kitchen, selected a blunt knife and thrust it under the tongue of the lock, levering it gently upward. Still it resisted. She tried more force. Then a little more.

With a pop the lock sprang open as if it had been waiting to open itself to her all the time. Whether she had broken the lock or merely released it she did not know. Nor care.

The box was full. On top was pressed a layer of newspapers as padding. By the dates they had been put there by Kit Langley himself. Anyway, after Tim's death.

Judging by what lay underneath, Kit had just tumbled all Tim's possessions from the shelves into the box and put the newspapers on top. This would not represent carelessness on Kit's part, he would not have wanted to pry into Tim's life. Perhaps he had not wanted her to, either, because he had held back the papers in a gentle way.

And yet he had left her here with them in a box which was not, after all, impossible to open. Perhaps he was leaving it up to her: to open and read if she wished. That would be like Kit.

Just as to leave his possessions in a muddle was like Tim. He had left life in a muddle if she really faced up to it. Well, she was here now to tidy it up. Was this really her function in Tim's life? To meet him, to love him, to bear him a son, so that it was then all right for him to die?

Life couldn't be like that, could it? But it might be.

If it was like that, then there had to be some great muddle in Tim's life which she was to tidy up.

She had known Tim for two years; he had been Kit's friend first. She had loved him from the beginning, and he had responded, but looking back she could see she had been the initiator. If there had been a sexual war then she had been the aggressor. She had led, Tim had followed.

Beneath the newspapers was a collection of law books. These lay on top of files and notebooks relating to his cases in court. Underneath those were letters, some of her own, as she saw at once. Moving all these aside, she came upon a series of thick desk diaries, going back several years.

She took them out, one by one, flicking over the pages; as far as she could tell, they were a record of engagements both business and personal, a mere skeleton with initials and times, no more. She turned the pages till she found her own initials. Yes, there she was.

Satisfied, and yet frustrated at the same time, she put the books down. They only went back a few years.

At the bottom of the box was a large, sealed envelope.

Edwina took it up; it felt heavy in her hands, bulky. Interesting. She wanted to tear it open. Really not meant for her to see; sealed envelopes should be kept closed, no doubt, but she found she had very little inhibition about opening it. Her fingers did it for her without warning.

The contents fell out quickly, most of them anyway. Her fingers, at it again, must have given the envelope a quick shake.

Kit had known what she might find. It had been his hands which had sealed the envelope Tim had left open as if, any minute, he might add a bit more material.

Perhaps he had feared it, and this was why he had done away with himself. It was Kit's private belief that he had done away with himself. Or let himself go to death.

Edwina's eyes fell upon the newspaper cuttings as if they belonged to another world, another planet.

Just at first; then she began to read what she had in her hand as if she had always known it was there waiting for her.

One headline on a yellowed newspaper cutting fascinated her:

TEENAGE SWEETHEARTS IN DEATH TRAGEDY

That round young face could not be Tim's but certainly was, she recognised him. There was a bigger picture in another newspaper.

The word 'murder' appeared for the first time on the next cutting. Edwina read seriously, gravely, not feeling that she was prying into Tim's secret but was being instructed into something she must know. An initiate being led into an inner circle.

BOY LOVER STRANGLES SWEETHEART stood out in big letters. JURY'S VERDICT: GUILTY OF MURDER?

I'm not miserable or frightened or despairing as I read these, said Edwina to herself. Certainly not.

Well, that's a lie to start with. I am reading this stuff with a pain so extreme that I cannot yet feel it.

Would it be any better when the pain started? It would be more like life, anyway.

Better than dying. She would have to hang on to that thought, because she doubted now if Tim had agreed with it. He must have thought a lot about dying. In every possible way, causing death and being dead.

She went over what she had learnt: Tim had killed a girl he had been going with, he had strangled her, his motive was not clear, but the act had been deliberate if not premeditated. It may even have been that.

Tim had been young, but not so very young, old enough to go to trial, receive a judgement and serve a prison sentence.

Old enough to do all that and still young enough to come out, be educated, turn into a lawyer, and to meet her.

The factor of the child entered in now.

Tim would never have killed me, she thought.

But the writing on the papers told another story.

There was her own photograph and attached to it, or at any rate falling out of the envelope very close to it, a piece of writing paper with a scrawl: *I'm so frightened that I might kill her. I have done it once. Why shouldn't it happen again, and there might be no stopping it.*

These words appeared again on another piece of paper: *There might be no stopping it ... I am not mad, though.*

And alas, he wasn't, thought Edwina. She couldn't say he was, she had known him and he had not been mad. That would have been the easy way out.

There was a bit more to read: *I ought to clear out.*

Nothing more, but that was enough. Enough to open up perspectives in the mind. To ask yourself if a death might not be an accident but contrived?

Of course, people who said they were going to clear out didn't always kill themselves.

At the back of her mind was yet another thought that she was unwilling to formulate, telling herself that life was not like that. All the time lately she seemed to be telling herself what was normality and what was not, because she felt the approach of dark shades.

There was life, and there was death, and there might be life after death, but you did not want to think of it walking down the street after you.

She put the papers neatly back in Tim's box but did not drag the box back under the table. Instead she left it where it was.

It was impossible not to think about it, though, and after a bit Edwina gave up the attempt to work and went out to the kitchen to make some coffee. The place was as casually untidy and yet as efficient as everything in Kit's life seemed to be. The coffee tin was not labelled but it was next to the coffee machine. No milk, but some dried cream if you wanted it.

Edwina took a mug of coffee back to the sitting room. It was a small joy in her life at the the moment that coffee tasted good again. Sipping the coffee she sat thinking about Tim. How little she had really known him. But she

260

felt no anger (although that might come later), just pity and a sense of freedom. She was truly on her own now with the child and it was better so.

There was something else she had read in Tim's archives. She went back to the box, took out the envelope and opened it up again.

At the bottom of the second peice of paper, scribbled in pencil as if as a bitter afterthought, were the words:

Why can't they leave me alone?

Edwina put everything back and returned to her coffee. No, we didn't leave him alone, she thought sadly. She blamed herself. With her strong-minded friends and her gallery dedicated to the art of women, she had been too much for Tim, she could see that now. 'What a threat we are, no wonder we are resented. Hated even, in some quarters.'

Inevitably it was a troubled, restless day. She made some necessary telephone calls, received one from Lily and her father in Italy and persuaded them not to return. 'Who told you where I was?'

Lily laughed. 'Kit of course. He *cares*, Eddie.'

'I know.'

'Oh, you sound so *neutral*.'

'Better that way, Lily.' Kit's chances had never been lower.

'Well, I don't know. You get things wrong sometimes, my friend.'

'I know that too.'

'Look after yourself. Love from us both, you know that,' and she was gone, her light cheerful voice departing on a high note. Edwina's father never spoke himself on the telephone if he could help it.

Kit arrived home early, but tactfully preceded himself by a telephone call.

'Didn't want to alarm you.' He had brought home flowers, some wine and some cold food from Harrods' Food Hall, and tossed across her letters which he had collected from Dougie at the gallery.

'This is your home, damn it.'

His eyes took in the box left freestanding in the room.

'Ah ... you found them.' It wasn't a question. 'Read them?'

She nodded.

'You shouldn't have read them.'

'You left them there for me to read.'

'I thought it wise,' he looked at her, 'to give you the choice.'

'There was no choice.'

'No, I suppose not ... I'm sorry, Edwina. I'd like to spare you everything, you know that. Want to talk?'

'No. Not yet.' One day perhaps.

He went out to the kitchen. 'I see Mrs Vicars

262

came. Not a bad old stick is she? Give you some coffee, did she? I told her to make you some toast, you don't eat enough.'

'I eat plenty.'

He appeared at the door wearing a neat blue apron more like a fishmonger than a butcher. 'Melon with Parma ham? And then smoked turkey? I'm rather fond of it myself. And I make a good salad.'

'Lily telephoned. Said you told her I was here ... I'm surprised you knew where to find them, thought they were touring.' She was idly examining her letters: one with a Deptford postmark caught her eye.

'Oh, we keep in touch ... They worry about you.' Kit had obviously been keeping Lily and her father accurately informed of what was going on. He called from the kitchen. 'Clear the table, I'm coming in with the food.'

They had a comfortable meal; she surprised herself by eating.

'Coffee. I'll go and make it. Stay where you are.' He was pleased with himself.

While he was gone she bundled all her letters into her lap and began to open them. A bill, a receipt, a letter from an old customer hinting at a commission. Then she allowed herself to open the letter from Deptford.

Mignon Waters had put her best red hat on and written her letter *con brio*; she had really enjoyed herself, feeling that she had a foothold in a world she had enjoyed once and might enter again, the world of fashion and art, so superior in every way to the one she at present inhabited.

Dear Madam:
[She had discovered Edwina's name, but chose not to use it although, illogically, it would be on the envelope.]

On the matter of the gentleman who was enquiring after you. It may have been that I was more than a little discourteous to you on that occasion. I was not quite myself. It was the anniversary of the day my dear husband died.

[Let her think I celebrate his death with bad temper, decided Mignon, pushing her red turban from above one eye.]

The gentleman left behind him an umbrella which since it is an expensive article I am anxious to restore to him.

The name engraved on it is T. Croft, so now you know him, madam, as I am convinced he knows you. On this matter perhaps we can now come to terms whereupon I will hand over the umbrella. Address as above.

[The red turban slipped again on one side, making Mignon look like a panto pirate. Not money but a foot in her door, she told herself. Before I die I am absolutely determined to do something very worldly and very bold, and this looks like my chance.]

Edwina read the letter, then read it through again, more slowly.

'All right in there?' called Kit. 'You're very quiet.'

'Fine, absolutely fine.' Edwina put the letter back in the envelope and the envelope in her pocket.

In the kitchen Kit shrugged: whatever it was, she was not going to say now and he knew better than to press. She'd had so much to absorb, poor girl, better let her stay quiet.

I am safe enough here, Edwina thought. And then: Or am I?

♦

CHAPTER THIRTEEN

The clinic in Ladybird Lane seemed to change its nature every time Edwina went there, while remaining essentially the same. A paradox perhaps created by her own mind.

But the truth behind it was that although the essential décor remained the same with the scuffed plastic chairs, the margarine-coloured paint and the posters on the walls about the dangers of smoking and not wearing your seat belt, the clients and the medical staff were always different. You never saw the same doctor twice and rarely the same nationality; they never knew your name and you never knew theirs. Their advantage was that they had a card and case history with your name on it and you did not. But bad luck to you if they got the wrong case history. You were right to speak up and identify yourself but not encouraged to do so. During her first few visits Edwina had nourished revolutionary views of doing something about it and had even discussed it with a few other like-minded and pregnant souls, but since she never met them again, and inertia and an acceptance syndrome (now to be recognised as part of the package you picked up when you started on this business, along with depression, anxiety, fear and bursts of downright joy and happiness), had set in, she had done nothing about it.

Revolution was ticking away at the back of her mind now as she sat on a hard chair and waited for her appointment; she had waited an hour already and no real sign of movement in the queue. There ought to be a game called Waiting for the Consultant, she thought, then decided that, of course, there was and they were playing it now.

But her thoughts had a darker strain to them now. She had not yet replied to Mignon Wates's strange letter but some response she would have to make. The woman was an eccentric, no doubt of that, but there was some hard fact in the letter.

Never mind how Mignon Waters had got on to her, she now had an umbrella with Tim's name on it in her possession. There had been such an umbrella but how it had got to Deptford was a question to be thought about. Did it mean anything at all?

A voice broke into her thoughts. 'How do you get on with the exercises?' It was her neighbour, a small, dark, anxious-looking girl; still very young.

Edwina collected herself. 'I don't do them.'

'Oh! Don't do them?' The girl's eyes widened. 'Oh, you are brave. I wouldn't dare not. I do mine. My husband does them with me. Does yours?'

Edwina shook her head. 'No.'

'Oh you are lucky. I wish mine wouldn't. He does them better than I do.'

'He's not got the bump you've got.'

The girl giggled; her anxiety lightened a bit. 'He's getting quite a tum, a kind of false pregnancy. He says it's wind. Is this your first?'

'Yes.'

'Me, too. I'm terrified. Are you?'

Edwina thought. 'Underneath, yes, I believe I am.'

'Oh good, that makes me feel better. I can't stand these cows who say they've never felt better and it's life's most wonderful experience. If that's their best I'm sorry for them.'

Edwina considered again. 'I should think seeing its face might be a pretty good moment.'

'Yes, and counting everything to see it's all there. Does that bit worry you—it being normal?'

'Of course.'

'Me too. Still I'm all right so far.' A more tactful girl than she appeared, she did not ask if Edwina was. 'But I think it's better not to know too much. I'd rather be like my mother was, not knowing everything. I shan't ask what sex it is. If you've got to go through all that, I think you deserve a surprise at the end.'

'I'm not sure I like surprises,' said Edwina.

A nurse appeared at the end of the corridor. 'Mrs Matthews, Mrs Matthews, you are not wearing your robe. Will you go and change at once, please, Doctor wants you.'

Mrs Matthews gave Edwina an anxious look and fled, muttering apologies and excuses all round.

'You next,' said the nurse crisply to Edwina. 'Get yourself ready, please.'

In the cubicle allotted to her, Edwina sat on the stool in the corner and allowed her thoughts to surface.

The man who had been asking after her, her pursuer as she felt, had been carrying Tim's umbrella; the man who *might* have been following her on the way to her own flat two nights ago had been wearing clothes that reminded her of Tim.

Fantasy? Imagination? Seeing what you want to see? But that was rubbish. Tim was dead.

Or was he? All right, let your mind go free, indulge in a nightmare. Tell yourself that Tim did not die in a car crash in Inverness, was not dead and never buried.

He had loved and run because he feared he might kill her. Now he was back and after her.

That was the horror story.

It was a nightmare she could summon up in her mind but hardly bear to talk about. Who could she tell?

Not Kit, she decided, nor Cassie nor Alice, her closest friends, because there was another element in this horror story that she was making up for herself out of bits and pieces, and that was that this undead Tim might have murdered two other people. The deaths of Luke Tory and Miss Dover seemed an inextricable part of the problem. Somehow they fitted in and were part of it.

The pieces did not match, though, it was like trying to make a mosaic out of the wrong-sized bits of stone: you had the cartoon for the complete picture, but the bits you were handling were all wrong.

Unconsciously she had come to the same conclusion as the police investigating team. They were not privy to Edwina's horror story but they had one of their own: they were pursuing a perfectly orthodox investigation and were getting results; they thought they could see the murderer's face, but they were becoming aware that they had something very queer on their hands.

As with Edwina, the pieces of evidence did not feel right in their hands.

As the double police investigation team worked on, it came to focus on a possible name; thus they were able to direct their attention purposefully to the past history of one person. This person had attracted attention by being in everyone's life, crossing all paths. Digging into the character's past brought confirmation of what they suspected from strange places. And Edwina and her adversary were now seen not to be, as thought, an irrelevance, but there at the very heart of the killer's life. A life now seen to have moved in and out of unlikely places.

'Talk about church and state,' joked one senior police officer. 'Prison and pulpit. Theatrical business, isn't it?' By which he meant that in his opinion publicity had been desired, because this was a revenge killing, and revenge could be like that.

They thought they had a murderer's name because this person was in every frame bar one and might yet prove to be in that, too. But evidence and proof was another matter. The bite, ah the bite, had let them down.

The odontologist who was providing forensic

back-up was having his own thoughts on the subject. He clung to his belief. He recognised that the teeth marks did not, after all, appear to lead towards the killer. Or, to put it differently, because the police team thought they had a good idea of who it was, the marks did not tend to confirm it. He was beginning to form an idea about it; he thought he might know which way to turn their thoughts to show them how the marks *could* be used to identify the murderer.

He communicated something of this in a discreet way to Sergeant Bill Crail who was a friend; they often met for a drink after work. Bill Crail had a restless and enquiring mind, he was a worrier, a happy worrier, who enjoyed his worries and saw the point of them: they pushed you forward. He was inclined to think, too, that he might have made a good forensic scientist. He might leave the police and take a belated science degree. If he was going to get anywhere permanent with Cassie (but did he want to?) he would probably have to do something with his career.

As he looked at the plaster models of teeth on the bar table in front of him, the grins of his suspects without their faces round them, he was speculating that he could see where the solution might be, both to the bite problem and the perceived gap in their questioning net. Without knowing it, his mind was running on parallel lines with the odontologist. The same solution

271

might plug both holes. Or it might turn out to be just one hole. A hole in the tooth: joke, he told himself.

'Just pop over to have another word with that theatre troupe. Here today and gone tomorrow, that lot.'

'I might come with you. I've always been interested in stage make-up. From the technical point of view.' He thought that if he had not been a scientist he might have made a good policeman. Too late now. The odontologist gathered up his specimens and put them into his case, amongst others the assembled grins of Canon Linker, Bee Linker, Cassie, Alice, Edwina.

Edwina let her tongue run over her teeth; the doctor had suggested she visit her dentist. It had been, after all, a cheerful interview. The child within her was growing; he had made a spurt. Perhaps he would always be one of those people who developed in jumps.

But as he gained, so Edwina lost: certain vital minerals and metal traces were leaching from her blood. The doctor had also suggested more iron, more calcium, more vitamin tablets.

She had passed Mrs Matthews on her way to the consultation. 'This doctor's lovely,' was the message.

'You're doing fine, girlie,' he said, in a strong New Zealand accent, giving her a friendly slap on the shoulder. 'You and the little one. On your way.'

Immensely heartened, Edwina walked to the gallery to find Dougie in the process of selling a picture to a large lady in tweeds and a great deal of gold and pearl jewellery. He looked so pleased with himself that she walked past to her desk, tactfully letting him get on with it. But she knew the woman and knew that she would return the picture within the week and demand a refund. The signs were there already. She was pointing a finger at a portrait painted in 1930 of Gertrude Lawrence. 'Look at that,' she was declaiming. 'Detail is wrong. Any fool knows they wore gold jewellery in the morning and platinum in the evening.' Dougie would learn.

She sat down at her desk and started to examine the post. Presently Dougie came over and sat down beside her, his customer having departed leaving a cheque.

'Made a sale,' he said triumphantly.

'Clever you.'

'Nice to see you back. You look fine, more upbeat, somehow.'

'I am.' Amazingly it was true. Edwina was back to feeling she could take on the world. Anyway for a limited period. But she meant to tidy up her private life first. This child of hers must come into a world in which its mother had some control. Or understanding. She was working through the papers with some speed.

Understanding meant taking action and she

273

meant to do just that. She had been entirely too passive in this business so far.

'Will you be in regularly from now on?' Dougie was hopeful.

'Probably. But away for a few days first.'

'I see.' Things not quite back to normal yet then. 'What about the post? Send on or will Kit collect?'

'Hang on to it.'

'Ah,' Dougie nodded. Kit out of favour then, or some other little hiccup in his beloved employer's life? 'Will do.'

'But do me a favour.' She was typing rapidly:

Dear Mignon,
Hang on to the object in question. Here is a retainer. [She had estimated Mignon's temporary loyalty at twenty pounds. More would be required later. Or something else. Mignon wanted what she could get.]
I shall be claiming it in due course.

E.F.

'Take this in person . . . The address is on the envelope and let me know what you think of the old person who receives it. I'd like to know . . . And don't say anything.'

'Be glad,' said Dougie, holding out his hand. 'And where will you be?'

'I have a bit of journeying to do.'

'Ah.' He was reading something about her

274

that he did not like, that alarmed him. 'Can't I come too?'

'Nothing dangerous.'

'You alarm me,' and he meant it. Dougie was a sharp observer of his world and he didn't like what he saw. 'Want to tell? Me, or tell Cassie or Alice? Why not? Better to talk.' But from the look on her face he could tell she was not going to and this in itself told him a lot: she doesn't trust any of us.

'I've been the pursued long enough,' said Edwina. 'Now I'm going to do a bit of hunting on my own account.'

After a longish pause, he said, 'Are you going far?' But, of course, it was not movement in space that counted but movement in time, and from the look of her she might be going a fair distance there.

'Quite a way.' She smiled. 'Quite a way.'

★   ★   ★

The road to the north was crowded; a week ago, Edwina would not have had the strength to face the drive. Now she was enjoying it, the sun on her face, the wind blowing her hair. Didn't matter if the air smelt of diesel and petrol from the M1. Edwina was a reluctant driver, but one who got pleasure from it.

She was on her way to Northumberland to visit Tim's mother, and to see his grave. She ought to have been braver about it before; now she had to go, to lay this fantasy that he was not dead.

Behind her was a tricky interview with Kit Langley.

He had come upon her packing her things before departing yesterday evening.

'I didn't expect you back so soon.' She had raised her head from the case.

'Obviously.'

'I was going to let you know.'

'After the event? Oh come on, love. I know it's swings and roundabouts with you at the moment, there's probably a good physical reason for it that you can't help, but you might tell me what's up.'

She had not wanted to tell him her destination but with a short, brisk cross-examination he had it out of her: Northumberland; Tim's home; his mother.

'All right.' He relaxed a litte. 'Perhaps you're right to go. Are you going to tell her about the child?'

Edwina shrugged. 'Don't know yet.'

'She has a right to know.'

'I'll think about that.'

'You can be bloody, Edwina, when you like.'

But he was less angry now he knew where she was going; he knew enough not to ask if he could come. Anyway, he had an important case in court next day. Sometimes Edwina seemed to him immensely more important than any career point could be, and sometimes she didn't. Now the career was on top.

'Cassie or Alice going with you?'

'No.'

He didn't mind that, either. In his eyes it was no bad thing that the close triangle was breaking up.

'Let's have a drink then, and I'll take you to dinner.'

Food might settle her down. He thought of her as a bird or some winged insect. Sometimes Edwina seemed to settle in his hand so that he thought he had her there, then she was gone again. One day she might flutter off for ever. It was terrible to love anyone as much as he loved Edwina and yet not feel sure she could be part of his life.

Would he really want her if he got her? How ever would they live together? Hard questions demanding hard answers, but loving Edwina was a hard business.

There was something about Edwina that made you love her and fight against her at the same time. Provoking was the word.

'I'm not going to drink too much.' There she was, at it again, planting down an assertion like a blow. You could pick it up and return it, or ignore it. He ignored it. This time.

'Of course not.' He handed over a glass of wine. 'You wouldn't dream of it.'

Over the wine, a good white Burgundy, intelligently and deliberately chosen by Kit, she said: 'Are you in love with me?'

He looked at her and smiled. 'I'm thinking of letting it happen.'

She could not tell if he was lying or not; he was not a barrister, a kind of actor, for nothing. But she was thinking of him now as she drove. Her body told her to trust Kit, her mind said: Watch.

That was one of the disadvantages of being a woman and a pregnant one at that; you fluctuated so, your mind and your body frequently going in different directions. There was no question that your judgement was threatened. What was the equivalent for men? None, probably, that was the maddening thing.

If I was really a witch, she thought, as the M1 melted away behind her, instead of being called one by some, and thought one by others, I would concentrate my powers on seeing that men *did* have some similar situations.

Some form of infatuation would do.

'That's not bad, Eddie,' she told herself.

Behind her she had left a police investigation that was growing like a vegetable, a brachiate, with arms spreading out. One arm would soon reach out and touch Edwina: Miss Drury, recovering in hospital, had sent a message that she wanted to see her. Edwina had left, the message missed her, but was received by various

278

other people including the person who least wished to hear it: the murderer.

Another arm of the investigation had stretched out geographically, going to an open prison in Worcestershire near Bromsgrove. A couple of officers, one a woman, one a man, of equal rank, both sergeants but representing the two sides of the investigation team, had gone as a pair. (Two teams for the different areas were working on the related murders of Luke Tory and Miss Dover: later their co-operation was to be a textbook example of how to work together.) They knew the questions they had to ask, having been well briefed, and they had photographs to produce. It had been, in its way, a small *cause célèbre*.

They saw the prison governor, and afterwards the prison medical officer.

'Oh yes.' The governor knew at once what to say. 'I wasn't here, but I know the details. They met here. Just before my time, but I know the details. It started here, but I had no idea it was still going on.'

'Only in a way,' said the woman detective.

'Quick of you to pick it up.'

'The name was remembered.'

'Good thought ... One person here, our doctor, remembered them. I believe he introduced them. And bitterly regrets it.'

The prison medical officer was a small, sparse, anxious Scot whose whole life had been devoted to medicine and the theatre.

'It was through you they met?'

'Yes. And the biggest mistake of my life. Of course, the whole thing was put a stop to. I thought that was it.'

He'd been a bit naive, the young woman detective thought. Not the end. Not the beginning either. Of course, the whole story had been kept quiet, only the police and prison circles had known.

In her opinion he continued to be naive. 'In spite of what he'd done, he had quality, Tim. In this case, I swear he was unaware of the effect he was having. Young men like him draw a certain type of person. Sex hardly comes into it.'

Don't you believe it, thought the young woman. Naive, again. And wrong. 'Goodbye and thank you, Dr Fleming.'

'You've got what you wanted?'

'Yes. Some of it.'

Confirmation. Identity match. 'Yes,' Dr Fleming had said as he looked at a photograph, 'I recognise the face. Changed, but the same.'

*   *   *

Faces change but remain the same, moods change but underneath you still know where you are going.

A few miles short of her destination, a village called Eglington, Edwina stopped in a layby to think.

The countryside with its green, rounded hills, sparse of trees and yet managing to be a rich, domestic scene, was as beautiful as she remembered it. She had been this way only once before. With Tim she had driven north to meet his mother; he knew her father, now it was her turn to meet his mother, a widow. But at this spot, more or less, Tim had stopped the car, turned and driven back. He had refused to let her meet his mother. They had driven back south in silence, not quarrelling but not touching either. Not long after, Tim had been killed.

She could see now why he had kept them apart: he had not been ready to tell her about his own past.

He might never have been ready. It was possible that he had crashed the car with this on his mind. An accident.

One of those accidents that have to happen.

Like the child.

Yes, that too. Death for Tim and life for Edwina, and probably both not quite an accident.

Time to move on.

Within minutes she was driving into Eglington. Ahead lay a wide, quiet street of grey stone houses with sharp pitched roofs and tall narrow windows. They were homogeneous and looked as if they had been built as a unit. In fact they had; she remembered Tim telling her that the whole village had been part of the Tusmore estate and that the mid-Victorian earl had been an 'improving' landlord, who had rebuilt the village to his own taste.

At the end of the street stood the village church, also a monument to mid-Victorian piety but a pleasing one, a quiet construction, again of grey stone, with a low tower and a pointed porch. A low wall round the churchyard.

The churchyard was neat, with well-clipped turf between the tombstones. Edwina walked between the graves, looking about her with care. She soon saw that all the graves around her were old, some going back beyond the last century, older by far than the church itself. Some of the stones were so old that the winds and the frosts had eaten away at the lettering, leaving only unreadable runes.

The new graves were in a bleaker area like a field behind the church. Not so many here.

She walked slowly, studying each memorial carefuly. No stone bore Tim's name. He might lie beneath one of those rounded humps of earth still awaiting the stonemason's work. Poor Tim, it would be so like him to get left with bare earth, not even grass.

The story had gone that Tim's mother had taken his body home for burial in their own village churchyard.

'I don't think so, though. You're not here,

Tim, wherever you are.'

There was a bomb ticking away somewhere in her future, she was aware of it, never more so than now in this quiet, bare churchyard, and yet she continued to walk towards it with gentle determination.

Her walk brought her to the gate of Tim's mother's house. Tim had never described it, but she knew it all the same. 'My mother likes everything in order,' he said, 'and all paint black.'

She stood at the gate, looking towards the front door where a figure in an overall and a big dark hat came round the corner of the house wheeling a barrow full of leaves. Edwina opened the gate. The gardener and the wheelbarrow advanced towards her.

But Edwina was not deceived. 'It's Mrs Croft, isn't it? I'm Edwina Fortune.'

Mrs Croft put down her wheelbarrow and took off her hat, revealing a lean, tense, eager face with bright blue eyes in a tanned skin. She appeared civilised and kind, and to Edwina's intense relief, she in no way resembled Tim. She looked Edwina up and down. 'I knew you of course. What is it you want?'

'I've come looking for Tim. I wanted to see if he could be here.'

Mrs Croft hesitated. 'You'd better come inside.'

'I had a sort of fantasy,' said Edwina, her eyes searching the other woman's face, 'that Tim might be still alive, and here with you. So I came looking.'

'Some brandy, I think.' Mrs Croft turned away to a cupboard. 'You look as though you could do with it. And, after that, food. And you'd better stay the night.' She poured the brandy and handed it over. 'You don't look like the sort of girl to have fantasies to me.'

'No. There are reasons, but I'd rather not go into it now.'

'As you can see, he isn't here.'

'I'm so sorry to worry you like this.' Suddenly the enormity of what she had done came to her. 'You must think I'm mad, Mrs Croft.'

'No.' She shook her head. 'I've been down that road myself. Tasted a little madness.' She drank her brandy, neatly but cleanly as if she knew how.

And more than a little of that too, thought Edwina.

'It's like believing in UFOs or aliens beaming from some distant star—a kind of comfort.'

She drank some more brandy.

'That and gardening; I find turning the earth very soothing. That's where Tim is, in case you were wondering. He was cremated and I scattered the ashes myself. I'm not sure where exactly; it seemed better not to remember precisely, but somewhere on the hills where the wind is strong.'

Edwina wondered how much brandy she had had or would have during her day. It was an escape she herself had not thought of so far.

'I'm afraid I treated you very badly, but I somewhat hated you at the time. I thought it was because of you Tim died. Not a complete accident, you know, his death. The police were never quite sure. But in Scotland you don't have to have an inquest and the Procurator Fiscal thought no enquiry was necessary. Or kind.'

She put out a hand towards Edwina who took it and held it gently. 'Sorry,' she said. 'I don't think I was all that good for Tim, but I did love him.'

'And he loved you. And would have loved the child.' She squeezed Edwina: it was her only reference to the child. 'But there was a lot of fear and anger in him always. Well, you *know*.'

'I know *now*; I didn't.'

'He was afraid that violence in him would surface *again* and he would kill someone he loved. His father was a violent man. Violence breeds violence.

'That was why I hated you. I thought: if she'd left him alone, none of this would have happened. But it's not true. If it hadn't been you, it would have been someone else.' She turned her head away. 'In fact there *was*

285

someone—or had been. I think still was, if you want to know.'

Edwina drank some brandy while she tried to think of some words that did not sound too hurt. But hurt she was and badly. For the first time, she saw a likeness to Tim; both of them knew how to hurt.

'I'm not telling you this just to give you pain. I wanted you to know that it may have been from *this* person that Tim was escaping. There was the fear there—I had a letter after his death, written the day before. At the time I thought it was you he was worried about—it may still be that it was—the child and everything. But there is this other possibility—this other person.'

'Who is she?'

'You know Tim's history—they met in prison. Inmate and prison visitor, that's how it started. It went on from there—till it was broken up.' She shook her head. 'I didn't know till it was all over. But I just have this impression that this person resurfaced in Tim's life. Or perhaps never lost touch. Always followed him.'

They left it there. Mrs Croft took Edwina upstairs and showed her a small, quiet room with a bed covered in flowered chintz. 'Not Tim's room,' she said briefly. 'Come downstairs when you've settled yourself.'

Edwina washed her face and tidied her hair.

Over a simple meal of omelette and salad,

they talked at first on general topics, books and music. Afterwards Edwina told Mrs Croft of the death of Luke Tory, who was a blackmailer, and might have been blackmailing Tim. She told how Luke Tory had wanted to see her, Edwina, just before he died which was perhaps why he had been killed. She did not say how she and her two friends had been suspected of poisoning him. But she did briefly ·mention how Miss Dover had died, and how one murderer was suspected of both deaths.

Mrs Croft poured some wine and let Edwina tell her about her own particular problem: the man who harassed her. She shook her head. 'All one. It has to be.'

Then Edwina said, 'Who is she? This other person. I do want to know.'

Mrs Croft got up. 'I'll make some coffee. You say—she—as to the sex of the person, I was never quite sure.' She turned round. 'There, I've said it now.'

Edwina said, 'I find that hard to take.' Tears appeared in her eyes unbidden and rolled down her cheeks. 'Damn it all, why did you have to say that?'

Hesitantly, Tim's mother said, 'I don't know that Tim responded. About that I'm not sure. Somehow, I got the idea that the other person was—well—more of a kind of voyeur.'

That night Edwina lay in bed in the green chintz bedroom, which, in spite of what Mrs

Croft had said, probably was Tim's room since there appeared to be no other bedroom.

She was thinking of the story so carefully handed over to her by Mrs Croft. She did not understand it all, it needed contemplation, but she had certainly found Tim. Not quite the Tim she had expected and hoped him to be, but one she had to admit she certainly found recognisable.

But into the picture had moved another figure: nameless, faceless, sexless, but who might be her pursuer, and a double murderer.

She turned her head into the pillow and tried to sleep. Tomorrow she would go home.

After breakfast, Mrs Croft stood by the car as Edwina packed herself in. 'Tell you something,' she said. 'There is something I have remembered about the ambiguous person we discussed. There was a connection with either the stage or the Church, or perhaps both. That was the way to the prison-visiting.' She gave Edwina a kiss with more than a hint of whisky. 'Goodbye.'

As she drove south, Edwina thought: Poor old Tim, he had a lot of the qualities that women are traditionally supposed to have, and I have a lot that belong to men, and I don't know that we did either of us any good.

As she drove home to whoever awaited her there, she reflected that out of Tim's past she and Mrs Croft had created a double-headed monster. Like a child's puzzle where there is a face with menace when you look at it one way, and love when you hold it another. It couldn't be the way life was.

No, it was all a question of vision: see it properly and the two faces would fuse together and she would recognise it.

CHAPTER FOURTEEN

Miss Drury, having roused herself to issue her invitation to Edwina, settled back more comfortably to her convalescence, confident that Providence would bring Edwina to her. She was getting better fast, but still not talking much. She was oddly content; she had an idea the story was drawing to a close and that her friend would be avenged. She closed her eyes and drifted off to sleep, into a dream where vengeance, although complete and perfect, was somehow not painful. The police would write it all down in a notebook, and then come and tell her. Lovely.

The police too, although not asleep and most certainly not content, thought they could see their way to the end of it all. They were doing it the straight way: talking to witnesses, checking statements, placing people where they had been at the time of both deaths. Here the investigations of both police teams met. It was tricky work, a question of judgement and luck. But on the whole their mood was up.

They visited Cassie again, Sergeant Crail being advisedly elsewhere, the task went to another CID sergeant who was both his friend and his enemy. To Sergeant Crosby, Cassie said:

'Yes, we asked the Cardboard-Cut-Out players to send us two kings. And I had three other guests who, one way or another, counted as kings. Five kings in all, or so I thought, but only two dressed up. It was a joke. No, I don't know precisely whom they sent. Just the two. You couldn't see in that get up. Loose robes and so on. I paid the bill, that's all.'

The Cardboard-Cut-Out troupe were in a good mood: their patron and principal paymaster had handed over a good contribution to clear their debts. They were polite to Sergeant Crosby, and interested to see a new face and not Crail whom they had been educating in their encounters to their own system of being kind to actors. Bill Crail they liked, this chap they did not take to, so their replies to him were cautious, accurate and kind. But reserved.

'Just the two of us. I went and Joly,' said Hal Everett, the leader of the troupe, if such a democratic group had a leader. Joly gave a confirmatory nod.

When he had gone, not entirely satisfied, Joly

said nervously, 'Do you think we should have said?'

'No.'

'But I'm sure I saw three kings: you, me and one other.'

'An optical illusion.'

'I can count,' said Joly sulkily. 'At one point; I swear.'

'Think how much champagne you'd had. No, forget it.'

Quarrelling cheerfully, because they were really feeling much happier now, they got down to discussing their next production, *The Flood and Mrs Noah*, for five actors and a donkey. Nina had agreed in her absence to play Mrs Noah, traditionally a part for a man but Nina was tall.

Leaving them behind, the police enquiry passed on, Sergeant Crosby throwing out a high deck of questions with the one ace carefully hidden amongst them. Canon Linker was no help to him. 'I left the wedding reception early; I had work to do. I returned in time to take my aunt home. Didn't notice all that much.'

But Bee Linker smiled. 'I can't see, so you will be surprised that I can answer your question. Yes, I would say there were three different kings present at that wedding. I felt and smelt and heard three different people.'

I wonder how that would stand up in court? the sergeant asked himself. But he was grateful to Bee. She'd be a sincere witness who believed in her own evidence.

All the activity was low-key, nor was there much communication between the people in question. The Cardboard-Cut-Out Theatre troupe knew what they had been asked, and Bee Linker knew what she had said.

She had uttered with deliberate, sad thought, 'Sometimes you have to betray even your nearest and dearest.' As a theologian of repute, her nephew Canon Linker would bear her out in this. The temptation to have said nothing, and to cling on to the person who enabled her to have life and identity, still was strong, but had to be resisted.

Miss Drury rested comfortably on her pillows, awaiting the return of Edwina. She was dreaming of a king's hands. I will tell Edwina, she told herself, to look for a strong hand with square polished nails, she must watch out for that hand.

None of this was known to Edwina as she telephoned around her group of friends to tell them she was back. It was their usual way when one or other had been away: you reported in. But they all knew the old closeness was gone. Edwina had started it, but the other two were naturally and simply drifting loose. Cassie was involved with Sergeant Bill Crail, while Alice ... But it was not clear about Alice. Alice, as usual, was keeping her own counsel. She was probably still after Kit Langley. Kit Langley, in Cassie's opinion, was hopelessly lost to Edwina. For all three, their cosy, private Garden was opening up and letting the aliens in.

Kit Langley was not answering his telephone, but Edwina kept trying. His chambers said he was away on a case in York, but they expected him back. His clerk did not seem to recognise Edwina's voice; she felt saddened, chilled. Perhaps Kit too was moving away. Just when she wanted him close.

*   *   *

'Why are you telling *me*, Ginger?' asked Edwina. She had got to the hospital at last; it was the day after her return, and she still had to see Dougie.

It wasn't one of Ginger's better days, she seemed to be drifting in and out of sleep. Why not the police? was what Edwina meant, but she had lost Ginger by then and had to wait for her to surface again.

She looked around as she waited, glad to sit, she was beginning to feel her weight. It was a pleasant, sunny hospital ward; and she would have no objection to being in one when her time came. She was beginning to think ahead about that appointment not to be broken. A natural childbirth? Or all the painkillers she was allowed? She was enough of a realist to expect she'd go for the latter.

Ginger woke up. 'Did I drop off?'

'Only for a minute,' It had been fifteen. 'Can you remember what you were saying?'

Ginger looked thoughtful. 'Hands. I was telling you. And you said: why me?' She reached out and took Edwina's wrist. 'Because you are *it*. That's what Pickles said: It's Edwina who's it.'

'But what did she mean? Don't go to sleep again, Ginger.'

But Ginger already had: she had told Edwina to look out for hands with peculiar-shaped nails and by them she would know the murderer. Satisfied, her duty done, Ginger slept. 'Tell the police tomorrow. You tell them.'

'Tell them what?'

'Tell them that it is you that is the victim; Pickles said so.'

The gospel according to Pickles having been delivered, Ginger settled back.

Then, before Edwina could go, she woke up again, looking surprised at herself for being asleep at all. Aren't I funny? her look said. But think nothing of it. The old Ginger is back here with you.

Edwina waited. I like the old duck, she thought.

'Something else I meant to say,' said Ginger. 'Come back to me now. Think it might concern you ... I saw someone sitting in one of those photograph booths. You have to sit, you know.'

'I know.'

'To me he looked like the chap who was such a trouble to you. Nasty, I thought, now he's getting his phiz taken, and what's he going to do with that?'

He sent it to me, thought Edwina.

'So I told Pickles, and I think Pickles guessed who he was, and that was one reason she was killed. She was clever, my poor old Pickles. Not quite honest, but clever.'

'Do you really think that was the reason?'

'One of them. The other being I think he may have hated Pickles. You *could* hate her. Even I did sometimes, and I loved her.'

Her eyes closed, but she managed to say loudly, 'Darling, don't forget the hands.'

Edwina gave her a kiss on the smooth innocent cheek. 'You big baby,' she said, 'leaving it all to me.' But what rubbish it was. Hands indeed. Was she to look at hands and teeth now?

Dougie was not in the gallery when she got there, leaving Alison, their fragile assistant, in charge, but he had left a note of explanation on her desk.

Have gone to an EGP. [This stood for an Extremely Grand Party in Dougie's parlance and meant the presence of either a megastar or HM herself.] Vital to go, expect to do business. Look on my desk for a letter from Kit; he wanted to be sure you got it. Also note the other *object*?

Edwina went across to Dougie's desk, orderly and clean as usual. On it rested a long, thin object wrapped in brown paper with another note from Dougie attached.

I bought this from a weird old biddy in a red hat: she said you'd asked for it. When I say 'paid' no money passed hands, but she's coming to your next private view. I think you've got her for life.

I think so, too, decided Edwina, as she unwrapped Tim's umbrella. Nor did she mind; predestined, a thing that had to happen. As with the child. She quite looked forward to a future of knowing Mignon Waters.

The letter from Kit was short, but somehow commanding. An end to nonsense, he was saying, let's wind this up.

Darling Edwina, I love you. Quite seriously, and what used to be called honourably, words which, I suppose, people don't use now, but you know what I mean.

You need this year to yourself, I see that, but at the end of this time . . . ?

There were more sentences, but Edwina put her hand over them as if they were bright, and must be protected. She wouldn't forget them because Kit's sincerity burnt the page. There was a legal sound to one or two of his phrases. Edwina laughed as she put the letter back in the envelope. The old thing would probably end up on the Woolsack. Life with Kit could be good, but she'd have to see; she might prefer to go it alone. But he was right, he deserved an answer. He certainly sounded as if he meant to have one. He always did. Perhaps that was what worried her about Kit: his force. Or whatever it was, something strong certainly—I want to love and trust you, Kit, she said, but I did that once with Tim and it was dangerous. You could be dangerous, too. You knew Tim; he was your friend; you lived together. Perhaps like called to like.

There was one other note from Dougie. It said:

The typing bureau could not complete the catalogue, *Actresses in Paint: 1900-1984*, so Janine offered. She will bring it round tonight when finished.

'Damn,' was Edwina's reaction. She had intended to finish her work on the *catalogue raisonnée* that night.

She worked on in the gallery as late as she

could, sending Alison across to Tuttons to bring her pâté and salad before letting her go home. She drank a glass of white wine as she worked, and while she worked she thought.

One of her fantasies—that Tim was still alive—had ebbed away, disappeared like a nightmare in daylight.

The way Tim's umbrella had turned up in Deptford was disturbing. Kit's story was that he had lost it. He also said he had given all Tim's clothes to the Salvation Army.

She believed it, but it suddenly struck her that she could have proof. She could ask Janine.

Somewhere she must have the telephone number, but it was not to be found. But Bee Linker must know, and the telephone was always answered in the Linker household.

'Jim Linker here.' He listened to her request. 'Of course. I don't know myself but I'll ask Bee.' Presently he came back with the number. 'How are you, Edwina?' His voice sounded deep and quiet.

It was strange how the telephone emphasised certain qualities in people's voices. Because he was celibate she had not thought of Jim Linker in terms of a man, but he was very much one, she now realised from his voice.

'I'm fine, feeling really well.' She said hastily, embarrassed by her own thoughts, 'I'm just going to ring Janine.'

She could hear Janine's telephone ring out;

she had never been there but Dougie had and he reported it as a snug little outfit over a shop and Janine living above that, all cosy.

It always took time for her telephone to be answered, as if she had to come running downstairs. She answered at last, not breathless, just quiet.

'Janine? Edwina here. I need to talk to you. Come to my flat, will you? Not the gallery. I've nearly finished here, then I'll go home.' When Janine hesitated, Edwina said, 'I'll come to you, if you prefer. Oyster Row, isn't it?'

'Oystead,' Janine corrected. 'But no, I'll be over. It would be better. I was planning to, anyway, as you know. But what is it you want?'

Edwina let the receiver rest in her hand. Why can't I ask a straight question, here and now?

Because I am frightened of what I might hear.

'Do you want to talk now?' Janine sounded concerned, anxious as if somehow she knew what Edwina wanted and was not surprised.

Perhaps she does, judged Edwina, perhaps everyone knows all the questions and some of the answers too. Cassie, Alice, Kit, not forgetting Sergeant Bill Crail, all with their bits of answers.

To Janine, she said, 'Let's talk when you come. I'd rather.'

For after all, it's such a silly-sounding question. I shall have to work up to it. 'Did Canon Linker give you any clothes belonging to

Tim from Kit to give to the Salvation Army?'

And if he did not, was it Kit who was lying? Just tossing off an easy answer to keep her quiet?

She did a little more work, then tidied her desk before leaving. A tidy desk, a peaceful mind, she told herself. Yes, nanny, good little Edwina.

As she was turning to go, the telephone rang on her desk; she was nervous about answering. Life had been quiet lately but she sensed it would not stay that way. For the moment she was to be left alone but not for ever.

'Hello?'

'It's Bee Linker here. Jim is coming round.'

'Bee—I won't be here; I'm just going home.'

'He's coming,' repeated Bee, as if she had not heard, as if she was saying: I didn't say you wanted him, I said he was coming. 'Oh, Edwina, I've suspected for such a long time . . . Look after yourself, Edwina.'

Then the telephone went dead. Telephoning was not one of Bee's skills, it was an effort for her to do it. Her fingers remembered certain places on the dial but she did not always find them. It had taken her some minutes to reach Edwina.

Edwina hurried home, debating what Bee had meant. It had alarmed her considerably. There were still people about, the curtain had just come down at the Opera House and the audience was beginning to trickle out. As always at this time of the night, in this place, there was a happy atmosphere as of a party near at hand. No sense of anyone following troubled Edwina.

She was almost at the top of the long flight of steps to her flat when she heard footsteps below. A few more steps, and she had her front door open.

She stopped, turned to listen. Something about the sound of moving feet was familiar.

'Kit?'

No answer, but the feet stopped for a minute, and then came on, more slowly.

Edwina went down a few steps and called again. 'Canon Linker, is it you?'

Jim Linker turned the corner of the stairs. 'Edwina—I've been following you . . .'

Edwina had never seen his face look so sombre, so dark. So frightening. Suddenly she saw him for what he was: a menacing male figure.

'Are you alone? Is anyone with you?'

She retreated backwards up to her own front door. Someone else was coming up the stairs, hurrying.

'Janine,' she said with relief. 'Thank goodness you've come.'

Janine was carrying a shallow tray with two copies of the catalogue. Over her shoulder swung her bag. She came hurrying up, her face absorbed, abstracted.

Then she saw Jim Linker and Edwina confronting each other and she stopped in surprise.

'Please, Janine.'

'Wait a minute.' Jim Linker put his arm out. Janine slid past and up towards Edwina. The two women stood together. 'I want to talk to you.'

His long legs took the last two steps in a bound.

Edwina spun round, dragged Janine with her, and banged the door in his face.

She was shivering, and for a moment it was all she could do to control her breathing. With a gulp, she said, 'I'm so frightened of him.'

Janine stared at her as if she could not believe what she was hearing. 'Of *him*?'

'Yes.' Edwina took hold of Janine's arm and drew her away from the door, which had gone quiet, but behind which Jim Linker must be standing, and into the living room. 'I'm so glad I've got you.'

'If you say so.' Janine's voice was polite but sceptical as if she could not quite believe what she was hearing.

Her calmness, coldness even, braced Edwina. 'Yes, I'm being ridiculous. I've overreacted. It's the way I am at the moment. He can't get in.'

'No, indeed.'

Edwina listened. 'It's all quiet out there, isn't it?' She looked at Janine. 'But I don't think he's

302

gone.'

The front-door handle rattled as if someone, Jim Linker, was trying to get in.

Edwina started to tremble again. 'I must control this, but I think he's done something terrible to me, destroyed a bit of me, I think. Eaten it away.' In a high voice, she said, 'That man is eating me up.'

She looked at Janine's incredulous face. 'You think I'm being hysterical?'

Janine made a slight movement as if to speak, and then thought better of it.

Outside there was a banging on the door. 'Edwina are you there? Answer me.'

'Take no notice,' said Edwina. 'I'm going to telephone the police.'

Janine stopped her. 'Not without telling me a bit.'

'I think he killed Luke Tory because Luke was blackmailing Tim, and strangled Miss Dover because she knew. I'm not sure how she knew. There's something about a photograph. Or she may have guessed some other way. She was sharp. And why was Luke blackmailing Tim? Well, I do know but I'm not sure if I want to tell you.' Tim, poor Tim, what lies he must have told to get his foot on the legal ladder. Kit would have kept a still tongue, but somehow Luke Tory had found out. 'Now he has turned on me.' She could hear Ginger's voice telling her that Pickles thought *she* was it all the time;

Edwina shuddered. 'God knows what he wants of me or what he thinks I am. But it's a kind of revenge, I believe, because of Tim. In a terrible kind of way he must have loved Tim. I don't know how it happened or when. I don't dare to think what the relationship was.'

'You're very unlucky,' said Janine.

'And Bee's so good, so kind, it's going to be terrible for her. I mean, to know he is *evil*.' She shivered.

'She's tougher than she seems, is Bee. I shouldn't worry about her.'

'No, but even so.' Edwina was remembering Bee's voice: not so tough as all that, she thought. Who is? Love is pain. What do you do when someone you love turns into a predator?

She had a picture of Jim Linker flinging on the robes of a king and using the wedding reception to poison Luke. Of him appropriating Tim's clothes to make a dead man live. And strangling Pickles Dover because she had sold him the poison and recognised him. Scum, she thought. Dirty, obscene, mad.

Outside all was quiet as if Jim Linker had gone away.

'Do you think he's gone? Or just sitting there waiting?'

Janine shrugged. 'Want me to look?'

'No.'

'So?'

'I shall phone the police.' She moved towards

her desk.

Janine gripped her wrist. 'No. Leave it.'

Edwina looked down at Janine's hand and saw how large Janine's hand was, how strong the fingers and square the nails. She tried to move her wrist free, but Janine did not let go. If anything, her grip tightened.

In a sudden panic, Edwina pushed at Janine who staggered backwards, her shoulderbag opened and the contents spilled out on to the ground. The first thing that attracted her attention was the photograph. *That* photograph. She stared from it to what else had fallen out. A purse, a lipstick and a pink plastic object, gleaming, mouth-shaped with three teeth top and bottom. An actor's device. A shell to slip in over the natural teeth.

The bite of the murderer without the face.

Edwina took in what she saw with horror. Not Jim Linker, but Janine. All the things she had imagined were true, but true of Janine. Not a man hunting her, but a woman who could act the man, with cheek packs and false teeth.

And she was shut up in the flat with her.

She said the first thing that came into her head. 'That photograph, it's you.'

'Yes, and Pickles knew it was me.'

'Why a photograph?'

'It was a frightener,' said Janine. 'Didn't it frighten you?'

Edwina did not answer; she was having

305

trouble breathing.

Janine bent down and picked up the mouthpiece with its teeth. Not joke teeth from Davenport's, but old, theatrical prop teeth, such as you never saw now, from a theatrical production of the 1920s in which Janine's father had played. Old Thespians never die. She seemed to hesitate for a moment between putting it in her mouth to grin at Edwina or into her handbag; she slipped it into her bag.

'I heard you once talk about the murderer as two-headed. I'm two-faced if you like. Nina, at the Cardboard-Cut-Out Theatre, and Janine when I type. The typing bureau is how I keep going. It provides the cash. A lot of actresses have two jobs; have to have.'

The rapid reversal of all she had been feeling made Edwina dizzy. 'You on the phone? Yes. You used your voice very cleverly. I really thought you were a man.'

'I am an actress. I have a natural low register to my voice.'

'Cassie wondered. She heard something in the voice that made her wonder.' I didn't, she thought, I didn't wonder enough. I believe I wanted too much to believe in the reappearance of Tim. You see what you desire to see, hear what you long for. 'So it was you that hated me so?'

'Yes. Of course. I wonder you couldn't feel it. I used to send waves of it across to you, but you never did. I must be a worse actress than I knew. I've hated you ever since I came to London to make contact with Tim and found you. I've always kept in touch. I met him first when I was teaching drama to long-stay prisoners, poor beasts. We loved each other. Don't you believe otherwise, but they took him away from me. As you did. I always got back to him again.' Now that she had come out into the open, her vocabulary was changing slightly, she was more of the actress and less the neat, quiet Janine. It was as if she'd come alive, and been reborn on the spot. 'I wanted to let you learn a few things: that I was here, all the time, that I came back into his life, and that he knew it. Well, I've taught you. Haven't I? Answer now. Say Yes or No.'

'Yes.'

'I really hated you: you and the women who had buggered up Tim's life and always would do.'

As if she wasn't one of them, thought Edwina. The worst probably. Would Tim have had the accident that killed him if it hadn't been for Janine, with all her pressure?

Suddenly she had a thought. 'What about the whisky? Did you mean it for me? Or was it really for Luke? Or was Luke's death an accident? It's like a play, a drama called *Who Must Die in the Garden?*'.

Janine said, 'Did you think I meant the

whisky for you and Luke got it by accident? I was the other paper-king, you know. It was so easy to dress up. Oh no. Nothing is by accident. And yet there are layers and layers to intention. It was for Luke to drink but, by God, if it had gone down your throat, I wouldn't have minded. Yes, I admit it, when I bought that particular poison I had you at the back of my mind. You should burn with love. Then, I thought: no, Luke; him first. Let him have it.'

Her voice fell to a whisper.

'And then—I kind of fell in love with you myself.' Her hands came and rested lightly one on either side of Edwina's neck. She felt their pressure. 'That was a shock to me. I always thought I was straight, and then I loved you.' Her hands trembled.

'Well, to hell with you,' Edwina said, knocking the hands down and pushing Janine back. She fell to the ground, dragging Edwina heavily with her.

Outside they could hear Jim Linker's voice.

'Let me in. Open that door.'

Winded, Edwina lay there for a moment, then rolled over on her side, struggling to get her breath. 'Coming,' she panted. 'Hang on.' Inside her, a snake-like pain began below her waist and wriggled down her back.

But Janine did not wait. She got to the door first, wrenched it open, and was past Canon Linker and pounding down the stairs before he could stop her.

Edwina could hear her feet running. Running, running.

★ ★ ★

'You should have stopped her.' Edwina let Jim Linker hold her hand while they waited for the ambulance. 'She'll kill herself.'

'Oh no.' His face was stern. 'People like Janine don't kill themselves. She'll just go on running. Then, one day, she'll stop and cry to us for help.' From the look of him, his mercy, when she got it, would be unsentimental.

'I've never seen you so hard.'

'Not hard, no.' His tone was matter-of-fact. Goodness, she saw, had a practicality of its own. 'But not soft either. Come along now, my child, let's deal with you.'

Everyone was very kind to Edwina after her death.

It felt like a death; she was sucked down into a vacuum like a black hole in the universe where matter is digested and spewed out in altered form. Or never seen again. But Edwina came through, after several days, having lost a good deal of blood, but as she said herself in a surprised way, 'Still mother and child'.

'She could have killed you,' said Kit. 'I wish I'd been there.'

'Yes. It was touch and go.' Edwina soberly

assessed what had happened. 'Not here and now, I don't mean, but in that room.' She gave a shudder. 'I'll never live there again. She as near as nothing strangled me, I could feel it through her fingers. Oh yes, she wanted to kill me all right. She probably wanted to kill Tim, too, a lot of the time.'

'She managed it.'

'No.' Edwina was decisive. 'His death was an accident. I've decided, and that's the way it's going to be. I can live with that.'

Her room was full of flowers, and Dougie, who in some ways knew her better than anyone, had brought her in a pile of new books and a bottle of Dior's L'Eau Fraiche—'Love it myself, dear, and it's the *best*, when you're not feeling quite yourself. Sprinkle some on the pillow.'

Kit also knew her well, and himself better, and his offering he slipped in front of her: an elegantly handwritten letter with a New York address signed Alicia Titmarsh, saying that she was coming over shortly and after all she'd heard from Kit thought she would be discussing Edwina's handling of her next European exhibition. Also, could she paint Edwina?

He would never tell her that Tim's real nightmare had been that he would kill Edwina. Not Janine, but Edwina. You only kill those you really love.

With quiet satisfaction, Edwina pocketed the

letter. 'Clever Kit.'

'The old girl's a friend of my godmother. I've been saving this up. Did you read my letter?'

'Yes. Just before Janine—No easy answer, Kit. Not yet.' But she held out her hand and he felt the promise in it.

'I'll be back this evening: your doctors say I can.'

Alice and Cassie came every day, had done since the first, effortlessly establishing a domination over doctors and nursing staff so that they were always let in even if not welcomed. The three had almost, but not quite, re-established the old close triangle. Underneath it had changed and they all knew it.

'Our horoscopes say up from now on,' predicted Alice brightly; she had to get over Kit somehow, and good humour seemed the best way.

'They're letting me out on Wednesday.' It did feel like being in prison, charming as the whole nursing staff were.

'Ah yes,' Cassie looked thoughtful. 'In case you were worried, Bill Crail gave me some news. He said to pass it on.'

'Janine?'

'Yes, Canon Linker was quite right. She did stop running. The police picked her up in Southampton yesterday. She asked for both the Linkers, Jim and Bee.'

'Thanks.' So that was one more detail tidied

away. One life for Janine was ending and another beginning. 'How is Bill?'

'Oh, we go on,' said Cassie. 'Yes, I really think we do.'

Coming from Cassie that meant a lot.

When they had gone, Edwina reflected on the past months in which love and death seemed to have been inextricably entwined with each other. It was good to know the nightmare of being hunted was over, not to hear the telephone in the dark. But she know also that a figure still flitted through the landscape of her mind: a double-headed figure with Tim's face on one side and Janine's on the other.

The door opened; a strong breath of 'Madame Rochas' told her it was not the nurse.

'Lily.'

Lily, her streaky fair hair swinging forward, sparkling blue eyes discreetly hidden behind dark spectacles.

'Your Dad's outside. But he's let me come in first.'

'Darling Lily. Let me look at you. Are you happy? Yes, I can see you are.'

'Recommend the state, love. Only pick the right person this time.' She gave Edwina a worried look. 'But we won't dwell on that. I never guessed about Tim and Janine, but, of course, I knew about Luke's little ways. He tried to blackmail me.'

'What for, Lily?' Lily lived such an open-plan life.

'Only a little love affair. But he said he'd tell your Dad. Go to hell, I said, told him I'd get in first with the telling. Of course, I didn't have to.'

Lily was always so shrewd.

'Can't see my father minding.'

'Ah well—he might have minded this—it was with a woman.'

Edwina gave Lily a look.

'For me it was a nothing. Just an experiment that didn't work. Might have meant more to the other person.'

The two women exchanged a glance.

'I think I can make a guess.'

Lily said, 'All's well that ends well.'

For me it has not quite ended, thought Edwina, I am a beginning as well. She knew the sex of the child about to be born. 'I shall be a good mother, because I've seen how you can go wrong.'

'What are you going to call the child?' asked Lily. 'Do tell, Edwina.'

'That's my secret,' said Edwina.

Photoset, printed and bound in Great Britain by
REDWOOD BURN LIMITED, Trowbridge, Wiltshire